Divine Rebel

Tom Wallace

**A Wings ePress, Inc.
Mystery Novel**

Wings ePress, Inc.

Edited by: Jeanne Smith
Copy Edited by: Joan C. Powell
Executive Editor: Jeanne Smith
Cover Artist: Trisha FitzGerald-Jung

All rights reserved

Wings ePress Books
www.wingsepress.com

Copyright © 2020 by: Tom Wallace
ISBN: 978-1-61309-571-3

Published In the United States Of America

Wings ePress Inc.
3000 N. Rock Road
Newton, KS 67114

Dedication

This book is dedicated to Marilyn Underwood, Julie Watson and Sarah Small. Three strong, brave, marvelous ladies.

* * *

One

The sun, a bright orange globe nestled within reddish-blue clouds, dangled dangerously above the edge of the horizon. In a matter of minutes, it would disappear completely, leaving darkness trailing behind while bringing with it the promise of tomorrow for those on the far side of the world. Every sunset was beautiful in its own way, but this one was majestic.

Over the years, I have often been asked this question: If I could have been anyone who ever lived, who would it be? My answer is always the same: Adam on that first morning. Kabbalah teaches that when Adam opened his eyes, he could see from one end of the world to the other. I doubt that's true, but does it really matter? One can't help but wonder how Adam must have felt, standing there alone, bathed in God's holy light. Surely, he marveled at what he beheld.

Of course, I don't believe the Garden of Eden/Adam and Eve story. Nor do I believe in a serpent that talks, the Cain and Abel murder mystery, the Tower of Babel, or Noah and the Great Flood. And I chuckle when told Methuselah lived nine-hundred-sixty-nine years. They are myths and tall tales, wonderful fiction written for us to read, study, enjoy, and learn from. Fabulous fables with a serious purpose.

For countless millions, myself included, our history begins when Abram answered Yahweh's call to leave his homeland and begin a journey that would eventually result in the world's three great religions... Judaism, Christianity and Islam. By this time, Abram, which means "exalted father," had become Abraham, "father of a host of nations." Tragically, those nations, those three great religions, have been killing each other for thousands of years. I doubt Abraham would be pleased with his progeny.

Those are the kinds of thoughts I have when I drink too much, which for the past several years has been a frequent occurrence. Here's the irony: I'm fifty and I didn't touch a drop of alcohol until my early thirties. Not in high school, college, or during the first Gulf War. I stayed away from booze on all fronts, in every situation, no matter the crowd I was hanging out with. Jake Kaplan, an editor at Delacorte Press and a close friend since our days as Creative Writing students at NYU, opines that I'm now trying to make up for lost time. Hard to argue with that, based on the circumstances.

Here's a second irony, or mystery, if you prefer to call it that: I don't drink because of my great love for alcohol. Far from it. I drink because I'm bored. Having too much free time and too much money is a great catalyst for boredom. But I don't complain. Better to be a bored, rich drinker than a busy, poor alcoholic.

I'm sitting at the bar in the Old Salty Dog on Siesta Key. This has been my favorite watering hole since I moved here seven years ago. The food is good, the drinks are honest, and the majority of folks who come in, especially the regulars, are an interesting collection of Homo sapiens. The Old Salty Dog is only a mile or so from my condo on the beach, easily within walking distance, should I choose to walk rather than pedal over on my bicycle.

When I mentioned that the majority of regulars were interesting, I wasn't referring to Rory Killion, who was currently sitting next to me at the bar. Unlike most of the regulars who see me as I see myself...a very lucky fraud...Rory was overly impressed by my past. He thought

I was big cheese. That's because Rory, who claimed to have studied acting in New York City, had seen the one play I had written—*Divine Rebel: An Evening with William Blake*. Every conversation with Rory invariably came around to the subject of my play. Or more specifically, to the actor who portrayed Blake...Anthony Hopkins.

"So, tell me, Nick, what was Sir Anthony like?" Rory asked, bestowing upon the actor his full title. Rory was drinking his usual gin and tonic. I had long ago lost count of how many he'd already consumed but it was at least a half-dozen. "Is he a regular dude, or a pompous asshole?"

"He was a nice guy," I answered, hoping my terse reply might shut down the conversation. It didn't. And I knew what Rory's next question would be.

"When you were with him, did you get the feeling you were looking at Hannibal Lecter? That had to be weird, wasn't it?"

"Actually, I saw him as William Blake."

"Still, though, weren't you ever tempted to get him to say, 'I ate his liver with some fava beans and a nice chianti'? I would have pleaded with him to say that line."

"If you see him, Rory, you do that. I'm sure he's only heard it a million times."

Thanks to Hopkins agreeing to take the role, my one-man play was a big success, financially and critically. Another superb actor, Jonathan Pryce, took over for Hopkins, first as his replacement on Broadway, and then when the play moved to England. *Divine Rebel* earned a Tony nomination for Best Play, as did Hopkins for Best Actor. Neither won, but like they (usually the losers) say, it's the nomination that counts. I wasn't excluded when praise was being passed around by the critics. I received great kudos for writing the play, which I'm not sure I deserved. While I did structure the play, and add a few connecting paragraphs that moved things along, every word of dialogue came straight from Blake. If anyone deserved praise, it was him.

Rory had been silently nursing his drink for the past ten minutes, fueling my hope that our little chat was finished. Didn't work out that way. I may as well have been hoping Charlize Theron would stroll into the Old Salty Dog, spot me, walk over, give me a kiss, and then take me by the hand and lead me outside and into her waiting limo.

"Hey, Nick," Rory said, "you spent all that time in film land, you must've been big pals with some of those movie stars."

"Not really," I said.

"Ah, come on, man, don't be so modest. Share the juice with me. Did you know George Clooney or Brad Pitt? What about Sean Penn? He's one of my favorites."

"Never met any of them."

"You write all those movies and you want me to believe you don't know any of the big stars? I don't see how that's possible."

"Working with an actor doesn't mean you know him or her. Those big stars reside in a galaxy far away from the lowly writer. They rarely ever notice us."

"Okay, I get it," Rory persisted. "Then tell me about that war movie you wrote. I love that damn flick. It's a true classic."

"Can't do it, Rory. See, when you contract to work on a big movie, the producers and studio executives require you to sign an NDA—a nondisclosure agreement. Legally, that binds me to silence. If I ignore the NDA and talk about the movie, they could force me to return the money I was paid. Plus, they could also charge me with a crime. I could end up broke and behind bars."

I have to admit that's one of my all-time best lies. That one should earn me a plaque in the Liars' Hall of Fame.

"Ah, shit, Nick, you're no fun," Rory complained. He ordered another gin and tonic, took a sip, and began to sulk. How long this period of silence would last was anybody's guess.

Now don't get me wrong, Rory's not a bad guy; he just can't let go of the movie shit. He's obsessed with it. That's why every conversation with him begins in the Old Salty Dog and eventually ends up in Hollywood, where I spent ten years of my life working in the film industry, just not in the capacity Rory claims I did. I never "wrote" movies. I was that mysterious creature known as a script doctor.

~ * ~

While I achieved my greatest critical success with *Divine Rebel*, it wasn't the play that padded my checking account to the extent that I could afford to buy a beachfront condo on Siesta Key. It was the decade spent in Los Angeles that made me a wealthy man. Those Hollywood folks hand out cash faster than Texas judges hand out death sentences.

Let me backtrack and explain how it all came about. After mustering out of the Army, I spent the next three months writing a novel, a detective mystery. I landed an agent, who pitched the book to several publishing houses. One of the smaller houses quickly agreed to publish the book. It was only a modest success (and that's being generous), but it did garner some positive reviews.

Even more important, it was noticed by a movie producer, who quickly secured the rights to the book. Naturally, when that happened, dreams of glory ran rampant in my head. I'm thinking Scorsese or Spielberg or maybe Oliver Stone as director. You know, one of the giants. The cast? Big-name stars for sure. And in my scenario, the movie would play in theaters all across the country.

Man, did I overreach on that one. None of that stuff happened. The producer was always about two hours away from bankruptcy, the director was a lush, and the screenwriter was a butcher. As for the cast, well, they signed one mid-level actor whose claim to fame was portraying a doctor on one of the daytime soaps, and then surrounded him with a bunch of no-name performers looking for a big break. And did the movie play in theaters? No, it didn't. It was seen on the Lifetime Movie Channel. Talk about a dream deferred. That was mine.

However, despite my personal disappointment with the entire experience, the movie wasn't all that bad. It was certainly a far cry from the story I had written, but I'm not the first author to complain about his or her book being poorly translated to the movie/TV screen. And I won't be the last.

But out of that mixed-bag experience came the call that altered the course of my life. (And lined my pockets with big bucks.) A major movie producer/director, Benjamin Schiller, had read and appreciated my novel. He especially admired my prose and my ear for dialogue.

Ben told me he had two movies in pre-production but still wasn't completely satisfied with either screenplay, both of which had been worked on and altered many times over the years. He wanted to know if I would be interested in making the trip to L.A., to see if I could make some improvements that might save the two films. He estimated I could get the job done in three weeks. Those three weeks turned into ten years, during which I worked on—or "doctored"—more than fifty screenplays.

Along with doctoring scripts, I also answered the call when an actor, almost always a male, wasn't satisfied with his role in a particular movie. Really, what the actor wanted was more screen time alone. This translated into wanting his role expanded. Either he or his agent would contact me with a request that I write the actor a couple of big speeches that would put him front and center of whatever action was taking place within the movie at the time. It wasn't much of a challenge, and I didn't get much joy out of doing the work, but the money was too great to turn down.

A script doctor is seen as a court of last resort. He's the ninth-inning closer a baseball manager brings in to seal the deal. The script doctor may be valuable to the producer or the director, but he is typically considered the enemy by the original screenwriter, who almost always thinks his work is perfect and therefore in no need of being "improved." Probably I would feel the same way if I were in his shoes.

But after ten years of laboring over works done by other writers, I decided I'd had enough. I was burned out and worn down, and I'd accumulated more money than I could ever hope to spend. Also, I had a fierce desire to be creative for my own purposes. As William Blake said, "I must create a system, or be enslaved by another man's." With that in mind, I once again put my fate in my own hands.

So, I packed up, relocated to Florida, bought the condo on Siesta Key in the Sarasota area, and went back to work on the Blake play, which I had begun several years earlier.

I finished it within six months, and the rest, so the saying goes, is history.

As Rory turned to hit me with another question, I was saved by my buzzing cell phone. I lifted it off the bar and checked the caller ID, which said Unknown Caller on the screen. Next, I checked the number. I didn't recognize it, but I did recognize the area code—270. That's the area code for where I'm originally from. Curious, I answered the call. That turned out to be questionable judgment on my part.

Remember what Martin Sheen's character, Captain Willard, said early on in *Apocalypse Now*? "I wanted a mission, and for my sins they gave me one."

That line didn't come to mind at the time, but later on it would. Overly dramatic? Probably. Self-centered? You bet. But factual nonetheless. No one knows the future, or the secrets it keeps hidden. We live our lives bound within the confines of certain mysteries. We have no choice but to wait until those mysteries, those secrets, are eventually revealed to each of us, as they surely will be.

But little did I know at the time that future events would closely conspire to echo Captain Willard's lament.

Two

After paying my bill, I pushed away from the bar, bid Rory a perfunctory "catch you later" farewell, stepped outside into the blistering heat, pressed my phone against my ear, and answered the call.

"This is Nick Gabriel," I said, already sweating profusely.

"Is this the legendary 'Slick' Nick Gabriel I'm speaking with?"

"The one and only," I said. "And unless I'm badly mistaken, I'm talking to the best third-baseman who ever covered the hot corner."

The call was from Mike Tucker, a classmate of mine through our twelve years in school. He was also a longtime baseball teammate, and a damn good one. Friend or not, if tradition held true, I suspected he was about to get in some kind of a dig against me. I wasn't wrong.

"More like I 'survived' the hot corner when you were pitching. I always felt my life was in danger during those games when you were on the mound. Did you ever strike out any batters, Nick? If you did, I don't remember it."

"That took too much effort, Mike. Think about it for a second. It takes a minimum of three pitches to strike out a hitter, as opposed

8

to one pitch that gets the guy to hit the ball to a vacuum cleaner third baseman like you. I was limiting the wear-and-tear on my arm."

"Once when we were on the way to a game against a veteran power-hitting team, I asked Coach if you were pitching. He said you were. So I asked him if I could wear the catcher's shin guards and chest protector. Coach thought I was joking. I wasn't. I was convinced my body would suffer grave damage that day."

That's a true story, and one Mike is never shy about sharing. We were sophomores and we got beat 8-1, which wasn't bad, considering we were a very young team that year. However, two years later, when we were seniors, we beat that team 2-1. I pitched a three-hitter and Mike provided the offense with a pair of solo home runs. That win qualifies as the pinnacle of our baseball success, which tells you all you need to know about our careers as athletes. Essentially, we were over the hill at eighteen.

I hadn't seen Mike for eleven years, not since we both attended our coach's funeral. This call, coming out of the blue, caused me to wonder if a former teacher or one of our classmates had passed away. Would I soon be on my way to another funeral? God, I hoped not. Friends who died, especially those in my age group, were stark reminders that we only have a finite number of days on this earth.

"What prompted this call, Mike, and where are you calling from?" I asked, fully expecting to be hit with grim news. But I was wrong.

"I'm actually in your neck of the woods," he said. "On Longboat Key, specifically. I was wondering if we could get together tonight for dinner. That'll give us the chance to reminisce about old times. Are you available?"

"Absolutely, that would be great. What brings you to Longboat Key?"

"My wife's sister and brother-in-law own a condo here. They are on vacation in Greece, so they asked if we'd like to stay in the condo while they are away. Naturally, we jumped at the chance. We'll be here for another five days."

"What kind of food do you and your wife prefer?"

"Anything works for us. We're not picky. Since you're familiar with this area, you pick the place. We'll be there."

I had only met Mike's wife once, briefly, and for the life of me I couldn't remember her name. I felt bad having to ask Mike what her name was, but luckily for me he bailed me out of an embarrassing situation.

"Karen does prefer Italian," Mike said. "Me, I'm your basic meat-and-potatoes guy. But it's your call, Nick. You lead, we follow."

"Karen's in luck. Caragiulo's is a great place to eat, certainly my favorite. I'm usually there at least once a week. It's on Palm Avenue in downtown Sarasota. You won't have any trouble finding it. What time did you have in mind?"

"What about seven? Will that work for you?"

"See you at seven," I said.

I was already heading home when we ended the call. The temperature had to be approaching one hundred degrees, if it hadn't already passed that mark. The heat was like a blanket of fire that smothered you. I was drenched in sweat. Walking home in this heat, even for only a mile or so, wasn't particularly pleasant. Some would even argue that it was dangerous. But I found it to be beneficial. It kept my weight in check, while the excessive perspiring helped eliminate some of the alcohol I'd consumed at the Old Salty Dog. It was like attending an AA meeting while strolling around in a giant steam room.

I was excited about seeing Mike again for the first time in years. He's a hometown guy, one of those lifelong friends who, even if you haven't seen them in ages, you wouldn't hesitate to trust them with your life. I'm sure strong bonds forged among childhood friends exist in every city, but in a small town like the one Mike and I grew up in, it's just different. Those older bonds rebe especially strong. Practically unbreakable, I would suggest.

Mike's father had been a coal miner, a job he wanted his son to have no part of. He didn't want Mike working a lifetime digging coal only to end up suffering from black lung disease. Or worse, dying in a mining accident. Mike went to college, earned a law degree, then opened a practice in our hometown. I heard from someone back home that Mike had been elected county judge executive. I had no idea what Karen did for a living, or if she even worked at all. I do know they had two kids, a boy and girl, but I didn't know their names or ages or where they lived. I'd probably learn all those details at dinner tonight.

~ * ~

Four hours later, after cooling down, showering, and getting dressed, I was sitting at a table in Caragiulo's waiting for Mike and Karen. I knew Mike wasn't a drinker, and I had no idea whether or not Karen was, so I ordered a soft drink. Better to go the safe route than risk offending someone.

Karen and Mike showed up at exactly seven. Mike scanned the restaurant until he saw me waving. A big smile creased his face. He tapped Karen's shoulder, pointed me out to her, then the two of them made their way to our table.

The years had treated Mike well. With the exception of a few extra pounds around his waistline and a slight touch of gray hair making an appearance above his sideburns, he looked like the guy I had grown up with. He looked fit enough to handle the hot corner like he had in the old days.

Seeing Karen failed to jog my memory of her, which was surprising, given that she was a real looker. I tend to remember gorgeous women, a category she easily fit into. This caused me to wonder if I had actually met her in the past. But I was certain I had. Most likely at Coach's funeral.

Karen was maybe five-eight with medium-length dark hair parted in the middle. She had a sleek figure...no excess weight anywhere on her... tan skin, full lips, and what I would call a Roman or Greek nose. She was dressed in white capris, a blue sleeveless top, and flat shoes. If she had on any make-up, it was subtle. In my opinion, she didn't require any help. Based solely on her physical appearance, I'd say Mike had struck gold when he hooked up with Karen.

I stood and exchanged an old-fashion handshake with Mike. No fist bump, no chest bump, no phony hug...just an old-school greeting. Very unhip in today's world, but, hey, current trends don't always translate to superior. I did the same with Karen once Mike introduced us. Formalities taken care of, we all sat down.

"You haven't changed at all, Nick," Mike said, settling into his chair. "I mean, not one bit. You look just like you did in high school. Do you work out a lot?"

"Less than three, four times a week, if I get motivated, which isn't a constant," I replied. "And I don't kill myself when I do."

"Must be the sun, sand and surf that are keeping you fit. Whatever you're doing, stay with it, because it's working."

When the waitress came to leave menus and take our drink orders, Mike asked what I was drinking. I quickly said a soft drink, and he said he'd have one as well. When it came time for Karen to order, she surprised me with her response.

"Would you please bring me a glass of your best Merlot?" she said, answering the question I had silently posed to myself. And the way she said it made clear that this wasn't the first glass of wine she'd ordered. I had a sneaking suspicion Karen was no stranger to the fruit of the vineyard.

One of my goals tonight was to make sure Mike and I didn't dominate the evening with a trip down memory lane. Given our shared past, such a journey was bound to happen sooner or later. I imagine Karen had already resigned herself to being a silent partner during dinner. But I had other ideas, so I made the decision early on to engage Karen in conversation. She deserved better than sitting silent as a statue while Mike and I rattled on like a pair of auctioneers.

"Where are you originally from, Karen?" I asked, feeling bad that I didn't know more about her.

Karen seemed startled...and pleased...that I had kicked off the night with a question directed at her.

"Batesville, Indiana," she said. "It's a small town located between Cincinnati and Indianapolis."

"Where did you meet this bum?" I said, nodding at Mike.

Karen waited until their drinks arrived before answering. After taking a sip of her Merlot, she said, "I was an undergrad at the University of Louisville when Mike was in law school there. A mutual friend introduced us at a party. I supposed you could say events proceeded from that point."

"What she neglected to say is that she was a freshman and I was in my last year of law school," Mike explained. "Meaning I'm several years her senior."

"Her senior, maybe, but I'm guessing you're not her superior," I said, casually getting in my dig at Mike.

"Oh, man, you got that right," Mike agreed.

"Do you work, Karen?" I asked.

She nodded, replied, "I teach high school English, and I also teach a literature class at the local community college. So I'm a busy lady."

"And what about your kids? You have a boy and girl, if I remember correctly."

"We do. Darren recently graduated from the University of Kentucky with an accounting degree. He has accepted a job with a firm in Lexington. Shelly, our daughter, is now a sophomore at Western Kentucky University. She's studying to be a teacher."

"Sounds like you guys did okay as parents," I said.

"It hasn't always been easy," Karen admitted. "Kids today don't comply with authority like we did. They challenge you on anything you say. Ask a kid to do this or that and they'll want to know why. And good luck getting a kid to put down or turn off the cell phone. That's like asking them to put out their eyes. Technology has its good points, but it should not become addictive. And for most people today, young and old, it most certainly has."

The waitress returned to take our orders. Mike and I had chicken parmigiana, Karen went with eggplant parmigiana. As the waitress started to walk away, Karen asked us if we'd like calamari as an appetizer. When Mike and I quickly responded with indifference, Karen told the waitress we would pass on the squid.

In my experience, the passage of time impacts memory in one of three ways: The memory being recounted is close to the truth, the memory is greatly exaggerated, normally to the benefit of those within the tale being articulated, or the memory is totally forgotten. Of course, there is a fourth category—the tale being told is absolutely false, which if that's the case, it's not really a memory, it's a piece of fiction.

After the food arrived, and as we ate, Mike took over and did most of the talking. He brought me up to date on former classmates...two of whom had passed away, and another, an ex-athlete who recently had serious back surgery and was confined to a wheelchair. Several of our old teachers had died, while another was a prisoner to Alzheimer's. Despite how I'm making it sound, not all news was grim or depressing. There was some upbeat news along the way, if beating cancer can be termed upbeat. According to Mike, three of our classmates had done just that. Their cancer was in remission. Personally, I find nothing relating to cancer, even if it is in remission, qualifies as good news. Remission generally means the cancer is just biding time until it shows up in another part of the body. Good news is when you don't have cancer.

My contribution to the conversation was generally limited to answering questions posed by Mike. And as I expected, most of those questions zeroed in on my decade working in the film industry. How did I get into the business, which of the movies I worked on was my favorite, and did I know certain actors? Things along those lines. My answers, though honest, probably disappointed Mike. People seemed hell-bent on hearing me say I am close pals with Jennifer Lawrence or Ryan Gosling. That's simply not the case.

One subject Mike didn't touch on was my failed marriage or my daughter. I kept waiting for him to bring it up, but he never did. Initially, I figured he was being respectful and didn't want to scrape the scab off of an old wound. But the more I thought about it, I began to wonder if Mike was even aware that I had been married and had a daughter. That all happened when I was in Los Angeles...the marriage, divorce, the birth of my daughter. The marriage ended twelve years ago, and while we were still together, my wife and I had never once visited my hometown. So, there was a good chance Mike had no clue about any of that.

As the evening wore on, I kept waiting for Karen to join the conversation but she never did. As a literature teacher, it would have only been natural for her to bring up William Blake at some point, maybe to discuss his poetry or some of his allied writings. Her failure to do so got me thinking that perhaps I was giving myself too much credit, that maybe she wasn't aware that I had written *Divine Rebel*. I mean, let's be real here. Broadway plays aren't a standard topic of conversation in Kentucky. But at no point during the night was Blake's name mentioned once.

Instead, as Mike droned on, or when I responded to one of his questions, Karen remained silent, content to finish off her meal and a third glass of Merlot without uttering a word. As we talked, the expression on her face ranged from mildly interested to no interest at all. But all things considered, she was certainly a good sport.

I chalked up her indifference more to being respectful and less to boredom, although that may have been a misguided judgment on my part. I certainly could have been misreading her. Maybe she was thinking, "Okay, guys, how about we bring this trip down memory lane to a halt? I'm tired of sitting here like a mannequin, a captive audience to your blast from the past." But like a dutiful, loving wife, and the obvious grownup at the table, she kindly allowed the two kids to ramble on for nearly three hours.

Then, just as the waitress cleared away our plates, and I handed her my credit card, Karen broke her silence with a statement that changed everything.

"Tell Nick about the murder," she said to Mike.

Three

"Murder? What murder?" I asked.

Mike looked around sheepishly, like he was fearful of getting into trouble. Like a kid who was someplace he shouldn't be and was worried about being caught. "Maybe we should continue this talk somewhere else," he said. "We've been here almost three hours already. I feel guilty sitting here, taking up space, while we're no longer eating."

I caught our waitress' attention and signaled for her to come over. When she did, I ordered two Diet Cokes and another glass of Merlot. The waitress nodded, smiled, and left to get our drinks.

"There, you happy now, Mike?" I said. "We are once again on the side of the angels. We're paying customers, which means we can stay here until they run us out."

"Yes, I do feel better," Mike said seriously.

"So do I," Karen chimed in, "although after four glasses of wine I may have to be carried to the car."

After the waitress delivered our drinks, I handed her a twenty-dollar bill and told her to keep the change. I'd already settled up for our dinner, which included a generous tip. She smiled, thanked me, and hustled away.

"Okay, Mike, back to the murder," I prompted. "Tell me all about it."

"Well, it happened about two months ago," Mike said, after taking a drink of Diet Coke. "Do you remember Steve Brown?"

"Sure I do. He works for the gas company. Or at least, he used to. He's a good guy. Are you telling me he was murdered?"

"No, no, it wasn't Steve. His eighteen-year-old grandson, Todd, committed the murder. He beat up the victim pretty bad, then stabbed him multiple times with a knife. From all accounts, it was a gruesome and horrific scene. The police zeroed in on Todd from the very start—I don't know how or why—but when he was arrested, he was wearing the victim's ring. To get that ring, Todd had to sever the guy's finger. Like I said...gruesome."

"Who was the victim?"

"Luke Felton."

"I know Luke. He's a cop in town, isn't he?"

"Not for years now. He left the police force, gosh, maybe fifteen years ago. Or it could be he didn't leave, he retired. I don't know. Recently, he'd been working as a free-lance photographer. He would shoot ballgames, band contests, school events, beauty pageants, automobile accidents, fires...things like that. I think he had a deal with the local newspaper. He'd photograph various things and they would pay him for his work."

"Where did the murder take place?" I asked.

"In an abandoned stripper pit out in the county. Luke's body was on the ground next to his car. A couple of teens out parking discovered the body."

"Luke is several years older than we are. He has to be in his sixties."

"Sixty-eight at the time of his death," Mike stated.

"Which begs the question: Why would an eighteen-year-old kid be hanging out with a sixty-eight-year-old guy? Or vice versa, for that matter."

"Can't say for sure, but my guess is drugs were involved."

"Drugs? Really?"

Karen said, "Drugs have become a huge problem in our town, Nick. In the entire county, if you want the truth. Pot used to be the hot-ticket item, but not so much now that you can buy it legally. Now we're dealing with truly nasty stuff... meth, cocaine, oxycodone... very addictive drugs that can kill you if you aren't careful. Drugs have become a serious epidemic in our part of the world."

"Damn, I hate to hear that," I said.

"It's not the same town you and Mike grew up in," Karen said. "Or even since Mike and I got married and moved there. Much has changed, and not for the better."

"And it's not unique to our hometown, either," Mike added. "Every community in the county has been impacted in a negative way. Since the coal mines shut down, the economy has gone to hell. Unemployment is sky high, and people's hopes are more shattered than a broken egg. The Great American Dream is a distant memory for most of the folks back home."

Mike looked away before continuing.

"The mines' closing was a huge blow, no denying that. But in my opinion that wasn't what sounded the death knell for our area. No, it was school consolidation that landed the killing blow. When we were growing up, there were seven high schools in our county, all located within ten miles of each other. Remember how fierce the competition was among those schools? Losing a basketball game, a baseball game, or a band contest to one of those rivals was like losing our country to the communists. Community pride was always at stake. People celebrated each victory and suffered with each loss. Schools and churches are the beating heart of most communities, large and small. Take away those schools and you forever wound the soul of that community. The pointy heads and scholars and educators call it progress, but you have to ask yourself, what price progress? Is what they've done truly for the good? Or is it yet another failed experiment that results in destruction for those on the far end of someone else's glorified dream? Who can say, right? First, we consolidated into two schools, now there's only one. And what's left for those communities who saw their schools shut down and boarded up? Skyrocketing unemployment and a crushed spirit, that's what."

Mike's story was interesting and depressing, but my thoughts were still locked in on the murder. I wanted to hear more about that. For whatever reason, perhaps because I knew and admired and respected Steve Brown, I was intrigued. As I listened, a certain plan was already beginning to formulate in my mind, a plan Karen had apparently thought of before I did.

"You should come back home, Nick, and write about the murder," Karen said. "There probably won't be enough for a book, but you might round up enough interesting material to write a nice magazine article. Maybe for *Vanity Fair* or *Rolling Stone*. You know, one of the more popular publications."

Magazine article? No way. I'm thinking much bigger than that, something more along the lines of *In Cold Blood*, Capote's masterpiece. Too grandiose a dream? Maybe. But how would I know unless I gave it a shot?

Based on the little time I'd spent with her; it was obvious Karen was extremely intelligent. Much more so than me, for sure. And I'm not a guy who is shy about picking the brain of individuals with more on the ball than I have. So I asked Karen a logical question. It was my way of testing to see if she and I were on the same page. As it turns out, we were close.

"What would be your angle if you were writing the book?" I inquired.

She was silent for a few moments, then said, "Well, it wouldn't be the murder itself. Now don't get me wrong, you certainly have to write about the murder. That's a given. But it would almost be an ancillary issue. The heart of the story would be the Brown family. Steve and Mary Sue Brown are terrific people. We all agree on that. His son and daughter-in-law are loving, devoted parents. They have three kids, two boys and a girl. Todd graduated from high school last year. He had the brains to be an excellent student, but he was content to simply scrape by. His sister, who will be a junior next year, is a brilliant student... major colleges are already offering her academic scholarships. She is arguably the best student I've ever taught. The third child is twelve or thirteen, and I've heard he is also a terrific student. So, you have three kids living under one roof, with outstanding parents and terrific grandparents, each child given the same love, attention and support, and, yet, two of those kids turn out to be model citizens, and one becomes a murderer. How does that happen? What causes one child to go so wrong? What contributing factors sent him down that errant path? Who do you blame when it does happen? Do you blame anyone, or was it simply a matter of fate? Ask those questions and try to find some answers. That's the approach I would take if I were writing the book."

Karen and I were thinking along similar lines, and I agree that the angle she was pitching was a solid one. But our thoughts didn't perfectly mesh. Somewhere in the back of my lizard brain, I kept coming back to the murder. For me, that was the heart of the story. Karen's angle concerning the family dynamics was the ancillary part.

"When is Todd's trial scheduled?" I asked Mike.

"There won't be a trial. Todd confessed."

"Is he in prison?"

"Yeah, he's incarcerated in the Green River Correctional Complex."

That's the new prison that opened in our county in nineteen ninety-four.

"What was his sentence?"

"Life with no chance for parole."

"Will he remain there?" I wanted to know.

"I'm not sure. All I can tell you is that's where he's located at the present time." Mike finished off his Diet Coke and stood. He was ready to go. "Are you seriously thinking about coming home and doing research for a book? If you do, you're welcome to stay with us."

"I don't know. A lot would have to happen before I did, beginning with finding a publisher willing to back the project. I won't write a book on spec."

"I just assumed you had a publisher."

"Nope."

"Do you have any publishing connections you can approach?" Mike said.

"Actually, I do," I said, thinking about Jake Kaplan. "A friend of mine is an editor at Delacorte Press. He'll be the first person I contact."

"I think it would make one helluva book," Karen said, slightly slurring her words. She stood, shakily, and hooked her arm into mine for balance. Based on her unsteadiness, it was obvious that her fourth glass of wine had been one too many. "God, I can't recall the last time I was this buzzed. Forgive me, Nick, I don't normally drink this much."

We walked to the front door and stepped outside. Almost ten at night and the temperature hadn't dropped more than a few degrees. It was still a scorcher. Mike and I teamed up to make sure Karen got to their car without falling. Once we arrived at the car, Karen leaned up and gave me a kiss on the cheek. After we got her situated and buckled up, Mike and I shook hands, and then he got in behind the wheel, started the motor, and drove off for Longboat Key.

I headed to my car, thoughts of a murder running wild in my head.

~ * ~

I drove straight home, went inside, fixed a scotch and soda, picked up my phone, and placed a call to Jake Kaplan in Manhattan. Jake answered, and judging from the background noise, I suspected a party was underway.

"Wait a second, Nick, and let me step into the bedroom so I can hear you." A few moments later, noise silenced, Jake said, "What's on your mind? Nothing bad happening, is there?"

"Everything is great," I said. "If you have time, I'd like to run something by you. Shouldn't take too long."

"I'm all ears. Go for it."

For the next ten minutes, I pitched the book idea to Jake, who listened without interrupting me once. I laid it all out for him, the murder, drugs, the area's socio-economic woes, the family dynamics. It was a quick, succinct briefing, but I omitted nothing. I even tossed in the Capote book as a template for what I had in mind. Finished, I waited for Jake's response.

"You truly believe there's enough there for a book?" Jake said.

"Yes."

Jake was silent for a long while. Long enough that I began to wonder if he'd passed out or dozed off. But that wasn't the case.

"Obviously, Nick, I have to get approval from upstairs before I can give you the green light," Jake said, breaking the silence. "Given your background, I'm fairly confident I can get the okay to move forward. However, I'm not sure how much of an advance I can get for you."

"Don't worry about an advance," I said. "Once I'm there, I have friends I can stay with. And should I choose to stay in a local motel, it shouldn't be all that expensive. There aren't many five-star joints in that area. We'll worry about money later. If you do get the deal approved, draw up a standard contract and send it to me. I'll agree to whatever terms Delacorte Press sets."

"Do me a favor, Nick. Just to be on the safe side, work up a proposal and shoot it my way. I'll go ahead and take your idea upstairs, but in case I get some pushback, having a proposal in my corner could be beneficial. Can you do that for me?"

"Not a problem, Jake. I'll get you one within the next couple of days. And hey, thanks for your help, no matter how things work out."

For the next three hours I worked on writing up the proposal Jake requested. I finished it at a little past two, and sent it as an attachment via email. It wasn't a first-class proposal, certainly not one I would submit to most publishers, but I felt it was good enough in this instance. If they requested something more detailed and fine-tuned, I'd get it to them. Anyway, like Jake said, he probably wouldn't need a proposal to get the okay to push forward.

He didn't need it. Jake woke me at ten the next morning to inform me that I was good to go, and that an official contract would be emailed to me before close of business. He asked me to sign it electronically, but to also print out a hard copy, sign it, and get it to him via snail mail.

At a little past noon, my phone buzzed. The call was from Mike. He said Karen was spending a couple of hours shopping on St. Armands Circle, and he, having no desire to accompany her, wanted to know if

I was game for another visit. I said sure, gave him the address to my condo, and told him I'd be there, waiting. He showed up forty minutes later.

"Pal, I hate to be a nuisance, but shopping with Karen is not high on my list of things I want to do. It's a painful experience, if you want the truth," Mike said. "Hope I'm not putting you out by showing up."

"No, not at all. It's nice hanging out with you," I said. "You up for a walk on the beach?"

"You kidding? Let's go."

~ * ~

Minutes later we were on the Siesta Key beach, the Gulf waters blue and calm and glistening in the sun, a soft warm breeze kissing our faces. Mike bent down, scooped up a handful of sand, and commented on how fine and powdery it was before letting it flutter away in the breeze.

"Here's the neat thing about this sand," I said. "It's ninety-nine percent quartz. That keeps it cool regardless of the temperature. Unlike most beaches, when the sun is frying everything in sight, you'll never have to do the hot-sand shuffle here. Footwear is not necessary when walking on this sand."

We walked for maybe a half-hour before returning to the cool of the condo. I pulled a couple of Diet Pepsis from the refrigerator and handed one to Mike. Then we moved into the den and sat, Mike on the sofa, me in a chair, just two old friends comfortable in each other's company.

"Are you seriously contemplating writing a book about Luke Felton's murder?" Mike asked.

"Well, I'm definitely going back home to do some research," I said. "I've been given the green light by a publisher to proceed with the book. Whether or not I can pull it off will depend on how much information I come up with."

"Karen is convinced that won't be a problem. That's all she talked about when we got to the condo last night. She's convinced there's plenty enough for you to write a book."

"I won't know until I look into it."

23

"When are you planning on coming home?"

"If I get a few things squared away here, probably within the next week," I said.

Mike took a sip of Diet Pepsi, then said, "How well did you know Luke Felton?"

"Ah, you know, he always seemed to be around. I remember seeing him quite often in the pool room. And he came to some of our baseball games. He was just one of those older guys I knew and spoke to. Why are you asking about him?"

"Luke was divorced and had two grown kids when he was murdered. And he was an ex-cop, you know, supposedly a tough guy. But rumors were floating around that he was gay, which has caused some people to wonder if that figured into what happened to him. I don't know if the gay thing is true or not, but it is intriguing."

"Is Todd Brown gay?"

"Karen says he definitely is not, and she had him in class, so she should know. In fact, she claims he was quite the ladies' man."

"The gay angle is something I'll have to look into," I said.

Mike stayed around for another hour before heading back to hook up with Karen on St. Armands Circle. Before he left, our conversation eventually drifted away from the murder and back onto more familiar turf. We talked about a couple of big baseball victories we were particularly proud of, or a certain female classmate we both had the hots for who rejected both of us in a most convincing manner. What hurt back then, we could laugh about now. Time might not heal all wounds, but it does heal some.

After Mike had gone, I sat at the computer and thought about areas I needed to explore once I did return home. I didn't have much to go on, but what little I did have was more than enough to get my writer's blood cooking. However, before I could write a single word, my plan was interrupted by a phone call.

And this one not only changed my immediate plans, it also broke my heart.

Four

The call was from Patrick Mackenzie, who proudly announced that he was an attorney with some pretentious-sounding four-partner law firm located in Carmel, California. Since Patrick's name wasn't among the four he mentioned, I suspected he was a second- or third-tier guy situated no higher than mid-level on the firm's depth chart. The fact that he was calling to deliver this particular message solidified my belief.

"Are you Nicholas Ray Gabriel?" Patrick Mackenzie asked, his voice full of self-importance.

I had no idea why an attorney from California would be calling me, but having been a writer in the film business, my first thought was that someone was hitting me with a lawsuit.

"I'm Nick Gabriel," I finally said. "What's this call about?"

"Were you formerly married to Katherine Marie Sparks Gabriel?"

"Yes, Kate and I were married for ten years. Why are you asking about our marriage? That's ancient history."

"Mr. Gabriel, I'm sorry to inform you that Katherine is deceased. She passed away two nights ago."

There are times in life when you hear something loud and clear but you don't remember hearing it. It's like a stream of water that runs just below the surface. You know it makes a sound, yet it doesn't quite register with you. This was one of those times.

Kate? Dead? How could that possibly be? She was a year younger than me, a true health nut who took care of her body. She ate right and exercised regularly. Never smoked, drank alcohol, or did drugs. And now she's dead? Why? How? An accident, a long illness? Surely, if illness were the case, even though we hadn't spoken in years, someone would have informed me before now. Wouldn't that be the decent thing to do?

"What was the cause of her death?" I said.

"She took her own life."

I wasn't prepared for that answer. It stunned me. Suicide? Hard to believe.

"How?"

"She swallowed an entire bottle of prescription sleeping pills, then washed them down with a bottle of whiskey. She went to sleep and never woke up. Karen had been deceased for several hours before she was found."

My concerns immediately shifted to my daughter, whom I had not seen since the divorce. "And Angel? How is she doing?" I inquired.

"Angel? I'm not sure who you're referring to," Mackenzie said.

"Samantha. My daughter."

"Oh, yes, Samantha. Well, as you might expect, she is devastated by what happened. Finding your mother dead has to be among the worst things that could possibly happen to a person. Just an absolute shock, a true nightmare. I have to believe it's especially heartbreaking for a nineteen-year-old woman."

Call me selfish, but heartbreaking was having a nineteen-year-old daughter you haven't seen since she was seven. Heartbreaking and unforgivable.

Patrick Mackenzie said, "The reason for this call, Mr. Gabriel, is to let you know that in her will your ex-wife bequeathed several items to you. I have no idea what those items are, but if you will give me your address I'll box them up and ship them to you."

"Has a service been scheduled?" I said.

"At her request, your ex-wife was cremated, but yes, there will be a memorial service in two days."

"Well, then, I have a better suggestion. You give me the time of the service and the address where it will be held and I'll be there. That will save you the trouble of shipping the box to me."

Mackenzie paused, then said, "Your daughter has requested that you not attend the service."

I doubt it's possible for words to be more hurtful than those I had just heard. They might as well have been a dagger being plunged deep into my heart. Rejected by my own daughter? I could only imagine how much she despised me.

"You tell Angel...Samantha...that I'm going to be there. Like it or not, she'll just have to deal with it."

"Well, Mr. Gabriel, I'm not sure—"

"Now, please give me the time and address for Kate's service."

When the call ended, I immediately phoned the travel agent I'd dealt with in the past and booked a non-stop flight from Tampa International to San Francisco. The airline was United, and the flight departed early the next morning. That meant I had to leave Siesta Key before daylight in order to catch the seven-hour flight to San Francisco. Once there I would rent a car and make the two-and-a-half-hour drive to Carmel.

~ * ~

Travel arrangements taken care of, I had time to let what happened settle in. I wasn't sure if I was more depressed by Kate's death, or by my daughter's demand that I stay away from the memorial service. It was a damn close call, and I couldn't begin to tell you for sure which one got my vote.

Logic told me Kate had done a number on me with Angel. Why else would she hate me so much? But somehow that didn't ring true. Kate was not someone who had hate in her heart, not for me, not for anyone. She was a kind, loving woman. Yes, our divorce was painful, but there was no animosity between us. It went about as well as any divorce can, and certainly better than most I'm familiar with. She received a generous financial settlement, and although I was legally bound to pay child support until Angel was eighteen, I have continued doing so until this very moment. In fact, I mailed her a check two weeks ago.

So even though I haven't seen or spoken to Angel in twelve years, I never failed her financially. And it's not like I haven't tried to contact her. I have. I made many attempts over the years to reach out to her. But she never answered my calls, nor did she respond to the hundreds of messages I left. She simply erased me from her life.

Angel recently finished her second year at Southern Cal and was living with Kate in Los Angeles. Kate had remained in our old house in Brentwood, the one we purchased when I got my first big check from a movie studio. But she was originally from Carmel, that scenic beach city on the Monterey Peninsula where the actor Clint Eastwood had been elected mayor in nineteen eighty-six. Kate's father was a wealthy big-shot in the community, and her older brother, Jason, was currently a successful businessman. I had to wonder how Jason and his old man would respond when they saw me. We'd had no problems before the divorce. In fact, we'd gotten along well. However, since then I've probably been declared the enemy.

The pre-dawn drive from Siesta Key to Tampa was light on traffic, and the flight to San Francisco was quiet and uneventful. These days, getting in and out of the airport has become the worrisome aspect of air travel. But we landed without incident, for which I'm always thankful. I rented a car, loaded my luggage, got in, and quickly found my way to U.S. 101, the Pacific Coast Highway. In no time I was on my way heading south, leaving rain behind in favor of bright sunshine.

I had booked a room at the Wayside Inn, a cottage-style hotel on Seventh Avenue and Mission Street, approximately four-tenths of a mile from the ocean. I chose the place not because it was near the beach, but rather because it was only four blocks from the Church of the Wayfarer located on Lincoln Street and Seventh Avenue. It was a

Methodist Church. I don't recall Kate being a Methodist, so it had to be her family who made the call to hold the service there.

~ * ~

Because of the time zone change, my flight to the West Coast had given me three extra hours to kill. Did this also mean I was three hours younger in Carmel than I would be if I were still in Florida? Not a question that really matters, is it? Three hours either way...what difference would that make over the long haul?

To fend off on-rushing fatigue resulting from my cross-country flight, I decided to take a stroll around downtown Carmel, a city I'd never visited. Carmel is regularly ranked among the best places to live in the United States, though not many can afford to do so. It is also a city descended upon by thousands of visitors every year.

Seeing the downtown area was but one reason for my walk. My main goal was to get something to eat. I was starving. A bagel and a glass of orange juice were all I had before leaving my condo this morning. That seemed like a hundred years ago at this point.

Not long after leaving the inn, I stumbled on the perfect place to satisfy my hunger... Brophy's Tavern, an Irish pub located in a two-story house on the corner of Fourth Avenue and San Carlos Street. Pub food sounded good, and that, along with some booze, was exactly what I was craving.

There was a decent-size crowd inside, primarily consisting of younger, hip professional types seated at various booths, enjoying an after-work drink. None of them paid me any attention as I made my way to the bar. I ordered a scotch and soda and asked to see a menu. After briefly looking it over, I decided on a Reuben calzone, fries, and a Caesar salad. While waiting for my food, I ordered a second drink and looked around the bar, which was impressive in every way. It was easy to understand why this place was so popular.

The food came, I wolfed it down faster than was healthy, and enjoyed every bite. Finished, I ordered a third scotch and soda, figuring my walk back to the Wayside Inn would shake off any buzz I might be experiencing. And if I did get stopped, I could tell the officer that I had met Carmel's former mayor, which happens to be true. Maybe having met Clint Eastwood (very briefly, I must say) would serve as my get-out-of-jail-free card.

After finishing my drink, I paid my tab and got up to leave. At the same time a woman rose from one of the booths and began making her way in my direction. She had blonde hair, blue eyes and a deep tan. She wore a white Tee-shirt, cut-off jeans and sandals. The classic California look. I assumed she was coming to the bar to order another round of drinks for herself and her pals at the booth. I was wrong. She walked straight up to me, a big smile on her face.

"'Great things are done when men and mountains meet. This is not done by jostling in the street'," she said, reciting a famous William Blake quote.

"A Blake fan, I take it," I said.

"Well, I wasn't until I saw *Divine Rebel*. Which I thought was great, by the way."

I didn't know which was more surprising...her having seen the play or recognizing me.

"When did you see the play?" I asked.

"On a visit to New York City. I got lucky. It was Anthony Hopkins's last performance before leaving the show. He was beyond great."

"It's good to know you enjoyed the play."

"*Divine Rebel* is a wonderful title. But I'm curious. Why call Blake a divine rebel?"

"Because that's how I view him. Many people mistakenly identify Blake as a mystic, which is only partly true, at best. I'd say it's more accurate to call him a visionary or a prophet. He was certainly a genuine revolutionary artist. Keep in mind that most of his ideas were not embraced by the majority of people living at the time. Blake was always an outsider. In fact, some people considered him to be mad."

"I know you're about to leave," she said, "but would you do me a favor before you do?"

"Sure, if I can."

"Give me your favorite Blake quote."

"That's a tough call. There is no shortage to choose from."

"Come on, Mr. Gabriel. Just give me one."

"How about, 'every harlot was a virgin once'?"

"Why am I not surprised that you would pick that one?" She smiled, grinned, and touched my arm. "It was a pleasure meeting you, Mr. Gabriel."

"Likewise," I said, as she made her way back to her friends.

I arrived at the Wayside Inn just as the sun was sinking into the Pacific Ocean. It was the same sun I saw in the sky above Siesta Key, but it didn't look the same. Somehow, it looked bigger, brighter, more majestic. Maybe a little closer to the one Adam had seen on that first day. Lucky Adam.

I went back to my room, undressed, lay on the bed, and turned on the TV, a plan that only lasted a few minutes before my thoughts drifted in another direction. I turned the TV off and allowed those thoughts to take shape.

I dreaded tomorrow, knowing it would be an awkward, difficult day. My own daughter apparently hated me, and I had no way of predicting how Kate's family would react upon seeing me. Would I be welcomed, or would one of them throw a punch at me? I had no way of knowing what might happen.

However, those thoughts were quickly pushed to the background by the murder in my hometown. In particular, one aspect of the crime continued to baffle me... why would a man Luke Felton's age be hanging around with a young kid like Todd Brown? Was it drugs, as both Karen and Mike Tucker seemed to believe? Or was there another reason, maybe something sexual in nature? If what Mike said was true, that Luke was gay, that did give weight to the sexual angle. I knew Luke, not well, but I'd been in his presence multiple times, and he never gave off a gay vibe. But did that really mean anything? Maybe he was just very adroit at hiding it. As a once-married man and the father of two, maybe he felt compelled to keep it a secret. I suppose the answer was destined to remain unknown until I began investigating the case.

Those were my last thoughts before I drifted off to a deep sleep.

~ * ~

At nine-fifteen the next morning, I was sitting alone in the Church of the Wayfarer chapel. The interior was beautiful, quiet and holy, a perfect place to pray or contemplate or seek inner-peace. While I'm certainly no expert on houses of worship, I'd be hard-pressed to imagine a better site than this chapel.

Kate's gold urn was sitting on a table at the front of the altar. It was flanked by two 8x10 photos, one of Kate from several years ago, and a second that showed Kate standing next to Angel that had been taken several moments after Angel's high school graduation ceremony. Studying that photo for quite a while, I could only marvel at the beautiful woman my daughter had become.

Only then did the full weight of disappointment and selfishness and bad decisions come crashing down on me. Never had I felt this sadness, this acknowledgment of lost opportunities like I did at this moment. How had it to come to this? How had I been so misguided?

"Why are you here?" a female voice said.

I had been so absorbed in my own thoughts that I had failed to hear her enter the church. Although I had not spoken to my daughter in a dozen years, I instantly recognized her voice. I had no doubt who asked the question. Shifting in my seat, I turned and saw her walking down the aisle toward me. The photo next to the urn, taken two years ago, failed to do her justice. She was even more beautiful now than she was then.

Standing, I said, "Angel, I can't get over—"

"Don't call me Angel," she snapped. "I'm not a child anymore."

"You've always been Angel to me, from the moment I first laid eyes on you. When the nurse handed you to me and said I now had my own Angel Gabriel."

"And exactly when was that? Let's see. Oh, yeah, two full days after I was born. And where were you when Mom was giving birth? Shacked up in some motel with one of your lady friends, right?"

I had no rebuttal to that charge. Much as I hate to admit it, she was right. Sometimes there is no hiding from the truth.

"That was a long time ago, Angel," I said, weakly.

"I'm Samantha now, remember? But back to my original question: Why are you here?"

"Because I loved your mom, and I love you. And we're family. I should be here."

"Obviously, your notion of family is much different than mine."

"Look, I'm the first to admit that I messed up. Nobody has to tell me that. But I didn't walk away unscathed from that situation. Trust me, I paid a big price for what I did. You and your mom aren't the only ones who suffered. Angel, it's time to move on. All I want is for you to cut me some slack, maybe forgive me for the mistake I made?"

"Dream on, Dad. We both know it wasn't just one mistake. There were plenty of women on your date card."

"You're making it sound like I had a different woman every night, which is simply not true. I agree that one was too many. But you're wrong to think I was some kind of Casanova. I wasn't."

She sat down, then said, "Sorry, but I'm not like Mom. We're cut from different cloth. Want to hear something truly bizarre? She never stopped loving you. Never. I constantly pleaded with her to go out, find a good man, get married again, and live a happy life. She wouldn't even consider it. Mom was always emotionally chained to you, which I never could understand. She lived with the hope that you would come back into her life. If she were here right now, she would forgive you. Sorry, but I cannot."

I sat facing her. "Would you at least try?"

"No."

"Why?"

"Because I blame you for her death. When she finally gave up hope that you were ever coming back, that was the moment she surrendered. She swallowed the pills, drank the booze, and checked herself out. No more longing for you, no more disappointment, no more pain and misery. She traded her personal agony for eternal sleep."

"Sorry, Angel, but I refuse to accept the blame for Kate's death. I'll admit to causing her tremendous pain and agony and disappointment. I bear the brunt of those charges. But suicide? No, that's on her."

"Spin it any way that makes it easier for you to live with yourself. I know the truth. Hell, I *lived* the truth all those years. So I'm not buying into your lame bullshit."

"Camus said the act of suicide amounted to a confession, that the person who chooses suicide is confessing that life is no longer worth living. When Kate chose to take those pills and drink the whiskey, she was giving her confession. I think she proved Camus's theory has merit."

"I wonder if Camus would say the same thing if his mother had killed herself. Probably not, would be my guess."

"Angel, I'm sorry about what happened to your mother," I said. "And I'm doubly sorry you were the one who found her body. I can't begin to imagine how difficult that must have been for you."

"I need to go," she said, standing. "I should be with my family."

Before she walked away, I said, "Do you need extra money for school? USC isn't cheap. I can help, if you'll let me."

"Thanks, for offering, but no thanks. Grants and scholarships cover most of the bills. When they come up short, Uncle Jason and Granddad provide additional assistance. My financial situation is taken care of."

"Well, if you do need money, or anything else, I'm only a phone call away. I'll help in any way I can. Deal?"

To my pleasant surprise, she had no negative comeback. Nothing wiseass or hurtful. I took that as a positive sign, a slight ray of hope.

"I do love you and miss you, Angel," I said. "Never forget that. My greatest hope is that you will somehow find it in your heart to forgive me. To let me be part of your life."

She walked away without responding. But I'm positive I saw tears in her eyes.

I sat alone in a back row during Kate's service, filled with feelings of sadness and regret. The service went well. It was respectful and dignified. Several speakers, including Angel, recounted stories involving Kate, and two songs were sung by a young woman identified as a classmate of Angel's at USC. She had an excellent voice and was a very talented pianist.

When the service concluded, I left without speaking to anyone. I wanted to say goodbye to Angel, but I didn't think the timing was right. I didn't want to risk being confronted by Kate's family. I had no idea how they might respond if they saw me. This was neither the time nor place for an incident of any type, verbal or physical.

~ * ~

My original plan had been to fly back to Florida in the morning. However, by the time I got back to the hotel I decided to leave sooner, provided I could catch an earlier flight. Back in my room I phoned the San Francisco airport. I got lucky. A flight to Tampa was scheduled to depart in four hours, which allowed me (barely) enough time to get to the airport if I hustled. I checked out of the Wayside Inn, got in my rental, and began the drive north.

On the ride to the airport, my thoughts again shifted to the murder that had occurred in my hometown. For both personal and professional reasons, I was eager to begin looking into what had transpired on that deadly night. To get the ball rolling meant speeding things up once I got back to Siesta Key. I decided to spend a day or two catching up on my rest, then once I felt fully rejuvenated, I would pack some clothes, grab my laptop and a tape recorder, and make the long drive to my hometown.

Only then could I begin to answer the many questions I had about that deadly encounter between Luke Felton and Todd Brown.

Five

My hometown, Central City, is located in Muhlenberg County in the western part of Kentucky. The entire county's population is approximately thirty-one thousand. When I was growing up there, the racial makeup consisted entirely of whites and blacks. There were no Asian-Americans or Hispanics. I doubt there are any Asian-Americans living there today, although that's probably not true concerning Mexicans.

If you're traveling on the Western Kentucky Parkway, you'll see an exit sign for Central City. As you approach the city limits there's a sign that says the population is fifty-five hundred, which is exactly what it was forty years ago when I was a kid. This leads me to conclude that in my hometown every death has been offset by a birth, thus accounting for the never-changing number of folks living there.

There is a chance you may have heard of Muhlenberg County, thanks to the late singer-songwriter John Prine, who mentioned the county in his early song "Paradise", his requiem for the Muhlenberg County of his youth before it had been ravaged by the Peabody Coal

Company. The song is a stark and vivid reminder of just how much damage strip mining had done to the county.

Prine was from Chicago, but his parents were originally from Muhlenberg County, where, as a child, he often visited during the summer months. He is but one of four musicians who belong on what I always enthusiastically refer to as the mythical "Muhlenberg County Musical Mount Rushmore." And Prine, popular and highly regarded as he is, is by no means the most-famous member of this quartet.

That distinction belongs to Don and Phil, the Everly Brothers, masters of exquisite harmonies and lovely melodies. Although both brothers are warmly embraced as natives by the locals, for the sake of accuracy it must be acknowledged that only Don was born in Muhlenberg County. By the time Phil came along, their parents, Ike and Margaret, had relocated to Chicago. In the history of pop music, it is impossible to overstate the world-wide popularity of the Everly Brothers, or their strong influence on subsequent groups like The Beatles, Crosby, Stills and Nash, and Simon and Garfunkel. The Everly Brothers' legacy is unlikely to ever completely fade away.

The first and oldest member of this fabled quartet was Merle Travis, an influential guitar player who also wrote many songs, including "Sixteen Tons," which became a number one hit for Tennessee Ernie Ford in the mid-fifties. Travis began his life in the tiny community of Ebenezer.

Muhlenberg County also contributed, albeit on a smaller scale, to Hollywood, courtesy of two marvelous character actors. The most-famous was Warren Oates, who was born in the rural community of Depoy. Oates, with his craggy face, shifty eyes, and scratchy voice was in dozens of movies, including *The Wild Bunch*, *In the Heat of the Night*, and *Stripes*. James Best, famous as Rosco P. Coltrane on TV's *Dukes of Hazzard*, hailed from Powderly. Although Best was lesser known than Oates, he actually had the longer-lasting career.

Those six Muhlenberg County natives left large footprints in the entertainment world. Not bad for a small Kentucky county.

When Merle Travis wrote songs like "Sixteen Tons" and "Dark as a Dungeon," he was writing about a subject he was very familiar with...

coal mining. Muhlenberg County was long recognized for producing coal, first with underground mines, and then with strip mining, a process that brought with it. Dual outcomes...devastation of the county's landscape, and tremendous prosperity for the communities and the people living in them. By the mid-sixties, when strip mining was at its zenith, Muhlenberg County was one of the top coal-producing regions in the world.

However, it was during my years growing up there that the tectonic plates supporting economic welfare had begun to shift. Things started to change, and not for the better. Joyous prosperity was replaced by a sense of dread, of impending doom. This monumental change came when a ruling by the Environmental Protection Agency judged the area's vast coal reserves to contain high levels of sulfur, thus rendering it environmentally unsuitable for use. Suddenly, coal, the engine that drove the local economy, was as lifeless as a dead baby still in the womb.

Naturally, given the circumstances, the EPA, or "APE," as it was derisively described by the local newspaper, became the villain in what was happening. Locals saw this as simply one more example of Big Government moving in to hand down a draconian dictate that impacted in a negative way those most seriously affected by decisions made by eggheads comfortably ensconced in cushy offices many hundreds of miles away. The end result of that ruling was the death of mining in Muhlenberg County. Almost overnight, miners traded a regular paycheck for a meager monthly unemployment check with a relatively short shelf-life. Those benefits ended after a certain length of time, replaced by welfare checks and food stamps intended to serve as a final lifeline, neither of which provided a family with its real needs... pride and dignity.

A handful of miners, the lucky ones, found work in mines located in bordering states. This was a double-edged sword for the men: it did provide a paycheck, but it also required the miner to either find a temporary place to live during the week, or to make the daily drive to and from the worksite, both of which were a hardship for the miner and for his family. Some ex-miners found jobs locally that paid nowhere close to what they had previously earned digging coal, while the rest, the majority, ended up unemployed, barely scraping by on those monthly subsistence checks.

In Muhlenberg County, David did battle with Goliath, and Goliath was victorious.

~ * ~

Pulling off the Western Kentucky Parkway, I was back in the very battleground where Goliath crushed David, thus relegating David to the dustbin...or coalbin, if you prefer...of history.

Turning left onto U.S. 431, I headed toward my hometown, which was less than two miles away. Several motels were to my left, including a Best Western, where I had made a reservation before leaving Siesta Key, two eating places, a Huddle House and a Mexican restaurant, and to my great surprise, a liquor store (more about booze later). I had entertained the idea of staying with Karen and Mike Tucker, but eventually decided against it. If my preliminary research into the murder proved fruitful, and I had to really begin digging into what transpired on that deadly night, the last thing I needed were distractions. My mind had to be zeroed in on a single purpose, trying to uncover a dark truth. I'm not suggesting Karen and Mike are distractions...they most-surely are not...but they are generous and friendly and kind, which would almost certainly require them to show me a good time on occasion. Also, given what I was looking into, a brutal homicide, they would naturally be inquisitive, meaning I was sure to be bombarded by dozens of questions about who I had spoken with, what I had learned, and what was my next step. Being entertained or constantly having to answer questions were not high priorities on my agenda.

Having already reserved a room, I decided to proceed into town to see how close it was now compared to how I remembered it growing up. Turning left onto Broad Street, it didn't take but a second or two to see that it in no way resembled the town I had left all those years ago. Nostalgia can distort, I openly acknowledge that, but what I saw today was sad and depressing.

Back in the day, Broad Street was a consistent buzz of activity and energy. Both sides of the street were lined with thriving businesses of all types, each one fully capable of meeting customers' needs, regardless of what product or service they were seeking. The success of those businesses was definitely buoyed by the booming coal industry and the TVA power plant located in Paradise. Yes, the very same Paradise mentioned in John Prine's song.

On Saturdays, the city population swelled dramatically with the arrival of folks from smaller communities who showed up to do their shopping, and to connect with friends they rarely saw during weekdays. It was a wild, rambunctious, energetic town back then, and a great place to live and to come of age in.

Sadly, those days were long past. Broad Street, once healthy and prosperous, resembled a decaying mouth with many missing teeth. Locations where those successful businesses once stood had given way to empty, vacant lots that dotted both sides of the street. Sure, there were businesses operating, including a handful familiar to me from my days living here, but Broad Street was only a shell of what it had been in its heyday. As for shoppers, I didn't see a single one. On this day Broad Street appeared to be totally abandoned.

Not unlike many small communities around the country, if you wanted to shop, to purchase just about anything under the sun, you were forced to make the short drive to Walmart. While it is undeniable that Walmart killed countless small businesses throughout this country, it is also undeniable that the giant retailer is now the heartbeat that keeps my hometown from going completely under. Like many things life hurls our way, Walmart is both a blessing and a curse.

Now back to the alcohol situation. Until very recently, my hometown, indeed all of Muhlenberg County, was dry, meaning alcohol sales were strictly prohibited. You could go to jail for selling booze. If someone desired alcohol, he or she had to travel to a nearby city to satisfy the urge. But don't be fooled—the wet/dry dynamic was in actuality a legal/illegal issue. True, it was illegal to sell alcohol, but that in no way meant booze wasn't readily available. It was, courtesy of the many bootleggers working in the city/county, two of whom were remarkably successful. One lived within the city limits, while his rival operated out in the county.

The hometown guy lived in a second-floor corner apartment at the far end of downtown. He was no longer a young man, so going up and down the stairs to make a sale had become an unpleasant experience. Having grown weary of conducting business in such a manner, he had looked for an alternative method, which he found by simply tying a rope to a bucket. Then after stepping out onto the balcony, he lowered the bucket down to the potential customer with the instruction to first put the money in the bucket. Cash in hand, our guy went into his apartment, retrieved the requested alcohol, put it in the bucket, and lowered it down to his waiting customer. Not a bad system for our bootlegger, who years earlier had been the town's chief of police.

His arch-rival in the illegal booze-selling enterprise conducted his business out of his house several miles outside of town. He made his sales via a drive-thru window on the side of his house rather than utilizing a bucket and rope. His preferred a method proved to be highly successful. On most weekends, he served more customers and did better business than the average McDonald's.

As I slowly circled through town, everywhere I looked many pleasant memories sprang to life. There was the pool room where I misspent much of my youth, a house where I courted a girl, and the cemetery where we played football. *Run down to the Gish monument, cut sharply to your left, and I'll hit you with a pass*, the quarterback ordered. The play seldom worked, but, hey, not every pass thrown by Joe Namath or Bart Starr resulted in a completion. It was the complex strategic planning that mattered.

I found my way to River Road and made the hilly ten-minute drive to Green River, where as a teen, I and my buddies would swim, oftentimes traversing the river in a daring race to avoid being crushed by the huge barges carrying coal to the steam plant. In retrospect, it was a dangerous thing to do; back then, blindly fearless, we gave no thought to potential disaster.

On the drive to the river, I had my first glimpse of the prison where young Todd Brown was currently incarcerated. Would he remain there, I wondered, or would he eventually be moved to another facility? I hoped for his sake that he stayed put. Being so close to his parents allowed them to visit on a regular basis without any undue hardships. That is, if you grant that seeing your son behind bars for life isn't considered a hardship.

Turning around, I drove back to town, to my hotel, and checked in. After schlepping my luggage and my laptop to my room, I splashed cold water on my face, sat on the bed, took out my cell phone, and called Mike Tucker to let him know I had arrived.

Karen answered and immediately invited me to join them for supper. I respectfully declined, deferring, truthfully, because I was eager to begin digging into the murder of Luke Felton. Karen accepted my rejection without challenge or argument. She did, however, elicit a promise from me to take a raincheck for supper at a future date. I gave her my word that we would get together soon, and then we ended the call.

I sat at the desk, fired up my laptop, and got down to business. Prior to leaving Siesta Key, I had searched for articles in local newspapers that related to the murder. Surprisingly, considering the murder occurred in a small town, I found several detailed, well-written accounts of the crime. My primary focus was on learning the names of the principal actors involved with the case. There had been no actual trial, but there was a sentencing hearing, and it was from reading about that meeting that I found the names of four individuals I wanted to interview:

* Mark Robinson (County Attorney)
* Anne Bishop (Brown Family Attorney)
* Robert Durham (Circuit Judge)
* Jimmy Martin (Chief of Police)

~ * ~

Jimmy Martin was the only member of that quartet I knew. He was a year older than me and attended a county school, but we competed on the baseball diamond on numerous occasions. I must admit to being surprised that he was the chief of police; knowing him back when we were young, my money would have been on him ending up on the wrong side of the badge. Despite whatever reservations I had about him, Jimmy was a cop, so I had no choice but to speak with him.

Those four names gave me a starting point, yet I couldn't help but feel there had to be others involved. For instance, was there an outside investigator? Almost certainly there had to have been. I couldn't envision Jimmy Martin being a skilled or competent homicide investigator. And what role, if any, did the sheriff's department play in the investigation? It was difficult for me to believe they weren't involved in some way. After all, the murder took place out in the county, not in my hometown's city limits. I made a notation to find out who was the sheriff.

The big question for me was who did I want to speak with first? My instinct was to get in touch with Steve Brown, whom I knew, and talk to him. But a part of me said that wasn't a good idea, not yet, that it was too soon to get his take on what had happened with his grandson. Speaking with Steve would have to be put on hold for the time being. Who, then? I made my decision after studying the list for a few seconds—Mark Robinson, the DA.

Grabbing my cell phone, I dialed Mike Tucker's number. He answered before the first ring ended.

"Change your mind about having supper with us tonight?"

"No, that's not why I'm calling. I need your help with something."

"Sure, what do you need?"

"Do you know Mark Robinson?" I said.

"Very well. In fact, his office is right down the hall from mine."

"I'd like to talk to him about the case. Can you arrange a meeting between us?"

"This ain't exactly Hollywood, Nick. No need to schedule a meeting. You show up at my office tomorrow morning and I'll introduce you. Mark's a great guy. Smart as hell, too. You'll enjoy talking with him. Come by around ten and we'll go from there."

"One more question. Who's the sheriff?"

"Perry Jackson."

"What's your scouting report on him?"

"I don't know Perry well, but...there are those among us who swear he'll never be nominated for sainthood."

"Gotcha. See you tomorrow at ten, Mike."

I ended the call, then added Perry Jackson's name to the list of people I needed to interview.

Six

Early morning had a strangeness to it that was disconcerting. Color seemed to have been washed away from the landscape. Bleakness ruled. Everywhere I looked was like viewing an old Mathew Brady Civil War photograph. All that was missing were the twisted, dead soldiers scattered across the blood-soaked terrain. The culprit for this weirdness was those thick clouds floating across the sky like an inverted ocean with its dark rolling waves. I could not recall ever being met by such an odd, colorless morning.

Although Huddle House was within easy walking distance of my motel, I decided to drive. Ten minutes later I was inside the restaurant, which was packed with customers. Every stool at the counter and every booth was occupied. After a brief wait I got lucky...a family of four vacated their booth. I grabbed it immediately and no sooner had I settled in than a waitress was at the booth taking my order. I went with an omelet, hash brown potatoes, link sausage, and orange juice. The food arrived in short order, and it was tasty. Finished, I paid, left a nice tip, walked outside, got into my car, and drove away.

The Judge Executive's office where Mike worked was in the courthouse in Greenville, which was seven miles from my hometown. This community of approximately forty-five hundred citizens also served as the county seat. It was there that virtually all county legal business was conducted. Among the offices within the courthouse were the Sheriff's Department, County Clerk, Election Office, PVA Office, and Deeds and Records. Most of those offices were located on the first and second levels. The third floor was home to the large courtroom.

It was only eight-thirty when I arrived at the courthouse. I parked, climbed the stairs, and went inside the big building that dominated the block. Instead of going directly to Mike's office, I took a detour, went up to the third floor to the courtroom, and sat in a back row. The large room was quiet, dignified, not unlike a church. It was, for me at least, a place that inspired reverence.

When I was a teen, my uncle Arthur Tyler was the circuit judge, and on several occasions, I had the good fortune to attend trials he presided over. He thought it would be a good civics lesson for me to get an up-close view of how justice was meted out when individuals violated the social contract by committing crimes ranging from homicide to theft to assault and battery to dozens of other felonies and serious misdemeanors. Uncle Art was always cool and collected, but no one doubted the courtroom was his. He ruled absolutely.

Sitting there, I smiled when recalling a story I was told about a trial Uncle Art was presiding over. The guy on trial, his name was Johnny, had been in and out of prison for a litany of petty crimes. However, this time the charge was far more serious. Johnny was on trial for setting fire to a barn that resulted in the death of several horses. With so many past offenses on his resume, he was considered a habitual criminal, which meant a guilty verdict could land him behind bars for a lengthy period. Now this guy's mother, Greta, was a real piece of work. She was pigeon-toed, cross-eyed, and had skin like sandpaper. She didn't walk as much as she shuffled rapidly forward. Greta was severely bent at the waist, meaning that wherever she went her head arrived three seconds before her ass.

After all the evidence had been heard, Uncle Art charged the jury, then sent them off to deliberate. When the jury was out of sight, Uncle Art looked up and saw Greta racing straight down the aisle toward the bench. Upon arriving, she said, "Judge Tyler, I want you to know how displeased I am with the way this trial has been conducted. Johnny is so upset that he hasn't had a bowel movement in a week." To which my uncle replied, "Well, Greta, you just wait until he hears the verdict this jury is going to come back with. He'll have a good one then."

How can you beat that for a civics lesson?

~ * ~

I had intended to silence my cell phone before entering the courtroom but had failed to do so. It was buzzing, sounding much louder than normal in this quietness. I wrestled it out of my pants pocket and checked to see who had the temerity to disturb the solitude. To my surprise the call was from my daughter.

"Are you okay, Angel? Is everything all right? Has something happened?" My flood of words was met by a long silence. I could hear her breathing as the silence extended. My fear was that she would hang up without speaking. "Talk to me, Angel. You phoned, you reached out. That tells me you are searching for something. Don't let this moment pass."

"Why is there no accountability for the sinner? Why does he get to walk away from the carnage left in his wake? What is his punishment for crimes committed?"

"Those questions are too serious to be discussed over the phone. That's face-to-face stuff. Look, Angel, I'm in my hometown. Come here and hang out with me for a few days. We'll talk about whatever is on your mind. Fly into Louisville, Nashville, it doesn't matter. I'll pay for everything. What do you say?"

"Your hometown, huh? Did you enter riding a donkey amid a chorus of hosannas from your multitude of worshippers?"

"Hardly. It was more like the prophet not being recognized in his own land," I said. "No, just about everyone I knew has either moved away or died."

"What's your reason for the visit? Business or nostalgia?"

"There was a murder that happened here recently. I'm going to look into it, see if I can get enough material for a book."

"Sounds interesting."

"Come and join me. I could use another set of eyes and ears."

"When did you ever need anyone, Dad? We both know you were the master at pushing people away, especially those you were supposed to love."

"Maybe I've changed. Did you ever consider that? And for the record, I never wanted to push you away."

"What was I, then? Collateral damage?"

"Yeah, unfortunately you were. But it's time I repair the damage."

"Let me think about it, Dad. I'll let you know in a day or two."

"I'll be waiting to hear from you," I said.

I smiled. Another small step for mankind. You take them when you get them.

~ * ~

After ending the call, I went down to Mike's office. He had just arrived, and after unlocking the door he instructed me to hang loose for fifteen or twenty minutes while he ran to the post office. I made myself comfortable in a chair across from his desk and reflected on my talk with Angel. It had gone well, I thought, about as well as I could hope. At least there was dialogue between us. That was a positive beginning. There were serious issues that needed to be addressed. Hopefully, if we really listened to each other, we might put aside past troubles. But that could only happen by communicating. Maybe if she came for a visit, we could work things out and improve our relationship. Maybe even get it closer to what it had been prior to the divorce.

A firm tap on the door startled me back to the present. I turned to see an attractive, well-dressed woman standing just inside the office. She looked to be in her mid-thirties, with brown hair, hazel eyes, and a slim figure. Her attire...blue business suit, white blouse and flat shoes... screamed attorney. The briefcase in her hand only added to that assessment.

"I was looking for Mike," she said. "Obviously, you're not him."

"No, Mike had to run to the post office," I said. "He should be back in a few minutes. Feel free to wait, if you like."

"Do you have business with Mike?"

"Not really. Mike and I went to high school together. I'm just here for a visit."

"Well, I'm pressed for time, so I'd better try to catch him later today," she said. "If you don't mind, inform Mike that Anne Bishop came by to see him. He'll know what it's about."

She was almost out the door before I realized I knew that name from somewhere. Then it hit me... she was the Brown family attorney, one of the four individuals I needed to speak with.

"Wait a minute, Anne," I said, standing and moving closer to her. "Didn't you represent Todd Brown at his sentencing?"

"How do you know about Todd?"

"Mike told me about the case when he and Karen visited me in Sarasota a week or so ago. I was intrigued by what he said. Also, I knew Steve when I was a kid growing up here. Karen suggested that I come up and do some research into what happened. That I might find enough material to write a book about the case."

Pointing her finger at me, she said, "You're the guy from around here who wrote the movies, aren't you?"

"I was more of a script doctor than an actual screenwriter. But, yeah, I'm the guy. My name is Nick Gabriel."

"Sure, I've heard of you. You're kind of a half-assed celebrity around here."

I laughed and said, "Half-assed sounds about right."

"That was my half-assed attempt at humor and not a pejorative assessment. I meant no offense."

"None taken. Would you be willing to speak with me about Todd's situation?"

"Sure, but I can't do it now. Like I said, I'm in a hurry. But if you are free, say, around one-thirty, we could meet somewhere for lunch. Would that work for you?"

"That would be great. Where do you want to meet?"

"There's a place here called Philly's. You familiar with it?"

"Yeah, I passed it on the way into town."

"Good. Then I will see you at one-thirty. Don't panic if I'm a little late. My meeting might run longer than expected. But I'll eventually get there."

"I look forward to seeing you," I said as she hurried away.

~ * ~

Mike returned to his office a few minutes later holding a stack of letters in his right hand and a small package crammed under his left arm. He deposited his load onto the desk, removed his sport jacket, loosened his tie, and turned to face me.

"I bumped into Anne as she was leaving," he said. "She told me you guys have a one-thirty meeting at Philly's."

"That's correct," I responded. "She seemed more than willing to talk about the Todd Brown case."

"That was a fortuitous meeting, I must say. And a lucky one. It saved your morning from being a total disaster. Sheriff Jackson is out of town until Friday."

"No big deal. There are others I can speak with until he returns."

"Unfortunately, I won't be here to shepherd you around and assist with introductions," he said. "I'm leaving tomorrow morning for a conference in D.C., and I won't be back until Saturday afternoon."

"Washington, D.C. Land of sharks and gutless wonders. Be careful, or you might get sucked into the quicksand."

"I promise to hold my nose and keep a safe distance from the madhouse," Mike said.

"Is it possible to get far enough away to be safe in that town?"

Mike sat, said, "What are your plans for the rest of the day? And how can I help?"

"In a perfect world I would move my interview with Steve Brown to the top of my list. However, I think it's wise to hold off until I meet with Anne Bishop. It's important that I get her take on what happened that night and during the days following the murder."

"Sounds reasonable. Sorry I'm not going to be here to help you."

"I have names and addresses of those on my list. It shouldn't be a problem tracking them down."

"Three hours until one-thirty," he said. "What are your immediate plans?"

"Go back to the motel, gather my thoughts, make a list of questions I want to ask Anne."

"Okay, well, like I said, I'll be out of town until Saturday. But you can always call me if you need anything. And Karen is still planning on having you over for dinner. If she asks while I'm away, say yes. Don't let my absence influence you. She's a helluva cook. You'd be a fool to turn down one of her meals."

"I'll take that under advisement," I said, adding, "have a safe trip to D.C. And keep in mind what I said: Watch out for the sharks."

Mike gave me a thumbs-up.

I got back in my car feeling good about how the morning had gone. Meeting Sheriff Perry Jackson was not a high priority; meeting Anne Bishop was. It was dumb luck that she stopped by Mike's office while I was there. But if life has taught me one definitive lesson, it's this: luck is a roll of the dice that can come up seven or it can come up snake eyes. And trust me, I've been on both sides of the come-out roll. I've had hits, I've had misses.

Concerning this particular roll, I had the feeling a lucky seven was destined to hit.

Seven

Anne Bishop showed up at Philly's at one forty-five. She slid into a booth I had secured by the front window, apologized for being late, plucked a tissue from her purse, and dabbed at the sheen of perspiration that glistened on her brow. She gave the appearance of a woman always in a hurry.

"You should thank your lucky stars you didn't become a lawyer," Anne stated, shaking her head. "I've never been around so many attorneys... male and female who love nothing more than to hear themselves prattle on like old-time preachers. The only explanation is they must be filled with hot air. It's all I can do to be in their presence for more than a few minutes at a time. After that, it's like I'm hearing mosquitoes buzzing in my ears."

"If you hate being a lawyer so much, why not quit and do something else?"

"Oh, no, don't misunderstand me...I love being a lawyer. I've always considered it to be a truly noble profession. It's the darn *lawyers* I can barely tolerate."

"You can rest assured the thought of becoming a lawyer never once crossed my mind."

"I had some down time during my meeting earlier this morning and I checked you out on the Internet," she said. "You had one major accomplishment I didn't know about. I knew you had written for movies, but I wasn't aware that you wrote a successful play about William Blake. Movies, a play...that's an impressive resume."

Before I could respond by telling her that nothing I had done was all that damn impressive, the waitress came to our booth to take our orders. Anne went with a Caesar salad and a glass of iced tea.

"And for you, sir?" the waitress inquired.

"I'll also have the Caesar salad," I answered, holding up my glass. "And could I get a refill of Diet Coke."

"Absolutely. Your orders shouldn't take too long."

When the waitress was gone, Anne said, "In my faraway youth, back when I was in college, I dated a guy named Brett. He majored in English, and he idolized William Blake. Brett considered Blake to be superior in every way to most mortal human beings. He saw Blake as a God-like figure."

"I doubt Blake would have cared for that assessment," I pointed out. "He had a very uneasy relationship with God, especially with the Judeo-Christian God, who he considered to be a cruel and angry moralist. For Blake, I think, the human imagination was his god."

"Brett was forever quoting a line Blake had written. I can't remember all of it, but it had something to do with bricks and stones. Do you have any idea what Brett was referring to?"

"'Prisons are built with stones of law, brothels with bricks of religion.'"

"Yes, that's the one," Anne replied, chuckling. "I'm fairly certain Brett didn't have much experience with prisons, so I'm guessing it was the brothel reference he connected with."

The waitress brought our food and drinks and asked if we needed anything else. We said no, everything looked good. She told us to let her know if we did, smiled, and then hurried away to begin cleaning one of the just-vacated tables.

Neither Anne nor I spoke while we ate. The salads were excellent and we quickly consumed them. Finished, I pushed my plate away, while Anne nabbed a couple of croutons and nibbled on them.

Anne said, "So, you're here to gather material about Todd's case, because of...what? You're friends with Steve Brown?"

"That's not inaccurate, but there are alternative reasons I plan to explore. My hope is for the book to be about more than just a murder."

"What would those alternatives be?"

I shrugged, said, "I'm not sure at this point. I suppose it all depends on what events unfold. On what details I uncover. The story will be dictated by what I learn."

The waitress returned with a pitcher of iced tea and refilled Anne's glass. She asked if I wanted another Diet Coke; I said no.

"Let's talk about Todd's case," I said after the waitress left.

"Sure," she replied. "But first, you tell me what you've heard about the case."

"I heard that Luke Felton was found dead on the ground next to his vehicle and that he had been stabbed multiple times. I also heard the ring finger on his right hand was severed and a ring he wore had been removed. The next day Todd was asleep at his home when law enforcement arrived and woke him up. He was wearing Luke's ring. They also discovered bloody clothes on the floor next to the bed. Todd was taken into custody, questioned, he confessed, and was arrested. Weeks later, he was sentenced to life in prison with no chance for parole."

"That's clear, concise, and accurate...with a lone exception. The part about Todd confessing."

"He didn't confess?"

"Not exactly. It was more like Todd agreed that he had committed the murder. Sheriff Perry Jackson did most of the questioning, but Jimmy Martin was also in on the interview."

"Why would Todd agree? Why didn't he defend himself, say he hadn't killed Luke?"

"Now we have arrived at the weird part," Anne said. "Todd claims to have no memory of what transpired that night. Swears he can't recall a thing."

"You stab a guy multiple times, then cut off his finger? I'd think that would be hard to forget."

"Todd was so messed up on drugs I'm convinced he's telling the truth. Maybe he did murder Luke, although I'm uncertain he did. But I do believe he genuinely can't remember what happened."

"Was he tested for drugs?" I asked.

"Yes. And he was loaded with all kinds of nasty shit. Xanax, Oxycontin, Vicodin, and pot. And even after he'd been asleep for several hours, his blood-alcohol level was high enough for him to still be considered legally intoxicated. I'm not clear if the drugs were in his system before or after the homicide, but the ones I just listed were present in his tox screen."

"Jesus. Kid takes that much junk means he's got a serious problem."

"Tell me about it."

"Why didn't Todd have an attorney with him during the interview?"

"Todd didn't request an attorney, and his parents weren't informed of his arrest until later that afternoon. By that time, Todd had already signed his confession statement."

"Was the interview taped?"

"Yes, it was." Anne sipped her tea. "I've watched it at least fifty times, searching for anything that might help Todd's case. Thus far, I haven't come up with much. But I do have a complaint with the interrogation. There are moments when Perry appears to be leading Todd rather than merely questioning him. I find that disturbing."

"When did you get involved with the case?" I said.

"Late on the evening after Todd was locked up. Steve called and asked if I would represent Todd. I'd done some legal work for the Browns on several occasions in the past. That's how Steve knew me. I told Steve I would see what was happening. I also informed him that he needed to bring in a big-time criminal defense attorney. What Todd was facing required representation far beyond the scope of my capabilities. But after Todd confessed, it really didn't matter who his attorney was. His fate was already sealed."

"Look, Anne, I'm not an attorney or a homicide investigator, but I see two questions that are begging to be answered."

"Only two? I can come up with half-a-dozen. But go ahead, ask your two."

"First, what reason would an eighteen-year-old kid have for being alone in a car at that time of night with a man Luke's age? And second, how were the cops able to so quickly identify Todd as the killer?"

"The answer to your second question is easy—Todd's driver's license was found on the passenger side floorboard in Luke's car. That put Todd in the car at some point. As for your first question, I have no answer. That one is still a mystery to me."

"Did you ask Todd about it?"

"Of course I did. I've asked him many times, but he has no answer."

"Was Luke Felton gay?"

"Nothing conclusive on that question," Anne said. "Some say yes, others argue no."

"Did he deal drugs?"

"Yet another question I've asked Todd and another question he won't answer."

"I got the feeling from your earlier comment that you have some reservations about Perry Jackson," I said. "Am I reading you wrong?"

"Let me be as tactful as possible. He's maybe okay when dealing with small-time, petty offenses, but on a case of this magnitude, I feel he was in way over his head. A homicide investigation requires a more skilled, more professional individual than Perry Jackson. He's not that intelligent or that talented. That's my humble opinion, anyway."

"I'm sure being involved in his first homicide case was definitely overwhelming for him. It would be for any small-town law enforcement officer."

"His second."

"Second, what?"

"Second big homicide case."

"There was another one?"

Anne nodded, said, "Yes, about three years ago. The victim was a twenty-eight-year-old female named Sharon Anderson. Her body was found in the trunk of her car, which had been partially submerged in a pond. Seems the killer or killers attempted to push the car into the pond but they failed to get it all the way in. The man who owns the property went to do some fishing and saw the rear end of the car sticking out of the water. He called the police. They found Sharon's body, but her head was missing. It has never been found."

"And what about the crime? Has it been solved?"

"No."

"Is it still being investigated?" I said.

"You would have to ask Perry Jackson that question."

"Two homicides occur that close together, both involving amputations? Any chance they could be connected?"

"Think about your question, Nick. For those murders to be connected, you have to surmise that Todd, when he was fifteen-years-old, killed and beheaded a woman. Then three years later he murders Luke Felton. No way am I buying that."

"Maybe Todd's not the killer. Maybe he never killed anyone."

"Now, *that* part I can buy," Anne said.

"Is it possible for me to interview Todd?"

"Sure, that's not a problem. I can arrange it for you. However, I would like to sit in when you do speak with him. Will that work for you?"

"Yeah, I can live with that."

"When would you like to interview him?"

"In a couple of days," I said. "That will give me enough time to meet with several others that I want to speak with. What about sometime on Thursday?"

"I'll set it up, then text you the time. If it's okay with you, we should ride together. It's just simpler that way."

"That's fine with me," I said, placing a credit card on the table.

"No, no, this one is on me." Anne opened her purse, removed her wallet, and took out a credit card. "I'm an attorney. I can charge this to my expense account. Besides, you're a cheap date."

"I'll relent only if you agree to let me pay for the next one."

"Deal."

After she settled up, we walked outside together. It was almost three-thirty and the sun was already heading west. The temperature was still hot, but the early morning strangeness had melted away, replaced by sunshine. I thanked Anne, shook hands with her, and then climbed into my car. Checking my cell phone, I saw that I had a text from my daughter.

OK, Dad, I know this is insane but I'll give it a try. Flying into Louisville on Thursday. Will arrive around noon. I'll rent a car, then drive to your hometown. Should be there by three. Reserve a room for me where you are staying. See you in three days.

I immediately texted her back, telling her how excited and pleased I was that she was coming for a visit. I also told her I would reserve a room for her at the Best Western. She replied with a smiley face emoji.

I made the decision to call Steve Brown when I returned to my motel room. Hopefully, he would agree to meet with me sometime the next day. I also wanted to speak with Perry Jackson, but since he was out of town, that talk had to be put on hold. However, there was nothing to keep me from setting up an interview with my old baseball rival, Jimmy Martin. He was in on Todd's interrogation, so I figured he might have something valuable to offer concerning the case. I could always get with Perry when he got back in town.

Not much had happened since arriving there but I felt things were looking up. All I could do was interview people with knowledge of the case, listen to what they had to say, and then eventually piece it all together. Either I would uncover enough material for a book, or I wouldn't. The jury was still out on that one. At the moment, however, writing a book was of secondary importance to me. That project ranked far below getting a visit from my daughter.

Who knew? Maybe miracles really do happen.

Eight

In the solitude of night, alone, my thoughts often drift in bleak directions. Silent questions are posed, most of which go unanswered. Is it possible that no answers exist? Perhaps that's the most profound question of all.

Salvation through suffering is a dark formula. And yet, is there an alternate path that leads to salvation? I have long ago concluded that no such path exists. Therefore, an individual can only achieve salvation after experiencing his or her lonely hours in Gethsemane.

In my hotel room, wide awake at midnight, I filled yet another cup (my fourth) with more scotch and soda. My thoughts, those unanswered questions, were drowning in booze. At the forefront of my thoughts was Todd Brown, a kid not yet twenty who was destined to live out his remaining years, most likely decades, locked in a steel cage like a wild animal, absent any chance, any hope that whatever potential he once had would be realized. It had vanished in a single act of madness. There would be no great achievements, no outstanding accomplishments, nothing to write on his tombstone except his name and the years of his birth and death. How sad. Such a waste of time, potential, and talent.

William Blake believed in the concept that "everything that lives is holy." But was Blake right? I'm not sure. Todd Brown certainly wouldn't be inclined to agree. After all, is being locked in a prison cell for life really living? How is it holy? Seems to me it's neither living nor holy. Blake is not a man to argue with, but in this instance I maintain that he simply got it wrong.

In the Kabbalah espoused by the great 16th century Jewish mystic Isaac Luria, *tikkun* means to repair the world, to restore it to its original, perfect state before evil came into existence. The task of repairing the world falls squarely on the shoulders of every living human. To wait for God to perform the act of *tikkun* is to waste valuable time. As Kafka said, "the Messiah will come only when he is no longer needed." Therefore, if it is left to us, then how do we go about restoring the world to its former glory? Several ways, we are told, including meditation, performing righteous acts, praying, and by striving for a closer relationship with the Almighty.

But how does a man confined to a prison cell repair the world? What methods are at his disposal that will allow him to take even that first small step toward achieving such a goal? He can't; there are none available to him. What, then, is his alternative? To give up, to abandon all hope? The answer to that is yes, if his goal is to repair the world, but no, in thunder, if he desires to repair the one thing that remains within in his control…himself.

Through my alcohol haze, another thought keeps making its presence felt…what if Todd were actually innocent? What if he didn't murder and mutilate Luke Felton? What if, in *his* alcohol haze, he was present when the murder took place but didn't commit the crime? Is that such an outlandish possibility? True, the evidence is heavily stacked in favor of his being guilty. Maybe that's what troubles me. As I see it, that evidence came in a package that was a little too neatly wrapped to be accepted without being challenged. Or it could be that I just *hope* the kid is innocent. Hope, though, is a damn weak argument when pitted against a mountain of evidence, regardless of how neatly wrapped said evidence might be.

Todd's suffering—hell, *everyone's* suffering—might cease to exist if Kafka's Messiah would simply get off his lazy ass and make his long-delayed appearance. But after thousands of years in hiding, what hope do we have that he'll show up anytime soon? Not much, I would argue.

By mid-morning my head had cleared but my stomach felt like Mount Vesuvius ready to erupt at any moment. This had not been a pleasant morning, but not many are when I go to bed with a belly full of booze. No doubt, my liver would thank me if I chose to cut back on my alcohol intake.

~ * ~

Two phone calls within a matter of minutes had jarred me awake. Both came as a complete surprise. There was no way I could have expected to hear from either of the individuals on the other end of the call.

The first call was from Karen Tucker. She wanted to know if I would have dinner with her tonight. I thought this was an odd request, given that Mike was out of town for the next few days. I told her I wouldn't be free until later, but she persisted, saying if I couldn't make it for dinner, I should stop by when I was free and we'd have a few drinks.

"With Mike out of town," she said, "we can drink all we want, just like real adults. And we won't have to feel guilty or selfish while we're doing it. You up for it?"

I was hesitant to say yes...meeting her while Mark was away somehow seemed inappropriate... but in the end, I agreed to the visit.

The second call was from Sheriff Perry Jackson, whose voice and tone carried elements of anger and resentment. It was clear from his first words that he had no desire to speak with me. I couldn't help but wonder why.

"Mike Tucker left a message saying you need to talk to me," he grumbled. "Talk about what, specifically?"

"I was told you were out of town," I said.

"Well, now I'm back. I repeat...what do you want to talk about?"

"The Todd Brown case."

Jackson hacked a cough, then said, "That's ancient history. I have nothing new to say about that case."

"How do you know until you hear what I ask?"

"You want to know about that case, go to the courthouse and read the transcript. That's where you'll find everything you're looking for."

"I plan to do that," I said. "But still...I would like to hear your thoughts on what happened."

There was a long pause before Jackson finally responded. "I'm tied up most of the day, but if you'll come by my office at, say, four o'clock, I'll give you thirty minutes of my time. That's the best offer you'll get. Take it or leave it."

"I'll see you at four," I said, ending the call.

What an asshole.

~ * ~

I showered, dressed, and gave some thought to an early morning scotch and soda... the old hair of the dog remedy... but decided that it probably wasn't a great idea. Instead, I found the phone number for Steve Brown that Mike had given me, and I punched it in. Since Steve knew me, I felt good about my chances that he would agree to talk about his grandson's terrible situation. But those chances were seventy-thirty at best. I had to remember that Steve was still grieving, so it was just as likely he might tell me to go straight to hell, friend or not.

When Steve answered and I identified myself, I received my third surprise of the morning. He not only seemed genuinely pleased to hear from me, he also knew the reason for my call. Apparently, word spreads faster in my hometown than a California wildfire.

I didn't ask Steve how he found out I'd be calling. That really wasn't important. What did matter was that he sounded upbeat and eager to share his thoughts concerning what had occurred with his grandson. That's more than I could have hoped for.

"I'm still trying to process what happened and I'm finding it nearly impossible to do," he said. "We are all still in shock, still reeling from what Todd supposedly did."

Supposedly did. What a peculiar choice of words.

"When is a convenient time for us to meet?" I asked Steve.

"Mary Sue and I are visiting Todd at the prison this afternoon from two until four," he replied. "Why don't you come over at four-thirty? We should be home by then."

"That won't work for me, Steve," I said. "I'm scheduled to meet with Sheriff Jackson at four. What about sometime tomorrow?"

"No, no, come see us after you're finished with the sheriff. We'd love to see you."

"You live in Gaslight Park, correct?"

"Yes." He gave me the street and house number. "I look forward to seeing you, Nick."

~ * ~

After ending the call with Steve, I left the motel and went on an expedition to find something to eat. My stomach had finally settled to the point that it was prepared to accept food without a major rebellion. Like every community in the United States, large or small, my hometown has a McDonald's, a Wendy's, and a bunch of familiar pizza places. I had a choice to make, although I quickly ruled out pizza—my stomach hadn't settled *that* much—so I flipped a coin between Mickey D's and Wendy's, and Wendy's won. I had the chicken sandwich, fries and a Diet Coke. A tasty meal, although I must admit I much prefer Mickey D's fries to Wendy's.

When I finished eating, I put in a call to Mark Robinson, the county attorney I had originally gone to the courthouse to see before I was hijacked by Anne Bishop. Robinson's secretary answered, and after I identified myself, she transferred the call to her boss. Unlike Sheriff Jackson, Mark Robinson was more than happy to speak with me, adding that he would be available all afternoon. I told him I'd be in his office in half-an-hour.

Mark Robinson looked like a county attorney straight out of central casting. Tall and thin, with dark hair just beginning to edge toward gray, he was dressed like Gregory Peck on a good day. He had on a starched white shirt, blue tie, black slacks held up by red suspenders, and shiny wingtip shoes. Even his deep voice and the precise way he pronounced every syllable sounded like Peck's Atticus Finch defending Tom Robinson in *To Kill a Mockingbird.*

"Todd's case was the easiest and the saddest one I've ever been part of," Mark said, after we were seated in the small conference room. "Every homicide committed by a teen is tragic in multiple ways. Two families are shattered by what happened. And as the person elected to ensure that justice is served, which in this case meant sending a kid to prison for life, well, it takes a toll on you. For sure, it took a toll on me."

"But there wasn't an actual trial, was there?" I asked.

"Wasn't necessary. Todd confessed."

"Before he had legal representation, right?"

Mark chuckled, said, "You've spoken with Anne Bishop, haven't you?"

I nodded.

"Yes, that's true," he said. "But he had plenty of time to ask for an attorney."

"He was eighteen."

"Eighteen-year-olds are considered adults under Kentucky law. It was up to Todd to ask for an attorney. Sheriff Jackson was under no obligation to make Todd aware of his right to have an attorney present."

"Maybe not, but it doesn't pass the smell test for me."

"From start to finish, everything about this situation was shitty. But Luke Felton was dead and Todd admitted killing him. Don't lose sight of that little detail. My hands were tied. I had no choice but to prosecute Todd to the fullest extent of the law. Same goes for Anne Bishop once she jumped in and got involved. Her hands were also tied. Like I said, it was a sad situation all around."

"According to Anne, Todd doesn't remember anything about that night. Any chance he might be telling the truth?"

"Only Todd knows the answer to that question," Mark said. "Why? Are you saying he might be innocent? And before you respond, let me remind you there is a mountain of evidence stacked against him."

"I've heard about the evidence and it does appear to be overwhelming. Still, there are a few questions I'd like answered. Perhaps you can help me."

"Let me hear them. I'll see what I can do."

"Am I right to assume the murder weapon was a knife?"

"Yes."

"Was the knife found, and if so, were Todd's prints on it?"

"The knife has never been located," Mark said.

"If Todd rode to the murder site in Luke's car, and if the car was still there when his body was found, how did Todd get back to his house, which was a good six or seven miles from where the murder occurred? Did he walk, hitchhike, what? How did he cover that distance in the dead of night?"

"Todd claims he doesn't remember how he got home. Or where he disposed of the knife."

"Explain to me why a kid Todd's age would be spending time alone with a man pushing seventy."

"This is only a guess, but I suspect it had to do with drugs. In case you haven't heard, Todd was a heavy drug abuser."

"So I've been told." I was silent for a moment, then said, "Drugs could account for his memory loss. Maybe he experienced a blackout."

"I have to be perfectly honest with you, Nick. I'm not buying Todd's amnesia act. It comes across as a little too convenient for me to believe."

Checking my watch, I realized I only had time for a couple more questions before I had to scoot out and get to my meeting with Sheriff Jackson. Lucky for me, his office was also in the courthouse, a floor below Mark Robinson's.

"Did you watch the tape of Todd being questioned?" I said.

"Several times, yes," Mark replied.

"Did anything about the interview bother you?"

"No. Why do you ask?"

"Anne says there were times when it looked like Todd was agreeing with Sheriff Jackson's statements rather than answering his questions. If that's true, it might indicate the sheriff was leading Todd in a certain direction, perhaps one he wanted Todd to travel."

"That's hogwash, Nick. Anne is desperate to find any flaw that will exonerate her client, which is what she's paid to do. I get it. I'd do the same thing if I were in her shoes. But she's dead wrong to claim Sheriff Jackson bullied Todd into confessing. That didn't happen. Perry acted in a professional manner. So did Jimmy Martin, who also sat in on the interview."

"How wsould you describe your relationship with Sheriff Jackson?"

"Strictly professional."

"That's a rather subdued assessment."

"It is what it is."

"I've heard whispers that Luke Felton was gay," I said. "Any truth to that?"

"Here's what I know. It is true that Luke spent a lot of time in the presence of younger boys. Whether he was gay, or whether he was just a friendly guy who acted as a mentor to young boys, I can't say with any certainty. But...I will admit I do find it to be disturbing behavior on his part."

"Did you question any of those boys?"

"No, why should I? Luke was deceased and Todd confessed to the murder. Luke's sexual proclivities were irrelevant."

"I'm not sure I agree with you, Mark," I said, standing and offering my hand. "Thanks for taking time to answer my questions. I really appreciate it."

Shaking my hand, he said, "Mike tells me you're planning to write a book about the case. Is that true?"

"I'm leaning that way, yes."

"Can't be as exciting for you as writing all those movies. Hell, I'd consider that a dream job."

"Working in the film business isn't necessarily what it's purported to be, I can promise you that."

"Maybe not, but it sure beats the hell out of slaving away in this county." He opened the door and shook my hand a second time. "If you have additional questions, or seek more information, feel free to give me a call. I'll help in any way I can."

"Count on it," I said, as I left his office.

~ * ~

As I started down the stairs leading to the sheriff's office, I was struck by the realization that the Todd Brown case had begun to haunt me. It had seeped into my soul. Without any evidence whatsoever, I had come to suspect that Todd was innocent. But was that little more than wishful thinking on my part? Was I allowing my heart to rule my head? And by taking Todd's side on the matter, was I being unfair to Luke Felton? Someone had murdered him, and regardless of how I felt about Todd, I couldn't lose sight of that fact. The dead, especially victims of a violent crime, deserve our respect. I knew Luke, and I also knew he'd been a cop for many years. He'd paid his dues, earned his stripes. He had served with honor. While I may never learn the truth about why he was with Todd on that deadly night, I did know he never should have died in such a horrible and violent way.

But the truth is, no one should.

It didn't matter that I was ten minutes early for my meeting with Perry Jackson. The man wasn't there. When I walked into his office, one of his deputies informed me that Jackson left an hour ago to take care of some business at his house, and that he wouldn't be returning until tomorrow morning. I didn't bother asking the deputy what constituted the sheriff's business; I knew the man was lying. Sheriff Jackson had no interest in speaking with me. That had come across loud and clear during our brief phone chat earlier in the day.

Walking out of the office, I was convinced that if I had any hope of questioning Perry Jackson, I would have to catch him by surprise. Otherwise, he'd keep finding ways to avoid seeing me. But time was on my side, I knew. Sooner or later, come hell or high water, I would get my interview with the man.

I had an hour or so to kill before it was time for my visit with the Browns, so I decided to drive back to my motel and type up notes from my conversation with Mark Robinson, a man I found to be honest, forthright and professional, but perhaps somewhat dismissive in some areas. Once I finished that task, I'd head out to Gaslight Park for my meeting with Mary Sue and Steve Brown for what was certain to be an emotional evening. Given the situation, how could it be anything but emotional? And yet, my hope was that somewhere in the midst of all that emotion, I'd get a much clearer picture of Todd Brown.

Hope.

There was that word again.

Nine

When I was a kid growing up here, Gaslight Park was the new upscale place to live. It took serious money to purchase a lot and build a house on the property. Initially, there were only a scattering of houses, all very pricey for the times. But like everything else in my hometown, this was no longer the case. Very little was as it had once been and that included Gaslight Park. The area had expanded… there were many more houses… but the more recent ones lacked the size and elegance of the original structures. These days, the "in" place to live was out by the country club and the golf course.

Steve and Mary Sue Brown lived in a four-bedroom, two-bathroom brick home located on a corner lot. It was one of the more expensive houses built by the second wave of settlers in the neighborhood. There was a small front yard, a larger backyard, and a two-car garage. I wasn't sure how long the Browns had resided here, but I did know this wasn't where they lived when I was growing up.

Steve greeted me at the door, gave me a gentle pat on the shoulder, and invited me inside. Mary Sue, whom I didn't know nearly as well as I knew Steve, surprised me with a warm hug. Then she took my hand, led me to the den, and motioned for me to sit in a chair by the fireplace. She asked if I wanted something to drink, and when I declined she excused herself and disappeared into the kitchen.

Steve sat on the sofa across from my chair. The passing years had been kind to Steve. There were a few noticeable changes...his once-black hair was completely gray and a few wrinkles lined his face... but all things considered, he wasn't much different from the man I knew all those years ago. And considering the torment he'd gone through during the past couple of months, a torment reflected in his sad eyes, he had held up remarkably well.

"Are you sure you don't want something to drink?" Steve asked. "We don't have any alcohol, but we do have soft drinks. Or water, if you prefer."

"No, thanks, Steve, I'm good," I said.

"Been a long time, Nick. It's great seeing you again. And you look good."

"So do you, Steve. The years have treated you well."

"I'm sixty-six with no serious illness, so I can't complain. But I do feel like I've aged ten years since...what happened with Todd."

"I can only imagine how incredibly difficult that had to be for you and your family."

Mary Sue came into the room and sat next to Steve on the sofa. She took his hand in hers and gave it a squeeze. Her eyes were sadder than her husband's.

"What brought you back to town?" Mary Sue said.

"I'm exploring the possibility of writing a book about Todd's case," I replied. "That is, unless you guys disapprove. If you do, I'll take a pass on the project. I have no intention of going against your wishes. And that won't trouble me at all."

"What's left for you to write about?" Steve said. "Todd confessed and is incarcerated for life. Where do you go from there?"

"Keep talking to people about the case, keep digging for information. I've already spoken with Anne Bishop and Mark Robinson, and I plan on talking to Perry Jackson and Jimmy Martin. I'm sure there are others I need to interview, and I will."

"What about Todd? Do you plan on speaking with him?"

I nodded, said, "Anne Bishop is setting that up for me."

"Good luck with that," Mary Sue said. "Todd swears he can't remember anything at all about that night."

"Do you believe him?"

Mary Sue seemed started by my question. "Why shouldn't we believe him?" she said. "What reason would he have to lie? So yes, I do believe him."

"I don't know how anyone could possibly forget something that traumatic."

"Neither can we."

"Has anyone suggested hypnosis?" I said.

"That was never brought up," Steve said. "Why? Do you think that might work?"

"I don't know, but it couldn't hurt to give it a try. If Todd is going to be locked up for life, wouldn't you want to be absolutely sure he actually committed the crime? I would, if I were in your shoes."

"If Todd is hypnotized, will he remember what happened?" Mary Sue asked.

"Look, guys, I'm not a detective or a homicide investigator, so maybe I need to keep my mouth shut. But from what little I've learned about the case, I definitely see some blank spaces that need to be filled in. Questions I'd like answered, beginning with how well did Todd know Luke Felton?"

"We weren't aware he knew Luke at all," Steve said.

"Okay, so what reason would Todd have for being in Luke's car that night?"

"In case you didn't know, Todd has a serious drug problem. Maybe he got his drugs from Luke."

"Has any solid evidence been uncovered that suggests Luke was a drug dealer?"

"None that I'm aware of," Steve said.

"What if Todd was never in Luke's car that night?"

"His driver's license was found in the car. Plus, Todd's clothes were covered with Luke's blood. How else can you explain that unless Todd was in the car?"

"It was all staged. A set-up to implicate Todd."

The look on the faces of Steve and Mary Sue was all it took for me to realize that I had better change course, and fast. To continue down this path would only lead to more disappointment for them. All I was doing was offering a glimmer of hope to two people who had accepted the darkness. I was shining a light into that darkness, yet it was a light that might easily lead to a deeper darkness. I had no desire to create hope only to see it crushed by further disappointment.

I braced for the inevitable question I knew was coming.

"Do you genuinely think there's a chance Todd is innocent?" Mary Sue asked.

"I'd be lying if I said yes." This was the only answer I felt I could give, even though I didn't think I was being totally truthful. "But if I have your blessing to continue gathering material for a book, I'll keep digging for answers."

"Yes, by all means, go ahead," Steve said. "You have our complete support."

"Just don't let your hopes get too high. There is a lot of evidence against Todd. But I'll talk to a few people, including Todd, and see if I can come up with anything new."

"We'll help you in any way we can," Mary Sue said.

"I appreciate that," I said, standing. "And I'll definitely keep in touch. If I learn anything new, you'll be the first to know."

We walked to the front door. Steve opened it, shook my hand, and said, "Good luck, Nick. And thanks for everything you're doing. I mean that."

Mary Sue gave me a hug, then silently watched as I headed to my car. Darkness had settled in, which somehow seemed appropriate to the occasion. I started the car and drove away, a portrait of Steve and Mary Sue standing arm-in-arm on the porch captured in my rear-view mirror. Two decent people had been put through hell and were still living there. My heart ached for what they were going through. And here I was, a hack writer, offering to help when there was little chance in hell that I could. Sometimes I let my mouth write checks my ass can't cover. This was, I'm sorry to say, one of those times.

My next stop: Karen Tucker's for a drink, which didn't at all seem appropriate.

~ * ~

Three hours later, after we'd had several drinks, Karen excused herself and went to the bathroom. She had done most of the talking, primarily asking questions about the time I spent writing for the movies. Like virtually everyone else, she greatly inflated the work I had done, and my importance to the overall process of making a movie. She had the misguided notion that I was on the set the entire time, always just a snap of the fingers away from being summoned by the director to rewrite or rescue a scene that was failing miserably. I would swoop in and somehow magically turn dreck into gold. Nothing could be further from the truth. As I explained to Karen, I was rarely on the set at any point during production, and on those occasions when I was, it was usually at the behest of a panicked actor who was dissatisfied with his dialogue, or else he wanted me to beef up a big speech he was about to deliver. I could tell Karen was surprised when I told her that, with a few notable exceptions, being a screenwriter was a thankless, unappreciated job. Most of what a screenwriter puts on the page is eventually rewritten, often many times over. That's different with playwrights; no word is ever changed without the playwright's permission.

As a script doctor, my work normally ended up on the screen, although few people knew it. As an example, which I pointed out to Karen, was the work I did on a war movie that garnered glowing reviews. The two men who got screen credit for writing the movie were nominated for an Academy Award for Best Adapted Screenplay even though I had written seventy-percent of the dialogue that ended up in the film. If most screenwriters are underappreciated, I told Karen, script doctors are practically invisible.

While I politely answered all of Karen's questions, my thoughts continued to linger on Todd Brown's situation, and more specifically on what impact it had on his grandparents, who by any standards had provided a loving, supportive family structure for their own kids and then for the grandkids. Until Todd, not one family member had ever been in serious trouble. Now he was behind bars for life, having been convicted of committing the worst crime of all... murder.

How did that happen? What caused him to go off the rails? And what could Steve or Mary Sue, or Todd's parents, Tony and Susan, have done differently that might have prevented it from happening? Nothing, as I see it. In life, we kid ourselves if we believe we are in charge? We aren't. Life is a cosmic crapshoot and we don't roll the dice. Try as we might, some...many... outcomes are beyond our control. We can only watch helplessly as the dice tumble toward a result we have no choice but to accept.

Karen came back into the room wearing a thin, silk see-through negligee. I hadn't anticipated her being dressed in such a provocative way, but I must confess I wasn't completely surprised. Deep down inside, I knew this was why I had been invited in the first place. With Mike out of town, what other reason would she have for inviting me? It wasn't to talk about movies or writing.

She leaned over and kissed me hard on the mouth. I knew I should pull away and say something inane like, "This is a mistake, we shouldn't do this, Mike is my best friend," but there was no way that was going to happen. Instead, I responded by pulling her closer and meeting her kiss with one of my own.

Karen knelt between my legs and began unbuckling my belt. Seconds later, she had unfastened my pants and was slowly working the zipper downward. At that point, my fate, shall we say, was literally in her hands. We had officially reached the point of no return. I knew what the ultimate outcome was destined to be.

One other thing I knew for certain: The pleasure I was soon to experience would almost certainly lead me straight to hell.

Ten

My Divine Rebel, William Blake, despite his iconoclastic opinions on many subjects, had a long and successful marriage. His wife Catherine was illiterate when they married... she signed the marriage certificate with an X—but Blake, through infinite patience and caring, taught her to read and write. He also taught her to paint and draw in a style very similar to his, a skill that proved to be beneficial to him professionally.

Blake's views were very liberal-minded and forward-thinking for the times in which he lived. He was a product of the Enlightenment, and many of his ideas, judged to be scandalous at the time, are viewed in a more favorable light in today's modern world. He detested child labor, particularly the abuse of young children forced by greedy profit-driven adults to slave away in London's '*dark satanic mills.*' He advocated sexual freedom and '*gratified desire*' for both men and women. (However, despite his liberal views on such matters, there is no record that he ever strayed from Catherine). He had enormous respect for Jesus, yet his assessment of organized religion was that its primary aim was to suppress man's natural desires and to stifle his imagination. Blake had little use for a God residing in the far-off heavens, saying in a statement that echoes a central Gnostic belief *'that all deities reside in the human breast.'*

I wonder how Blake would have judged my tryst with the wife of my best friend. I have a hunch he would have condemned it as misguided and foolish, but a living experience just the same.

For the next two days, Tuesday and Wednesday, the rain came down in wind-blown sheets. It was a monsoon. Tornado warnings were issued for the entire area, but thankfully, none materialized. With a single exception, an excursion to a grocery store to purchase food and drinks, I stayed in my hotel room. I was eager for Thursday to arrive. Anne Bishop called Tuesday morning to let me know she had scheduled a meeting with Todd at the prison for ten on Thursday morning. And later that day Angel should be getting here. I couldn't wait to see her, and to hopefully begin ironing out some of our many differences.

Karen Tucker showed up at my room at nine Wednesday night. Again, I didn't expect to see her, but I can't say I was all that surprised. She stepped into the room, held up two bottles of Merlot, and gave me a kiss on the lips. Every instinct in my body cried out for me to demand that she leave. But I didn't. And even if I had, I doubt she would have followed my directive. Obviously, she's every bit as immune to feelings of guilt as I am.

She stayed until a little past two and then departed for her house. There was enough wine remaining in one of the bottles for me to have two final drinks, which I did. I lay back in the bed and did my best to wipe out what had happened during the past five hours. I was only partially successful. Thoughts of my morning meeting with Todd, and then seeing Angel in the afternoon kept being interrupted by Blake-like visions of a disheartened Mike Tucker upon discovering his so-called best friend had violated his wife.

That was more than enough to keep me awake the rest of the night. Could be I underestimated my feelings of guilt.

Bleary-eyed but wired, I showered, dressed, grabbed my bag, and went down to the lobby to wait for Anne Bishop to pick me up. She had phoned to say she would be there at nine. I stopped at the area where breakfast was being served and had a cinnamon pastry and a cup of orange juice. Sitting at a table, I opened my bag and made sure I had plenty of tapes, and that my recorder was in good working order. I also had a legal pad and plenty of pens. Everything checked out fine; I was fully prepared for my interview with Todd Brown.

I had made a promise to myself that I wasn't walking away from my talk with Todd until he answered one or two specific questions I had for him. Whether he truly couldn't remember or was just bullshitting everyone was irrelevant. I was going to insist he provide something... anything... that would give me solid cause to remain involved. There was no good reason why I should invest my time and energy in writing a book if he wasn't willing to make the effort at uncovering the truth about what occurred that night.

~ * ~

Anne showed up a couple of minutes before nine. When I got in her car, I was surprised by how she was dressed... jeans, a denim shirt and sneakers. Her hair was tied in a ponytail, and her eyes were hidden behind sunglasses. She looked more like a convict working on a chain gang than an attorney. Considering our destination, perhaps that's the look she was aiming for.

Neither of us said much on the ride to the prison. For no particular reason, I checked the contents in my bag a second time. As I did, Anne committed what I regard as a cardinal sin... texting while driving. I've always considered driving to be a full-time occupation. I didn't complain, but I was fully prepared to take command of the steering wheel if a life-threatening situation arose.

Once we arrived at the prison and passed through security, we were led by a guard to a large open area and directed to take a seat at a long metal table. We were the only ones there. The guard said he would fetch Todd, then excused himself, and departed. Obviously, he had been made aware of whom we were there to interview.

Sitting there, I realized I had no idea what Todd looked like. I did know Steve was about five-nine, but did that really mean anything?

Perhaps someone on Mary Sue's side of the family was extremely tall, and that's who Todd took after. I suppose I would find out shortly.

I was startled by Todd's appearance when the guard led him into the room. He looked nothing like I had imagined. He was slightly shorter than Steve, very thin, had close-cut brown hair and alert dark eyes. His facial bone structure was exquisite. There was a gentle, almost-feline quality to his youthful face. Had he been female, he would have been described as beautiful. Todd Brown resembled a cherub, not a hard-core killer.

He sat across from Anne and me. We all remained silent until the guard shackled Todd's right handcuff to a steel ring on the table. He moved away, eventually sitting at a table several feet from ours. His hard eyes never left us the entire time we were with Todd.

Anne broke the silence. "Todd, this is the writer I told you about. His name is Nick Gabriel."

"Pleased to meet you, Todd," I said.

"What have you written?"

"I did some writing for the movies. I also wrote a play."

"Any movies I might have seen?"

I rattled off four or five that came quickly to mind.

Todd nodded, said, "Yeah, I have seen a couple of them. The one about war was really good. I liked it a lot."

"That's probably the best one I was involved with," I said.

"Anne tells me you may write a book about my case. Is that true?"

"Depends on what I learn today."

"What is it about me, my sorry situation, that interests you enough to write a book?"

"I knew Steve when I was growing up here. I always had a lot of respect for him. He's a good guy."

"Then why not write a book about him?"

"Because he's not in prison for murder," I said, perhaps more bluntly than I intended. "And because I also knew Luke Felton."

"Did you consider him a good guy?"

I dug into my bag and extracted the tape recorder. Placing it on the table, I said, "Are you willing to answer a few questions? If you say no, I'll pack up and leave right now. And there will be no hard feelings."

"Didn't Miss Bishop explain to you that I can't remember anything about what happened that night?"

"She did. But if you're willing, I'd like to take a stab at finding out what you do remember. How about it?"

"Sure, give it your best shot."

I turned the tape recorder on and eased it to the center of the table. Then I went back into the bag and took out the legal pad and a pen. "Okay, Todd, let's assume that I believe you are experiencing a total memory blackout about that night. What I—"

"Are you saying you don't believe me?" Todd asked.

"No. What I am saying is we set the blackout period aside for now. What I want to know is the last thing you do remember that day."

"I went to see a friend... who shall remain nameless... to score some pot."

"What time was this?"

"Four, four-thirty that afternoon."

"Did you get the pot from your friend?"

"Not from him...he wasn't home. I got it from his wife."

"Had you taken any drugs earlier in the day?"

"Of course."

"What about alcohol?"

"No, I had nothing to drink."

"Did you drive to your friend's house?"

"Yes."

"Was anyone with you that afternoon?"

"No, I was alone."

"Okay, so how well did you know Luke Felton?" I asked.

"I saw him around, but I didn't really know him," Todd replied.

"Did he ever sell you drugs?"

"Are you kidding? I'd never buy drugs from a stranger. Why? Did he deal drugs?"

"There's no evidence that he did. But I had to ask." I paused for a moment before continuing. "When did you hook up with Luke?"

"I don't remember hooking up with him. And there's no reason why I would. That makes no sense to me. Like I told you, I barely knew the dude."

It suddenly dawned on me that there was one detail no one had ever discussed. I turned to Anne, and said, "Where was Todd's vehicle located?"

"In the American Legion parking area," she answered.

"Do you belong to the American Legion, Todd?" I said.

"No."

"Were you at the American Legion that night?"

"Yeah, I was."

"Had you ever been there before?"

"No, it was my first time."

"You're too young to be a member, so how'd you get in?"

"I went with a friend of mine. He vouched for me."

"What's this friend's name?"

"Rodney Adcock."

"Rabbit?"

"Yeah, Rabbit," Todd said. "How do you know him?"

"We're the same age. We grew up together. How did you connect with Rabbit?"

"Purely by accident."

"Explain that for me."

"I was in Speedway buying a bottle of Ale 8. Rabbit came in, saw me, and we started talking."

Anne opened her briefcase, removed a pad and a pen, and began taking notes. It was obvious she was hearing this was information for the first time.

I said, "Do you often spend time with Rabbit?"

"Depends on how you define often, I guess. Rabbit's a fun guy to hang around with. I like him because he doesn't always abide by the rules. He tends to do what he wants to do, regardless of rules, or the law. He's kind of dangerous...a renegade, you know?"

"In other words, Rabbit hasn't changed over the years," I said. "Do you buy drugs from Rabbit?"

"Rabbit is an alcoholic but he never touches drugs."

"Okay, you're standing in Speedway. What happens next?"

"He suggested we go to the American Legion and have a drink. And that's what we did."

"What time was this?"

"I don't know, six-thirty, seven, maybe. It was just before dark."

"Was the place crowded?"

"No, not really."

"What did you have to drink?"

"Rabbit ordered us both a bottle of beer. When we finished with those, he ordered a second round. Only this time he also ordered us each a shot of bourbon."

"How much did you end up drinking?"

"I had one more beer and another shot, and that's the last thing I remember. Between then and when the cops woke me up the next day is a total blank."

I thought for a second, then said, "At any time while you were at the American Legion did you leave the bar?"

"Yeah, I went to the restroom after that second round."

"Before the third round, which is the last thing you remember, right?"

"Right."

"Think back, Todd. Do you recall how Rabbit got to Speedway? You say he came inside. Did you see anyone drop him off? See a car pull away?"

"No, I was buying the Ale 8, so I had my back to the front entrance," Todd said. "Why? What difference does that make?"

"Maybe no difference at all. But Rabbit had to get there some way, and I doubt he walked. If someone drove him, I would love to know who the driver was."

"I didn't ask and he didn't say."

"Are you gay, Todd?"

"Hell no."

"For a guy your age, you seem to hang around a lot with older men. I can't help but wonder why."

"Well, it's damn sure not because I'm gay, that I can promise you. And for the record, I spend very little time with older dudes."

"Todd, is there anything else, anything at all, no matter how insignificant you think it might be, that you recall about that day or night?"

"Not really, no."

"One final question, Todd. In your heart of hearts, do you truly believe you murdered Luke Felton?"

"I don't know, but...the evidence says I did. I mean, I had his ring, his blood was on my clothes, and my driver's license was in his car. What other conclusion could I possibly have?"

"You've regurgitated details I already know, Todd. What you failed to do was answer my question. Do you think you killed Luke Felton?"

Todd shrugged but didn't say anything.

I said, "You know, Todd, the evidence against you is awfully strong. Overwhelming, I have to say. Which leads me to conclude that you are guilty, wouldn't you agree?"

"Yes, I agree. But..."

"But what?"

"I can't imagine why I did it."

Eleven

"The way you manipulated Todd into agreeing that he's guilty was virtually an exact replica of how Perry Jackson did it," Anne said, as we drove back to town. "He managed to get Todd to agree three or four times that he killed Luke Felton."

"I'd like to watch the tape of that interview, if possible."

"That can be arranged."

"Were Todd's fingerprints found in Luke's car?" I asked.

"I'm not sure Luke's car was ever dusted for prints. If it was, I never heard about it."

"I have to tell you, Anne, I'd have to give this investigation a failing grade. I understand Todd confessed. But still, he deserved better than he got." I had no desire to pile on, but I wasn't finished venting. "A soft-spoken eighteen-year-old kid with no history of violence suddenly becomes a murderous butcher and no attempt was made to find out why? That's well beyond incompetent, that's criminal."

"You're absolutely right, Nick. The system failed Todd. Hell, *I* failed Todd. Everything about the investigation was sloppy."

"No, calling it sloppy gives it too much credit. Sloppy indicates the investigation took place but it was poorly executed. This investigation wasn't sloppy, it was non-existent."

There was no further conversation during the remainder of the ride into town. Under the circumstances, which had become somewhat tense, silence seemed the wisest option. And that's the one we chose. There was nothing to be gained by treading into areas we didn't need to go.

Timing is rarely perfect, but in this instance it was. Angel was checking into the motel when I walked in. Seeing her, it was all I could do to keep from running up and giving her a big hug. But I wasn't sure how she would react, so I restrained myself. No need to get things off to an uncomfortable start.

"What room are you in?" I asked after she finished registering.

"I requested one across the hall from yours," she replied. "If I'm to be your 'eyes and ears,' I thought it best if we were close together. Lucky for me, the room was available."

"How was your flight?"

"Boring."

"Was the Louisville airport busy?"

"Aren't they all these days?"

"Any trouble finding your way here?"

"No, that's what GPS is for."

Inside the room, I stood around while she unpacked her clothes. When she had everything in its proper place, I said, "I know you're probably hungry, but if you can hold off for a while, there's a place I'd like for us to visit."

"Does it involve the book you're working on?" she asked.

"Yes, it does."

"Then what are we waiting for?"

~ * ~

Although I had grown up in this town, I had never once set foot inside the American Legion. That's because neither of my parents were members, so I had no reason to be there. I had also never been able to understand why the Legion was allowed to sell alcohol when the rest of town was still dry. Even to a kid that seemed hypocritical. There is no shortage of stories about wild things that occurred there, but my favorite was one that involved my uncle, who, after coaching the American Legion baseball team to a victory, celebrated by taking the players to the Legion for a few beers. This was in the late forties, and those players were still in their teens. Can you imagine the outrage that would cause today? Parents would have had my uncle all but executed. Of course, those players worshipped the guy.

There was nothing fancy about American Legion Post 61. The building was one-story, brick, and square. Inside was about what I expected. There was a bar, several long tables, a pool table, dart board, and a stage that had been set up to accommodate local musical acts that regularly performed there. A large U.S. flag dominated one wall, while other walls were covered with hundreds of photos. No more than a dozen people were inside when Angel and I arrived.

The bartender was a burly guy with short blond hair, a Fu Manchu mustache, and tattoos on both forearms. He was standing at the far end of the bar when we entered but he slowly began moving in our direction once he noticed us. There was what could best be described as a wicked grin on his face as he surveyed us.

"Well, you're not a member here," he said, pointing at me. "And she's obviously underage. So, unless you can prove otherwise, you'll not be drinking here."

"Correct on both counts," I said, adding, "but we're not here to drink."

"What are you here for?"

"I'm looking for a guy and I was told he might be here."

"What's this guy's name?"

"Rabbit."

The bartender chuckled, said, "You don't look like a cop, so you must be with the IRS. Those are the folks Rabbit is usually dodging."

"No, I'm just an old friend of his. I'm in town for a few days, thought I would look him up and shoot the breeze for a while."

"Well, chief, your information is better than your timing. Rabbit practically lives here. It's not too far-fetched to say this place is his second home. Truth is, I'm surprised he's not here tonight. But it's still early. He'll probably show up later." He picked up a rag and wiped off the bar. "If you come back in a couple of hours, you'll likely bump into him. He don't miss many nights."

"Any chance you could give me his address or a phone number?" I asked.

"I wouldn't feel very comfortable handing out information like that to a stranger. Sorry."

"Fair enough. I may check in later this evening, see if he's here."

"If you do, don't bring her with you," he said, nodding at Angel. "I won't get hassled for having a non-member on the premises, but an underage kid? That's asking for trouble I don't want or need."

Angel was breathing fire as we headed to the car. "How does he know I'm underage?" she barked. "He didn't bother to ask for my ID. And if he had, I would have showed him a fake one that says I'm twenty-three."

"You have a fake ID?"

"Get real, Dad, I'm in college. Of course I have a fake ID. Several, in fact."

What could I say? My daughter, the budding criminal.

~ * ~

Back in the car I took out my cell phone and called Mike Tucker's number. The call went straight to voicemail. I left Mike a message asking him to contact me at his earliest convenience.

"Who's Mike Tucker and why are you calling him?" Angel wanted to know.

"Mike is one of my oldest and best friends. I'm calling to see if he knows where Rabbit lives. If he does, that will save me from having to pay another visit to the Legion."

"Why do they call him Rabbit?"

"You'll know why when you see him." I started the car and drove away. "Are you hungry?"

"Famished."

"There's not exactly a plethora of eating places to choose from, so don't set your sights too high. McDonald's, Wendy's, Mexican, pizza, barbecue…that's about the extent of your options."

"I vote for getting something from Mickey D's and taking it back to the motel," she said. "We can chat while we eat. Does that sound okay to you?"

"Better than okay," I replied.

We picked up our order at the McDonald's drive-thru window, then drove straight to the Best Western. I was also famished; I'd had little to eat all day. But it was the prospect of sharing this meal and speaking with Angel that I was truly looking forward to.

As we entered the motel lobby, a young woman rose from a chair and rapidly approached us. She was plump but not overly so, had brown hair, and wore cut-off jeans, a blouse, and white tennis shoes. She had a very worried look on her face.

"Are you Nick Gabriel?" she asked. "The writer?"

"Yes, I'm Nick Gabriel," I said, thinking she might ask for my autograph. "And you are—?"

"Heather Anderson."

"What can I do for you, Heather?"

"You're in town to investigate the Todd Brown case, aren't you?"

"No, I'm not investigating anything. I'm seeking material in hopes of writing a book about what happened. Who told you I was here to investigate the Brown case?"

"Karen Tucker. I'm in her weekend Lit class at the community college. She told me."

"Karen was mistaken. She shouldn't have given you that information."

Heather lowered her head. Tears dripped from her eyes. I could sense that there was more to her story than the Todd Brown case.

"Is there a particular reason why Karen told you about me?" I asked.

"She thought you might be able to help me," Sharon said, fighting back a new wave of tears.

"Help you how?"

"My older sister Sharon was murdered almost three years ago and her case has never been solved. I guess Professor Tucker thought you could look into the case, maybe get lucky and uncover some new evidence."

"Your sister's body was found in a car partially submerged in a pond, right?"

"Yes. How did you know about that? Did Professor Tucker tell you?"

"No, Anne Bishop told me."

"I don't know Anne Bishop, but I'm thankful she shared that information with you."

"I'm sorry for your loss, Heather. But I'm not a homicide investigator, so there's not much I can do to help you. Who were the original investigators?"

"Perry Jackson, if you call that asshole an investigator, which I don't. He's a useless piece of slime, if you want my opinion. But the other guy, the FBI agent, he was good. I liked him."

"Do you recall his name?"

"Greg Harkins. He's in the Owensboro office."

Owensboro is a town about thirty-five miles from my hometown.

"Is he still actively investigating the case?" I said.

"He says the case is still open, but...you know what that means," Heather said. "It's no longer a high priority for him."

"When was the last time you spoke with Greg Harkins?"

"Three days ago. I know I'm driving him crazy, and I understand that unless some new evidence pops up, there's not much he can do. But I can't let it go. I want justice for Sharon."

That last statement unleashed a flood of tears. Angel placed her McDonald's bag on a table, reached into her hip pocket, took out a package of Kleenex, and handed it to Heather.

"Thanks. I'm such a big baby," Heather said, after blowing her nose. "I know it's been almost three years since Sharon was taken from us, but I refuse to give up hope. I want her killer caught and severely punished."

I didn't know how to respond. Sharon Anderson's murder had been bouncing around inside my head ever since Anne Bishop told me about it. Anne had pooh-poohed the notion that the murders of Luke Felton and Sharon Anderson were somehow connected, and even though I had no logical reason to contradict her line of thinking, I couldn't escape the feeling the two homicides were linked. Maybe my imagination was playing tricks on me. But maybe it wasn't.

Either way, I couldn't give Heather even the slightest hint that I was thinking along those lines. I didn't want to get her hopes up unnecessarily. Besides, if the FBI couldn't solve the case, what chance did I have?

"Heather, my suggestion is to keep after that FBI agent," I advised. "He's your best chance for finding those answers you're looking for."

Heather nodded, handed the package of Kleenex back to Angel, and silently walked away. I had no idea when or if she would speak with Greg Harkins again. But after our conversation, two things shifted to the top of my to-do list. First, I wanted to watch the tape of Perry Jackson's interview with Todd Brown. I felt it necessary to judge for myself the quality and the fairness of Jackson's technique, which Anne had given a poor review. And second, I most-certainly would contact Greg Harkins.

Surely, an FBI agent should be able to address my notion that the two cases were linked.

Twelve

"God, I feel for that poor woman," Angel said, emotion in her voice. "Her murdered sister's body is left in a car the killer obviously attempted to hide in that pond. No wonder she's so upset."

"Partial body."

"What does that mean?"

"Sharon Anderson's head was missing. It has never been found."

"Thanks, Dad. That's just what I wanted to hear while I'm eating supper."

We were in my room. I suggested coming here so I would be close to my laptop. That way, if an idea or thought popped into my head, some tidbit I didn't want to forget, I could type it on the computer.

"Who is Anne Bishop?" Angel asked.

"Todd Brown's attorney. And the answer to your next question is, no, I've never slept with her."

Angel grinned, said, "Good to know."

"What do you say we talk about you for a while?" I suggested.

"Why? So you will be bored to tears? Okay, what do you want to know? And the answer to your first question is, no, I am not involved with anyone. Fact is, I don't have time to devote to a serious relationship. Next question?"

"What's your major?"

"I have yet to declare one. But that has to change when classes start this fall. The time for waffling has expired. I have to decide between psychology and, are you ready for this, creative writing."

"Really?"

"I'm not blind to the psychological analysis I'll get if I do choose creative writing. There will be those who'll say I'm doing it because I love my father and I want to follow in his footsteps, and others who'll say I'm doing it because I hate my father and my goal is to put him down by proving I'm the superior writer. Neither of those judgments would be entirely right, nor would they be entirely wrong. However, to avoid any criticism, the safe road would be to forget writing and concentrate on psychology."

"Why not a double major?" I said. "Students do that all the time."

"I've considered that, and it's a possibility. I love to write, and I think I'm pretty decent at it, but your shadow would always be hanging over me. How could I ever match your talent, your success?"

"Angel, I've got news for you... you are a far more talented writer than I'll ever be. And believe me, I don't cast that large of a shadow."

"Come on, Dad, you are incredibly successful. You've made millions as a writer."

"Success very rarely has anything to do with excellence."

"Easy for the millionaire to say."

"You learned to write before your fifth birthday. Are you aware of that? And you were such an observant child. You paid close attention to everything that was said in your presence. And then you would wander off and write one-page stories for me and your mother to read. Once, after I told you the story about the scorpion and the frog, you went into your room and an hour later you came out with your own version. In your tale, the frog and the scorpion have their talk, the scorpion promises he won't kill the frog, and they start out crossing the pond. Halfway across, seconds before the scorpion was about to sting his escort, the frog flips over and dumps the scorpion into the water. 'Why did you do that?' the drowning scorpion screams. 'It's in my nature to kill.' As the frog swims away, he croaks, 'True, but it's in my nature to live.' That was a very clever reimagining for a seven-year-old."

"I'm surprised you remember that."

"Remember? I have it framed and sitting on a shelf above my desk in Siesta Key. I look at it when I'm seeking inspiration."

"Wow, I'm stunned."

"Look, you've had a long day, Angel. I'm sure you're worn out. Go to your room, get some rest. I know you can use it."

"What's on the agenda for tomorrow?" she said, standing.

"I want to get with Anne Bishop and take a look at the tape of Todd Brown's interrogation. Then I'll try to meet with Mark Robinson."

"Who's Mark Robinson?"

"The county attorney."

"What about Rabbit? Don't you want to talk with him?"

"We can always find Rabbit. That's not a problem."

She came forward and gave me a big hug. It's the first time that's happened in twelve years. My heart soared with joy. I felt the wall between us was finally beginning to crumble.

~ * ~

William Blake haunted my thoughts, keeping me awake much of the night. A lone thought led the onslaught. Had I become so enthralled by Blake's belief in the sacredness of human imagination that I had allowed mine to travel a false path? I had to keep reminding myself that I'm no William Blake. He was a legitimate genius who genuinely believed the poetry he wrote was dictated to him by messengers from heaven. I'm a hack writer hoping to get information from a guy named Rabbit. Could the gulf between us be any wider? I doubt that's possible.

And yet I could not disconnect the murders of Sharon Anderson and Luke Felton. I was under no illusion that my belief had been sent down from a higher sphere, nor was there a shred of evidence to support my belief, but it had taken root in my mind and wasn't going to fade away.

Crazy? Insane? Improbable? You bet. I agree that those descriptions are accurate. But my imagination, rightly or wrongly, was as real to me as Blake's was to him. I can't escape that truth. In that respect, I suppose I do have something in common with the great William Blake.

Around four, thoughts of Blake faded and I was able to catch a few hours of sleep. At nine, after showering and dressing, I grabbed my computer bag and went down to the breakfast area. To my surprise, Angel was already there. She was sitting alone at a table cutting slices of a banana and putting them into a bowl of Frosted Flakes. An apple was next to the bowl, along with a piece of toast. I filled a cup with orange juice and joined her at the table.

I took out my cell phone and gave Anne Bishop a call. When she answered I asked if I could come to her office and view the tape of Perry Jackson's interrogation of Todd Brown.

"Sure, that's not a problem," Anne said. "But I can send it to your phone in five seconds. That would be quicker, and it would also save you from having to make the trip here."

"Maybe later you can do that," I responded. "But I would prefer to see it on a bigger screen, if it's not inconvenient for you."

"Not at all. Come anytime you want. I'll have it ready to go when you get here."

"Thanks, Anne." I put the phone away and looked up at Angel. "Are you about finished eating?"

"I am. But don't you want something more than a cup of orange juice? That's not going to last too long."

"Not hungry."

Angel dumped her empty bowl and the banana peel into the garbage, picked up her apple, and said, "Okay, Dad, let's book."

~ * ~

I was in no hurry to get to Anne's office, so I decided to drive downtown and point out to Angel some of the places where businesses operated back when I lived there. I doubt she was all that interested in hearing about those old days, but I felt it was something I had to do. I wanted her to know a little about my past, and the town where

I came of age. Blame it on nostalgia or sentimentality, I don't care. I was being hauled back into the past, and there was nothing I could do to prevent it. Like it or not, Angel was going on this journey with me.

I turned onto Broad Street and immediately began pointing to my left, telling her that's where the D&W Café was located. Then there was a florist shop, Winnie's Grill, an alley, J.C. Penney's, and the State Theater, those last two having been burned to the ground by a massive fire in the sixties. The heat from that fire was so intense it melted the J.J. Newberry's sign across the street. To the right, on the opposite corner, there had been a bank, a hardware store, and the pool room, where I spent much of my youth. The next block had been dominated by clothing stores, including Barnes, Cohen's, Vaught's, and the M&R Shoppe. Sadly, not a single one of those businesses were still in existence.

I curled around and headed up Morehead Street past where the elementary school once stood. Then I drove out to the prison where Todd Brown was confined and all the way to Green River. I turned around and went back to town, pointing out where the Coca-Cola Bottling Company once operated. Then we drove up the street and stopped in front of where the high school had been. It had since been torn down and replaced by a nice Convention Center. The old gym, however, was still standing, virtually unchanged after all these years.

Then I continued up Ryan Hill, eventually connecting with Highway 62. This entire area was totally different from how I remembered it. To the left was a small shopping center, to the right was Walmart, neither of which was around when I was a kid.

Angel's silence made it impossible for me to get a read on what she was thinking, although I can't imagine she was all that impressed. Remember, she had lived in cities like Los Angeles and Carmel, California. It would take a truly special place to make an impression on her. My hometown, then or now, certainly didn't measure up to the places where she had resided.

"Was your hometown a wild place to grow up?" Angel finally said.

"Not when I was a kid, no. But back in the old days, especially the thirties when alcohol was still legal, it had the reputation of being a rowdy town. At least, that's what a lot of the old-timers used to tell me."

~ * ~

We drove the rest of the way in silence. I spied a vacant parking spot right in front of Anne's office and pulled in. Her office was directly across from the courthouse. I planned to check in with Mark Robinson when my business in Anne's office was finished.

A young black woman sitting behind a desk welcomed us in. After I told her who we were, she introduced herself as Emma. I didn't know if she was a receptionist, secretary, or a paralegal. For all I knew, in a small office like this one, she might fit all those categories.

We followed Emma down a short hallway into a decent-size conference room. In the room there was an oak table surrounded by six high-back leather chairs, two on each side of the table and one at each end, and a metal stand at the end of the table with a large TV sitting on it. Anne came into the room seconds after Angel and I took seats close to the TV monitor. She started to speak, but stopped when she realized I wasn't alone.

Seeing a look of concern on her face, I stood, and said, "Anne, this is my daughter Samantha. She's visiting from California."

"It's a pleasure to meet you." Anne paused, then asked, "Do you prefer Samantha or Sam?"

"Sam works for me," Angel said.

"Pleased to meet you, Sam."

"Same here."

Anne picked up the remote device from the table and showed it to me. "This is a piece of cake to operate," she said. "Your choices are Play, Pause, Rewind, Fast Forward, and Stop." She handed it to me. "Take as long as you need. We'll chat when you're finished."

Instructions given, she and Emma left the room, closing the door behind them. I looked at the remote, hit the Play button, and the screen came to life.

Seeing Todd Brown on the TV screen was shocking. Sitting in a chair, dressed in shorts, a Tee-shirt and flip-flops, he looked much smaller than he did in person. But then, most people would if they were being hovered over by two hulking behemoths like Perry Jackson and Jimmy Martin. Perry stood about six-one and weighed at least two-sixty, while Jimmy was six-six and two-forty. Todd was what... five-eight and one-fifty? He resembled a child in the presence of two gorillas.

Despite the size disparity, Todd didn't appear to be intimidated or afraid. If I had to describe his demeanor, it would be defiant. He kept his eyes locked on the two larger men, not once looking away. Perhaps this was in preparation for how he would have to act if he were sent to prison. In that cruel world, looking away could be taken as a sign of weakness. Maybe he was just getting ready for what lay ahead.

It was less than a minute into the interrogation before Sheriff Perry Jackson began to browbeat Todd Brown. His tone became more forceful, and he moved so close to Todd that he was virtually in the poor kid's face.

PJ: You murdered Luke Felton, Todd, and I want to know why.

TB: I don't remember anything about what I did last night. It's all a blank.

PJ: Come on, Todd, no one will buy that pitiful excuse. You kill a man, you remember doing it. So...tell me why you killed Luke.

TB: I can't tell you what I don't remember. Sorry, I just can't.

PJ: You did this murder, Todd. Admit it.

TB: I can't. I swear. Why don't you believe me?

PJ: Here's why I can't believe you, Todd. You were in possession of Luke's ring, his blood was on your clothes, and we know for certain that you were in his car. Who else could Luke's killer be? You did it, Todd. Admit it...a great weight will be lifted from your shoulders if you do. You'll feel much better.

TB: But I don't remember doing it.

PJ: Well, you did, Todd. I know it, Chief Martin knows it, and deep down you know it. Confess. Things will go much easier for you if you admit what you did.

TB: But—

PJ: All evidence points to you and to no one else. You killed Luke Felton. Admit what you did.

TB: Okay, you're right, I did it.

PJ: Did what, Todd? Come on, say it. I need to hear the words.

TB: I killed Luke Felton.

PJ (patting Todd's arm): You did the right thing, Todd.

TB: What happens now?

PJ: I put the cuffs on you, read you your rights, get you booked and processed. Once that's taken care of, you get to make a phone call. Now, stand, turn around, and put your hands behind your back.

~ * ~

The tape ended then, before Perry recited the Miranda warning. I punched the Stop button and the TV screen went dark.

"That was no interrogation," Angel said, angrily. "That was an asshole bullying a child until he heard what he wanted to hear. The sheriff should be fired for behaving in such a cruel, unprofessional manner. That's totally unacceptable."

I couldn't disagree. I was as upset about what I'd just witnessed as Angel was. But I vowed to refrain from expressing my anger when Anne showed up. I'd already done that once before; doing it a second time would likely drive a wedge between us that couldn't be removed. I had no desire to alienate a potential ally.

Anne must have heard the TV being turned off. She came into the room, stood at the end of that table, and said, "A pretty sorry excuse for an interrogation, don't you think?"

Reining in my anger, I said, "It was much worse than I expected it to be."

"Like I told you, Todd didn't confess nearly as much as he agreed with Perry."

Fact is, I had a lot more to say about the interrogation... in particular, what was left out... but I would keep those concerns to myself until I had the opportunity to speak with Perry Jackson. Now more than ever, it was imperative that he and I have a serious chat.

"Thanks for letting us take a look at this," I said to Anne. "It was ugly, but helpful."

"Do you want me to send a copy to your cell phone?" Anne asked.

"Probably wouldn't hurt if you did."

Anne's fingers began typing on her cell phone. Seconds later, mine dinged, indicating her message had been received.

She walked Angel and me to the front door, shook my hand, and gave Angel a hug. "It was good meeting you, Sam," Anne said. "I'm just sorry it had to be under these dreadful circumstances."

"Well, dreadful times have a way of becoming good times," Angel said.

"That was a very California-like thing to say," I told Angel, once we were outside. "Almost Zen-like."

"What can I say? I'm a California girl."

Thirteen

As we stood on the corner waiting to cross the street, Angel suddenly pointed toward the courthouse entrance, and said, "That big guy in uniform. He's the asshole who bullied Todd, isn't he?"

"Yeah, that's Perry Jackson," I said, as we watched Perry disappear inside the building. "And I'm not leaving town until he talks to me."

"Now?"

I thought about Angel's question. My plan was to speak with Mark Robinson, the county attorney, to ask him for more background information about Sharon Anderson's murder. But that plan might have to be put on hold for the time being. I feared that if Perry got word I was in the courthouse, he would leave rather than meet with me. I'd had enough of him dodging me.

Not this time, Perry, I said to myself.

"Yes, now," I said to Angel.

We crossed the street, climbed the steps leading to the courthouse, went inside, walked down the hallway, then down the stairs to the lower level where the sheriff's department was located.

When we entered the office, the same deputy who had previously lied to me about Jackson leaving for a bogus family emergency looked up at us with disdain on his face. Unfortunately for him, he was in no position to lie a second time. Perry Jackson was clearly visible standing in his office.

"I'd like to speak with Sheriff Jackson," I announced.

He shifted his attention from me to Angel, keeping his eyes on her longer than I thought appropriate. His were the eyes of a predatory animal. I had no doubt what thoughts were running through his head. The same thoughts every scumbag has when he looks at a beautiful woman.

"Sheriff Jackson," I repeated. "Tell him I'm here."

The deputy, his nametag identified him as McElwain, cut his eyes at me, snickered, and slowly got up out of his chair. He ambled into the sheriff's office, stayed there for less than a minute, came out, and motioned us forward.

Perry Jackson sat behind his desk, the scowl on his face an indicator that he was none too pleased to greet visitors. Especially these two visitors. I sat in one of the two chairs opposite his desk as McElwain closed the door and departed. Rather than sit in the chair next to me, Angel opted to remain standing. I took this to mean she wanted to look down at the sheriff. Her desire to feel dominant had kicked in.

"Well, you finally got your wish," Perry Jackson said, sarcastically. "What was it you wanted to talk about?"

"Todd Brown," I noted.

"Nothing to discuss. That's ancient history."

"Maybe so. But I just finished watching the tape of your interrogation of Todd. There are a few points I'd like you to address, beginning with how you treated Todd."

"Why? Do you have a problem with how I handled it?"

"Yeah, Sheriff, I'd describe it as terribly unprofessional."

"But effective. Todd confessed."

"Only because you bullied him into saying what you wanted him to say," Angel said, forcefully. "You intimidated a frightened, confused kid. That's shitty."

"And you are—?"

"Samantha Gabriel."

"My daughter," I interjected.

"A feisty feline, a tempestuous tiger. Are you an angry pussy...cat?"

Angel's body tensed and she stepped closer to the desk. Her hands balled into fists. Sensing she was ready to erupt, I grabbed her arm and gave it a gentle squeeze. This wasn't the time for an all-out war.

"Cool down, Angel," I whispered. "I've got this."

Angel removed my hand from her arm, took a deep breath, and let her rising tide of anger subside. She was quiet, but still trembling.

"In your interrogation of Todd, there were several important details you failed to address," I said to Jackson. "I'd like to discuss those with you, if you don't mind."

"There is only one detail that really matters...Todd confessed to murdering Luke Felton," Jackson said.

"Ah, there's much more than that, Sheriff."

"Such as?"

"What about the murder weapon, the knife? Why didn't you ask Todd about it?"

"Wouldn't have done any good. You saw the tape. Todd claimed he couldn't remember anything about that night."

"Did you search for the knife?"

"Why waste time? I had his confession. That was good enough for me."

"But weren't you the least bit curious to know for sure whose prints were on the knife?"

"Todd's prints would've been on the damn knife. He knew that. That's why he confessed."

"What if Todd's prints weren't on the knife?"

"Are you telling me you believe someone other than Todd Brown killed Luke Felton?"

"I'm saying I'd like to know for certain. Wouldn't you?"

"I *know* for certain," Jackson said. "And I can't help it if you don't. That's your problem, pal, not mine."

"How did Todd get home from the murder site? His house was six or seven miles from there. That's a pretty long trek to make in the middle of the night. Did he walk, hitchhike, what? I think that's an important question that needs to be answered."

"I don't care if he walked, ran, hitchhiked, or caught a ride on Superman's cape. It doesn't matter. All I know is he was at home asleep in his bed when we showed up the next afternoon. He had Luke's ring and Luke's blood on his clothes. And if that's not enough evidence to convince you, let me remind you that Todd's driver's license was in Luke's car. Goddamn, man, when you add all that up, how can you possibly doubt his guilt?"

"It's not the outcome I question, it's the process used to arrive at that outcome that troubles me," I said.

"You need to get over it and accept the truth."

"Todd's car was found the next morning parked in front of the American Legion, right?"

"Yes."

"Todd wasn't a member, and he was too young to go inside, so why do you think his car was parked there?"

"Because that's where he probably hooked up with Luke Felton."

"Once again, I have to ask: Why would an eighteen-year-old kid hook up with a sixty-eight-year-old man? What could they possibly have in common?"

"Why are you so interested in this particular case?" Jackson asked, avoiding my question. "Hell, you're just a writer. You aren't a cop, don't wear a badge or carry a weapon. Why do you have a bee up your ass for this case?"

"Because I'm a huge fan of justice, that's why."

"What are you saying? That justice wasn't served in this case? Because if you are, then you're that lone voice crying in the wilderness."

"Quoting Isaiah...That's very good, Sheriff. I'm impressed."

"I'm no dumb hillbilly. Believe it or not, I have read a book or two. You're not the only intelligent guy to come from around here."

"Tell me about Sharon Anderson."

"She's dead."

"What can you tell me about her case?"

"Not much. The FBI came in and took over almost from the very beginning," Jackson said.

"*Almost* from the beginning? Does that mean you were in charge for a while?"

"Yeah, for the first day. I went to the crime scene and identified the body. Her purse was in the car, and her driver's license was in the purse. I ran her plates; the car was in her name. Then the next day the Feds showed up and booted me aside. That ended my involvement."

"Who contacted the FBI?"

"I couldn't tell you. If you want answers to those questions, check with that agent. His name is...hold on, it will come to me."

"Greg Harkins."

"Yeah, that's it." Jackson leaned back in his chair and put his feet on the desk. "Do you remember Billy Hughes?"

Talk about a surprising out-of-the-blue question. "Vaguely. Why?"

"The two of you had a fight in the alley behind the movie theater when you were teenagers. Billy was a big, strong kid, yet you beat the shit out of him. Means you must've been pretty tough."

"That was ages ago. Why bring it up now?"

"Billy is my cousin," Jackson said. "When I saw the damage you inflicted on him, I decided to hunt you down and give some payback. But Billy's mom reminded me that I was much older than you, and that an adult can go to prison for beating up a minor. You got lucky. Because of her, I cut you some slack."

"Based on how you treated Todd Brown, I'm surprised you did."

Jackson slammed his feet on the floor and leaned forward. "We're done here," he snapped. "You and your daughter have a nice day. Mac will show you out."

~ * ~

We left without speaking. Angel was still steaming and I can't say I blame her. What Perry Jackson said to her was nasty and uncalled for. She had every right to be pissed. Me, I was simply dissatisfied with Jackson's responses to my questions. They were little more than hollow and repetitious echoes of a story he had convinced himself was true. I didn't share that belief with him.

In the hallway leading to the stairs, Angel said, "So, Dad, you were a real tough guy, a badass, right?"

"Not really. I just chose the right opponent. It kept my winning percentage high and my injuries low."

At the top of the stairs, Angel said she needed to make a pit stop in the rest room. When she went inside, I leaned against the wall to wait for her. Moments later, Karen Tucker came out of Mike's office. She noticed me standing there, smiled, and began fast-walking in my direction.

"I can't believe this," she said, taking hold of my arm. "I was just thinking about you. We need to get together soon for more drinks. When can you come over?"

The rest room door opened at the exact moment Karen asked that question. I prayed that Angel didn't hear it. But she would have to be practically deaf to have not heard it.

"This is my daughter, Samantha," I said, taking a step back from Karen. "Samantha, this is Karen Tucker."

"Pleased to meet you, Samantha." Karen turned to me. "Your daughter is extremely beautiful, Nick."

"Yes, she is," I replied.

Angel eyed Karen suspiciously but asked me, "How do you two know each other?"

"Her husband, Mike. Remember, I told you he's an old friend." I shifted my attention to Karen. "You were coming out of Mike's office. Is he back in town?"

"No, he's expected back sometime Saturday. I was in his office to pick up some papers I need to sign."

"We should be taking off, Karen," I said. "It was good seeing you again."

"When Mike does get back, you two will have to join us for dinner one night."

"Give me a call. We'll be there," I said.

Angel was already halfway down the hall when I left Karen. I caught up with her and we descended the steps to the street together in a silence that continued until we were in the car.

"God, Dad, I cannot believe you," Angel said, buckling her seatbelt. "You are incapable of change, no matter how many promises you make. You slept with your best friend's wife? How slimy is that?"

How the hell did she know that? I started the car, fully aware that she was far from finished.

"I came here because you told me things would be different. And like the idiot I am, I believed you."

"It was only one time," I said. A lame defense, I'll admit, but what else did I have to offer?

"One time, five times or ten times...what difference does the *number* of times make? You want to know the correct number? Zero." She paused to catch her breath. There were tears in her eyes. "I should never have come here. Doing so was a mistake. If I had any sense at all I would pack my things tonight and head back to California."

"Don't do that, Angel. Please, I'm begging you. Having you here, spending time with you, it's the best thing that's happened to me in twelve years. Stick around. Give me one last chance at salvation."

"Like you really care about salvation. You of all people. Salvation for you is only a highway leading to a more glorious place. On Golgotha, you wouldn't simply be nailed to the middle cross. You'd be hanging there wondering what it takes to gain entrance into Paradise."

"That's a rather negative view."

"Yes, but in your case it happens to be true. Paradise through salvation would be too mundane, too common for you. No, you aspire to be like Elijah. Your dream is to ascend into heaven in a chariot of fire."

"No, what I want, *all* I want, is to be close to my daughter again."

"Well, I've got breaking news for you, Dad. I can't speak about Paradise, but your actions are not getting you any closer to your daughter."

Those were the last words she spoke for the rest of the day. Back at the motel, she went straight to her room and closed the door. I desperately wanted to speak with her, to continue pleading my case, but I doubt it would have done any good. Once again, I had blown a good thing.

Alone in my room, I sought to escape those dark feelings by firing up the laptop and beginning work on an early draft of what I hoped would be the first chapter of a book about the Brown-Felton murder case. I knew from experience that whatever I wrote tonight would undergo great change in the future. I was once told that good writing is rewriting. I have no reason to doubt that statement.

Well into the second page, I realized I wasn't writing an actual chapter; I was filling the pages with notes, thoughts, and further investigations I wanted to pursue. None of it was of much substance, and in reality, it didn't keep me from thinking about Angel, who I was almost certain had already packed and was prepared to leave at sunrise in the morning. The realization that she might leave hit me like a ton of bricks.

Sadly, I feared my hoped-for wall had been obliterated.

Fourteen

In the hollow of another sleepless night, my thoughts rambled from place to place before finally settling on something Angel had said prior to her mother's funeral service in Carmel. Angel told me that no matter what, Kate, my ex-wife, had never stopped loving me, and that she would always forgive my indiscretions. Even though I had not seen or communicated with Kate since our divorce, I didn't doubt what Angel told me. Whether I deserved it or not, and I surely didn't, Kate had and would always love me unconditionally.

The question was...why? What was in Kate's nature that allowed her to overlook my failures as a husband? To forgive my transgressions? Her capacity for forgiveness certainly didn't rub off on Angel. Forgiveness from her? Forget it. She crucified me, and rightly so. To me, that seemed more natural than Kate's way of looking at things. No human has the right to extend absolute forgiveness, just as no human deserves absolute forgiveness. That doctrine dates back to antiquity. None of the great religions believes in the concept of total forgiveness. They all have at least one unpardonable sin on the books. Commit that one and you're beyond help.

In hindsight, I could see that Kate was both a saint and a fool to love such an undeserving man as me. I also realized that I had been blind to just how lucky I was to have had her as my wife. Her death ended any hope that I had of redeeming myself in Kate's eyes. Hindsight may be twenty-twenty, but time never reverses direction. It only plows straight ahead.

My immediate plan for the day was to speak with Greg Harkins, the FBI agent working the Sharon Anderson murder. I phoned his office at nine. A man answered and identified himself as Greg Harkins. I didn't know if Greg's answering meant his was a one-person office, or if he was the first employee to arrive. It didn't really matter either way.

I gave him my name, let him know I was a writer, and that I was doing research for a possible book. He took all this in before responding.

"A book about—?" he inquired.

"Todd Brown's murder of Luke Felton," I said.

"Ah, yeah, the kid. I heard about that. He confessed right away. That's a lucky break for law enforcement. But I had no involvement in that case, so I don't think I can be of much help to you."

"Actually, I'm calling about a case you are involved in... Sharon Anderson's murder. I'd like to know what you can tell me about that."

"What's your interest in that case if you're planning to write about the Felton murder? They aren't connected."

I wasn't sure I agreed with that assessment, but I kept my suspicions to myself.

"I'm not insinuating that they are connected," I said. "But Sharon's sister Heather recently paid me a visit and asked if I would look into it. I'm doing it more as a favor to her than anything."

This was a lie.

"Yeah, Heather phones me about every two weeks," Harkins noted. "Poor kid. She's seeking answers I wish I had. But at the present time, I don't."

"Making no progress, huh?"

"At the moment I'm running in quicksand." I could hear the frustration in his voice. "How much do you know about the Anderson murder?"

"The basics," I said. "She was found in her car, her head was missing, and the car was partially submerged in a pond. That's about the extent of what I know. What else can you share with me?"

"Since she had been beheaded, cause of death could not be determined. There were no marks of any kind on her body, so the coroner couldn't be sure if she was deceased prior to having her head cut off, or if the beheading was the cause of death. God forbid that wasn't the case."

"Why do you think she was beheaded?"

"That's a great question. It certainly wasn't to hide her identity. Sharon's purse was in the car with her driver's license in it, the vehicle registration was in the glove compartment, and the car's plates revealed that she owned the car. Cutting off Sharon's head makes no sense, unless, of course, the killer kept it as a souvenir."

"What about drugs? Could that be the reason why she was killed?"

"There was a small amount of pot in the car. But I spoke with Sharon's family and close friends and they all agreed she was not a serious drug abuser. According to them, her vice of choice was beer."

"Was she married?"

"Divorced. And we ruled out her ex from the start. He was visiting Myrtle Beach when Sharon was murdered."

"Boyfriends?"

"We looked into a few names that popped up, but we came away empty." He paused before continuing. "Here's the bottom line, Nick. Unless we catch a lucky break, Sharon's murder will never be solved. That's just a sad fact. I'll keep working it, but I'm not hopeful."

"The perfect murder, is that what you're telling me?"

"The fact is, every murder is perfect until the killer is apprehended."

I thanked Greg for speaking with me and promised I would pass along relevant information should I happen to get any. He said any help would be appreciated, and then we hung up.

~ * ~

There was a knock on my door ten minutes after ending the call with Greg Harkins. The Do Not Disturb sign was in place, so it was unlikely that one of the maids was seeking entrance. I had no clue who it might be. Perhaps it was Angel, but after what happened between us last night, I wasn't going to hold my breath. I doubted it was my daughter, and I was right. It wasn't.

My visitor was Jimmy Martin, his six-feet-six inches and two-hundred-forty pounds filling up the entire doorway. He was dressed in his police uniform, his badge and weapon on full display. Standing there, I had conflicted feelings. I was happy to see him after all these years, but completely surprised that he showed up.

"Been a long time, Nick," Jimmy said, extending his hand. "How has the world been treating you?"

"Not bad, Jimmy," I said, shaking his hand.

"Mind if I come in? We have some things to discuss."

There was a second knock on the door before I could respond. This time, I figured one of the maids chose to ignore the sign and had come to ask if I needed anything. Once again, I was dead wrong. And completely surprised a second time.

The visitor was Angel. I opened the door, she walked in and was about to say something but stopped when she realized I wasn't alone. She looked at me quizzically.

"Samantha, this is Jimmy Martin," I said. "He's the chief of police in this town. Jimmy, this is my daughter Samantha."

Jimmy nodded, said, "Pleased to meet you, Samantha."

"What was it you wanted to discuss, Jimmy," I asked, as Angel sat on the side of the bed.

Jimmy glanced at Angel, the look on his face telegraphing his concerns about talking in front of her. I answered with a silent nod that it was okay for him to say what was on his mind.

"I hear you're in town writing a book about Luke Felton's murder," Jimmy said. "Did I hear right?"

"Not exactly. I'm here doing research for the book. If I fail to collect enough solid, interesting information, then a book is out of the question. At this stage, I suppose you could say I'm in limbo."

"And are you collecting enough solid, interesting information?"

"Too early to tell."

"How long do you plan on sticking around?"

"Too early to tell," I repeated. "Okay, Jimmy, fess up. Why are you really here? Clearly, you have a message you need to deliver. What is it?"

"You're beginning to rattle some cages, Nick. Starting to piss off a few folks."

"Let me guess, Jimmy. Perry Jackson has been whispering in your ear, right?"

"More like shouting in my ear."

"Why am I not surprised? He's not a particularly friendly guy, and he certainly doesn't like his interrogation technique challenged. My advice to him is get over it."

"Perry doesn't like to take advice, Nick. Trust me, I know that better than most people. I've been on the receiving end of his temper tantrums more times than I can count."

"Why? Do you two guys have issues?"

"Who doesn't?"

"You sat in on Perry's interrogation of Todd," I said. "What do you think of Perry's performance?"

"What do you want me to say, Nick? Perry got the kid to confess. That was his goal, and he succeeded."

"Only by bullying and intimidating Todd," Angel said. "That might be acceptable when interrogating a hardened criminal, but not when it's a kid. The sheriff was completely out of line with Todd."

Jimmy smiled, said, "Perry told me you were a hothead. I don't think he was wrong."

"So, what's the subtext of your message, Jimmy?" I said. "That I'm supposed to be scared, to back away from seeking information for my book? Is Perry trying to intimidate me? Did he send you here to threaten me?"

"You know me better than that, Nick. I'm not here to threaten you, only to make you aware that you don't want Perry Jackson as your enemy. He can be ruthless."

"You've warned me. But I'm not scared of Perry Jackson."

"Got it."

"Friend to friend, Jimmy. Are you one hundred percent convinced Todd Brown killed Luke Felton? Be honest."

"Nick, the evidence is stacked so high against Todd it would block out the sun. Based on what I know, what I've seen, my answer is, yes, he is absolutely guilty."

"Okay, Jimmy, let's say I concur that the weight of the evidence looks bad for Todd. But I'm still left with three questions that haven't been answered: Where is the murder weapon, and how did Todd get home after killing Luke?"

"That's two questions. What's your third one?"

"Why was Todd's car parked by the American Legion?"

"Those questions can't be answered because Todd claims he has no memory of what happened that night."

"*Claims*? You sound skeptical. Do you think he remembers?"

"Of course, he does. He claimed he didn't remember for one reason...it would help him get away with what he'd done. Even after that failed, he stuck with his story. It's bullshit. He knows what he did. You can bet on it."

"But a search for the murder weapon was a no-brainer," I pointed out. "That's on page one of the homicide investigation manual. Even though Todd confessed, why not look for the knife? It's the most critical piece of evidence."

"You'd have to ask Perry. That was his call," Jimmy said. "As for how Todd got home, your guess is as good as mine."

"Why was Todd's car at the Legion?"

"Same answer, Nick. Your guess is as good as mine."

"Did you know Luke when he was still a cop?"

"Yeah, he was chief of police when I joined the force. He hired me, in fact."

"Was Luke gay?"

Jimmy grimaced, said, "I don't know, Nick. That's...that's something I'd rather not talk about."

"Come on, Jimmy. You knew the guy. Was he gay?"

"I couldn't swear to it, but I always suspected he swung both ways. Don't forget, he had an ex-wife and two kids. So, he didn't exactly run away and hide from having sex with women. But there was scuttlebutt that he had a thing for boys. Young boys."

Jimmy looked first at Angel, then back at me. He took a deep breath, held it for a second, and slowly let it out. His brow was wrinkled and his eyes were troubled. I could sense he was about to reveal something he felt was important.

"Here's what I think happened that night, Nick. Todd met Luke in the Legion parking lot, maybe by chance, or maybe it was a scheduled meeting. Who knows? Todd gets in Luke's car and they drive away, eventually stopping at the place where the murder occurred. They talk, drink, do some drugs. Again, who knows for sure? Luke makes a play for Todd, promising him drugs or money in exchange for sex. Todd agrees to let Luke jerk him off or give him head. But something goes terribly wrong, maybe Todd changes his mind, he goes berserk and kills Luke. Then he whacks off Luke's finger and takes his ring. Anyway, that's how I see it going down."

Finally, a plausible theory that made perfect sense even though it wasn't what I wanted to hear or believe. And at this point, I didn't believe it. Jimmy's version only served to trigger another set of questions: Where did Todd get the knife? Did he bring it with him? Did it belong to Luke? What kind of knife was it? Pocket knife, switchblade, hunting knife? How long was the blade? Was it serrated or smooth? It would be helpful to have some answers, but lacking a successful search for the knife, it was virtually impossible to know for sure. That glaring oversight rests squarely on ruthless Perry Jackson's shoulders.

I couldn't help but wonder what else might be on Perry's shoulders.

Fifteen

When Jimmy was gone, I turned my attention to Angel, who was sitting quietly on the bed. Dealing with Jimmy, I hadn't had time to consider the fact that she had not only stayed in town, but was actually in my room with me. There were about a thousand things I wanted to say to her, but I felt it best to keep quiet and let her initiate the conversation. I moved closer to her and sat in a chair by the window. She had a pensive, almost enigmatic look on her face. I had no idea what she was thinking, or what she might say, but I was fully prepared to wait until she was ready to say what was on her mind, which she did after almost two more minutes of silence.

"Here's the deal, Dad," she said in a soft voice. "I have made the choice to stick around and continue working on repairing our relationship. Believe me, I'm more surprised by my decision than you'll ever be. And I didn't make it without serious consideration and some deep soul searching. But what I realized was that I really do want us to have a good relationship, to get close again. That can't happen if I leave."

I remained silent, knowing she wasn't finished speaking.

"Also, you're an adult, and that means I have no right to tell you who you can or cannot sleep with," she continued. "But I do have a question for you. Why is it that so many of your sexual conquests put innocent individuals in a position to be hurt? That's the part that baffles me. You were unfaithful to Mom, and now you sleep with your best friend's wife. What's that all about? Is it the risk of getting caught that excites you? Or could it be that you're hoping to get caught. Tell me, I'd really like to know."

"I have no good answers to your questions, Angel," I said. "But I can apologize. I'm sorry I hurt you. I was wrong and I admit it. Beyond that, all I can say is thank you for giving me another chance."

Again, a lame response, but I was thankful for the opportunity to say it. Her still being here was something I had given up on. I was convinced she was on her way to Los Angeles. I wouldn't have blamed her if she were.

I waited for her to comment, not knowing what to expect. When she did, what she said took me by surprise.

"How long have you known Jimmy Martin?" she asked.

"Since we were kids. Why?"

"Do you trust him?"

"More than some, less than others. Why are you asking about Jimmy Martin?"

"Because I don't think he was being truthful. I believe he came here to specifically deliver a threat."

"No question about that. But the threat was from Perry Jackson, not Jimmy."

"Come on, Dad. Does Jimmy Martin strike you as a mere messenger boy for anyone, even a *ruthless* man like Perry Jackson? I don't think so. The guy is big as a tree. I doubt many people frighten him."

"Jimmy was never inclined to back down from anyone."

"There you go. And remember, Jimmy sat in when Todd was questioned. And not all of the interrogation was taped. We have no way of knowing what Jimmy might have said to Todd. He could've been just as belligerent and bullying as Perry Jackson was. I'm telling you, Jackson and Jimmy...those two dudes are tight. No, Dad, that warning was from both men, I'm sure of it."

While I wanted to disagree with her and give Jimmy the benefit of the doubt, I couldn't do it. A voice inside my head kept whispering that she was right.

"Here's something else that troubles me," I said. "I've spoken with Jimmy and with Perry Jackson, yet neither man once went beyond acknowledging that Todd's car was parked by the Legion the morning after the murder. Neither one mentioned anything about Todd being *inside* the Legion. And nowhere in any of those talks did they bring up Rabbit's name. Why, I keep asking myself? Those are huge omissions."

"If Jimmy's theory is correct, Todd probably didn't go inside. He met up with Luke outside the Legion and they left."

"Yeah, *if* Jimmy's theory is to be believed. But that's a big if."

"You don't see it happening the way Jimmy laid it out?" she asked.

"Sounds good, but…there are too many holes in his story to satisfy me. And the so-called investigation? How shabby was that? Todd's car was found in the Legion lot, so why wouldn't Perry Jackson ask the folks inside if Todd was there that night? That would've taken, what, all of fifteen minutes? For any legitimate investigator that would be standard operating procedure in a homicide case. Yet Perry ignores it?"

Angel scrunched up her face, puckered her lips, and in a deep voice said, "It would have been a waste of time. The damn kid confessed," delivering a near-perfect Perry Jackson impression.

"Not bad, Angel," I said, chuckling. "You should be an actor."

"We need to speak with Rabbit," she said, getting serious again.

I liked how she said *we*. "He's definitely on our radar," I responded.

"You keep asking if Luke was gay. Maybe you're posing the wrong question. Maybe the better question is, was Todd gay?"

I shook my head, said, "He wasn't. Karen Tucker had him in class at school. She said he was a ladies' man, a real horn dog."

"Horn dog? Does that sound like anyone we both know?"

Give the kid credit. She knew when to plunge the dagger in and twist it. "I'll plead the Fifth on that one, if you don't mind," I said.

"Wise decision." She turned serious again. "You also keep bringing up the knife, how important it would be if it was located. So, why don't we go search for it?"

"Angel, that knife was never lost. Whoever killed Luke took it with him."

"Which means Todd could have tossed it on his way home, however he got there."

"If you believe Todd is guilty."

"You don't?"

"I'm still straddling the fence on that question. However, more and more I'm beginning to lean toward him being innocent."

"Okay, so how do we prove it?"

"We don't. Not tonight, anyway," I said. "I'm starving. What about you? Are you hungry?"

"Now that you mention it, yeah, I am."

"Good. Let's try the Mexican place next door. I'm craving a chimichanga."

"And a Tecate," she said.

"You're too young to drink, Angel."

"Fake ID, Dad. Remember?"

"I was trying not to."

~ * ~

The motel was close enough to the restaurant that we could have walked there. But we didn't. Angel wanted to drive, so we went in her rental. We ordered...she got her beer without having to flash her fake ID, and thus becoming a Kentucky criminal...and we ate what I considered an excellent meal. We stayed for almost an hour, never once discussing the Brown-Felton murder.

Mostly, we talked about Kate, and about how close she and Angel were. Angel admitted there were the normal mom-daughter adult-teen flare-ups, but none that were too great to overcome. Listening to Angel, I was once again reminded of the mistake I had made, and of how much I had missed.

Angel wanted to pay for dinner, but I waved her off. She asked if she could leave the tip and I agreed. When we got back in her rental, I suggested that we take another spin around town, which we did. I pointed out a few more places that were important to me when I was growing up, including where the old pool room had once been.

"There was an alley behind the place where plenty of arguments were settled," I said. "See that alley across the street? It ran between a restaurant and J.C. Penney's. That alley led up behind the old movie theater. That's where Billy Hughes and I fought."

"So, you were what...a hoodlum?" she asked.

"Far from it. I actually hated fighting. But, there were times when I didn't have a choice. Well, that's what I thought at the time. Looking back, I know there is almost always an alternative to fighting."

"Have you ever heard of Krav Maga?"

"Sure, it's a hand-to-hand combat technique developed in Israel. What about it?"

"I have a brown belt in it. And that's only one step below black belt."

"Really? What prompted you to do that?"

"I read somewhere that Sean Penn excelled at it. I like him, so I thought, why not give it a try? I did, and as it turns out I'm a pretty good student. I moved up the ranks really fast."

"How long have you been taking lessons?"

"Since I was eight."

"So, you're the real badass in the family."

"Let's just say, I do know how to handle myself in a tussle."

"Thanks for sharing that with me. I'll do my best to not piss you off."

"Again, another wise decision on your part."

We drove back to the motel and pulled in next to my car. There were no other cars in that part of the parking lot, which was in back of the motel. But someone had definitely been there at some point. Getting out of the car, I saw that all four of my tires were flat. It was obvious they had been punctured by a sharp object, maybe a knife, possibly a screwdriver. One thing was certain... four tires going flat at the same time was no accident.

Angel moved next to me, stared down at the wounded tires, and said, "Looks like someone sent you a second message."

"And this one can *only* be interpreted as a threat."

Sixteen

"Is writing a book worth this?" Angel asked.

"Searching for the truth is always a worthwhile goal," I answered.

"What if the truth is staring us in the face? Maybe Todd is guilty."

"If he is, why did someone send such a blatant message? What would be the point of doing this? There would no reason to. No, Angel, this proves Jimmy was right. We are beginning to rattle some cages."

"Yeah, and sometimes lions and tigers are in those cages." She kicked one of the tires. "Jimmy Martin came back after we left and did this, didn't he?"

I shook my head, said, "No, Jimmy wouldn't go this route. He's the face-to-face type."

"Then who? Perry Jackson?"

"I don't see Perry doing this; it would be too risky, even in this darkness. But he might not be above dispatching someone else to do his dirty work for him."

"Someone like McElwain? Mr. Personality?"

"He's the most likely candidate." I walked around the parking area and looked up at the back of the Best Western building. "No cameras. Why am I not surprised?"

"It's so dark back here, how can you know for sure?"

"Good point. I'll check at the front desk when we go in."

"What are you going to do about your car?" she asked.

"Nothing I can do until morning. Then I'll have it towed to a place that sells tires and have four new ones put on."

"You need to contact the car rental company."

"This isn't a rental. It's mine."

"You drove here from Siesta Key?"

"Yeah, I did," I said, using my key card to open the motel's back door. "Get some rest, Angel. We'll get my car taken care of first thing tomorrow, then we'll get some breakfast and decide what to do next."

Angel went to her room without argument. I think she was too tired and too worried to offer a challenge. I continued down the hallway and made a right turn into the lobby. No one was behind the desk. I was about to ring the bell to get someone's attention when a middle-age woman bounded out of the back office, all smiles and fully alert for so late at night.

"Yes, how may I help you, sir?" she asked, keeping the smile in place.

"Do you happen to know if there are security cameras in the rear parking area?" I inquired.

She suddenly turned serious. "Why? Is there a problem, sir?"

"No, no problem," I lied. "Just curious, is all."

Relieved, she said, "No, sir, there are no cameras back there. Do you think there should be?"

"Probably wouldn't be a bad idea. Just for security, you know?"

"I will bring that to the manager's attention just as soon as he gets to work this morning." The smile returned in full force. "Is there anything else I can do for you, sir?"

"No, I'm good. Thanks for asking."

~ * ~

Back in my room I sat on the bed and checked my cell phone. In all the confusion I had missed a call from Declan O'Connor. He left a message about an hour ago asking me to call him ASAP. Declan works for the company that is the licensing agent for my play. If someone wants to produce the play, they have to go through Declan's company to secure the rights.

A call from him at such a late hour could only mean he had good news to deliver. Although it was past one in the morning in Manhattan, I didn't hesitate to give him a call. Declan is a notorious night owl—rarely does his head hit a pillow before four a.m.... so I wasn't concerned about waking him up. And if by chance I did, well, he'd just have to deal with it.

"Nick, didn't expect to hear back from you at this hour," Declan said, sounding chipper and wide awake. "Did you just get back from a late-night stroll along the beach?"

"I'm in Kentucky, Declan," I pointed out. "That's a long way from the beach."

"What possessed you to make a journey to Kentucky? Vacation or business?"

"Doing research for a book."

"Good luck with that," he said, half-heartedly. Then: "I have great news for you concerning *Divine Rebel*. You're gonna love it."

"I'm all ears, Declan."

"In London, the Old Vic has agreed to extend the production for another six months with Jeremy Irons taking over as Blake. On our side of the big pond, the Mark Taper Theatre in Los Angles is planning a production with Brian Cox in the lead. And most exciting of all, Chicago's Steppenwolf Theatre is set to have a limited run beginning in September. Gary Sinise has agreed to direct and John Malkovich will portray Blake. Only death will keep me from seeing that one."

"This is terrific news. But still nothing in New York?"

Ever since *Divine Rebel* closed in New York and moved to London, there had been no production on or off Broadway. That was a big disappointment for me.

"As of now, no, but I'm working on it, so don't give up hope," Declan said. "But wait, there's more good news, Nick. Producers in Canada and Australia have made inquiries, and so have a half-dozen regional theatres in this country. Thanks to you, William Blake has been reborn."

"I appreciate the update, Declan," I said. "Keep me posted. And if you need anything from me, just call. I'm always available for you."

"I'll do what I can to keep the dollars flowing in, Nick. You know that."

More money, the play's additional exposure...that was great and I didn't downplay it. But not having a production in New York City robbed me of some enthusiasm. Realistic or not, I wasn't going to be completely satisfied until *Divine Rebel* was on or near Broadway.

I undressed, and after making a stop in the bathroom I set the alarm on my phone for six-thirty, pulled back the sheets, and got into bed. Too wired to get any sleep, I resigned myself to another restless thought-filled night. My head was buzzing. I was dead to the world two minutes later.

~ * ~

The tow truck was at the motel at nine the next morning. After the Lexus was hooked up and ready to go, the driver recommended taking it to Pace Tire Company on West Broad Street. I had no problem with that, and told him Angel and I would follow in her rental.

Pace Tire has been around since I was a kid, but I didn't know who owned the place or any of the current employees. Back in the old days, a guy named Tom owned it. When the tow truck pulled in and lowered the Lexus, a man dressed in coveralls and hard-toe boots came out to greet us. He identified himself as Rick Morgan. I had no way of knowing if he was the owner or just one of the employees.

"Four slashed tires," he said. "I'm gonna go out on a limb and say this wasn't the result of an accident."

"That's a keen observation, Rick," I replied.

Rick knelt, jammed his forefinger into one of the puncture holes, looked up at me, and said, "You chasing another man's hide?"

I could've sworn I heard Angel snicker in the background. Or maybe it was a groan. I couldn't tell for sure.

"No, not recently," I said, attempting to blend honesty with humor.

"Just asking, because this is the kind of thing a pissed-off husband or boyfriend might do."

"Do you have four good tires to replace these?" I asked, changing the subject.

"What's your price range?" Rick wanted to know.

"Cost is not an issue. Just give me the best tires you have."

Rick motioned toward a door, said, "Let's step into the office. I need to get some information from you."

After I had filled out the paperwork and paid in advance, I said, "Any idea how soon can you have this done?"

"We're slammed this morning, but I should have it ready by two, two-thirty at the latest. Will that work for you?"

"What time do you close?"

"Around six."

"I'll be here before then," I said, handing the car keys to Rick.

"Anything else you want us to do while it's here? Tune-up, maybe?"

"Just the tires, Rick."

Angel was already behind the wheel when I got in her car. "Do you think McDonald's is still serving breakfast?" she said.

"It's past ten-thirty, so I doubt it. But if it's breakfast you want, we can always go to Huddle House."

"You know what, Dad? I'm in the mood for a big delicious nasty burger and some fries. Sinful, I know, but you only live once, right? Besides, who's keeping score?"

"Mickey D's, it is."

~ * ~

Angel drove in silence but I sensed something was on her mind. She had a troubled look on her beautiful face. I worried that she was fretting too much about me, which I didn't want her to do. My problems were my concern, not hers.

Once we were inside McDonald's, placed our orders and taken a seat, she finally said what she was thinking. "Dad, don't you think it would be wise to move to another motel?"

Not a question I expected. "No way," I said. "Nobody is scaring me off."

"Relocating doesn't necessarily mean you're scared, only that you are being cautious."

"Where do you suggest we go, Angel? It's not like there's an endless number of motels around here."

"I don't know. Just some place other than Best Western. A location where no one knows we're there."

"We can always ask Mike and Karen Tucker if we could stay with them. I'm sure they would be more than happy to have us."

"*She* would, that's for damn sure."

"We stay where we are, Angel. I'm not running from anyone."

"That sounds like tough-guy talk."

"I don't have to be tough when I have Miss Krav Maga and her brown belt on my side."

"Don't be facetious, Dad. You just might need me before this is all done."

I started to reply with my acid wit, but stopped when I saw a familiar face walk in. Heather Anderson came into McDonald's accompanied by a woman of similar age and build. She marched straight to our table, leading me to conclude that she noticed us as she was preparing to place an order at the drive-thru window, parked instead, and came in to speak with me, her head filled with questions I had no answers for. I stood seconds before she arrived at our table.

"Mr. Gabriel, have you had a chance to look into my sister's murder?" Before I could respond, she said, "Oh, sorry, this is my friend Janice."

I acknowledged Janice with a nod and then motioned for them to join us. Heather slid in next to me, Janice next to Angel. "I did speak briefly with Greg Harkins," I said. "Unfortunately, he didn't have anything new to offer."

"Is he even working the case?"

"Yes, he is."

"Well, that's good to know," Heather said, not sounding placated by my response.

"He has a lot on his plate right now."

"I'm sure he does."

"Sharon was divorced, right?" I asked.

"For a long time now."

"What can you tell me about her ex?"

"Donnie? He's a selfish jerk. That's why Sharon split from him."

"Agent Harkins said he ruled out Donnie from the start. Do you agree with that?"

"Yeah, sadly, I do. See, Donnie knocked up a chick about four years ago and had to get hitched. Since then, he's fathered two more rug rats. He doesn't have time to murder anyone."

"Agent Harkins also told me Sharon was dating a few guys but none that was special or serious. Is that accurate?"

Heather looked at Janice before answering. "No, that's not accurate," she said, shaking her head. "Sharon had gotten serious about someone a short time before she was murdered. I think she was really ditzy about the guy."

"Do you know who he was?"

"I don't. She never mentioned his name, and I never saw them together. Which was really strange, because Sharon and I didn't keep secrets from each other. We shared everything."

"Why do you think she kept his identity secret?" I asked, knowing what her answer would be.

"Probably because he was married."

"How long had the relationship been going on?"

"Can't say for sure, but my guess would be at least three months."

"Did you share this information with Agent Harkins?"

"I didn't, no." Heather looked stricken by this admission. "I should have, but I—"

Tears filled her eyes and her nose began to leak. Janice came to the rescue, handing her a tissue and offering a gentle pat on her arm.

"I understand Sharon liked to drink beer," I said, hoping to brighten the mood.

This time it was Janice who answered. "Drink it?" she said. "It would be more accurate to say she guzzled it. Right, Heather?"

Heather blew her nose, wadded the tissue into a ball, and nodded her agreement.

"Where did Sharon do most of her drinking?" I asked, unsure which lady would answer.

"At home, my house, Janice's place, just about anywhere, really," Heather said.

"What about the American Legion? Did she ever drink there?"

"Yes. Sharon started going there when she and Donnie were married, and she still goes there quite often." Heather realized what she had just said. "I meant she *used* to go there quite often."

"Do you know Rabbit?"

"Everybody knows him."

"Could he have been Sharon's serious friend?"

"Heavens, no," Heather said, suppressing a giggle. "They were just drinking buddies, nothing more."

I had officially run out of things to say to Heather. No more suggestions, no more questions, nothing. Staying any longer would be a waste of time.

"I hate to break this off, Heather, but Samantha and I need to get moving," I said, standing. "I have an important interview scheduled in a few minutes and I can't afford to be late. So, if you'll excuse us, we'll leave you guys in charge of the place."

"I had no idea that I was taking up so much of your time," Heather said. "Yes, by all means, go. But I do appreciate all you're doing for me regarding my sister's murder. Maybe with a little luck, you or Agent Harkins will find out who killed Sharon."

Don't hold your breath, I wanted to say but didn't.

As we stepped out into the sunlight, Angel said, "Why did you lie to Heather? You don't have an important interview in a few minutes."

"That was no lie. I was being truthful with her."

"Who is this big interview with?"

"The bartender at the American Legion."

Seventeen

The Legion hall was extremely busy when Angel and I walked in. This came as a surprise to me. It was not yet one o'clock, yet vast quantities of alcohol were already being consumed. And make no mistake, no one was playing checkers, gin rummy, or throwing darts. They were here to drink.

The crowd consisted mainly of men, although four or five ladies were included among the early drinkers. Based on the ages of those on hand, it could safely be concluded that every American conflict from World War II through Iraq and Afghanistan was represented. Many of the men wore baseball caps that connected them to the war they fought in.

The same burly man who had been here on our previous visit was once again tending bar, although he had a different look about him— the Fu Manchu was missing. He had on a blue baseball cap with Navy Vietnam Veteran in yellow letters on the front. I doubted that I could ever be friends with the guy, but as a fellow vet, I should be able to summon a certain degree of respect for him.

He slapped a dishrag over his left shoulder when he saw us coming in his direction, turned his palms up, and shrugged, a shit-eating grin spreading across his recently shaved face.

"Thought we had reached an understanding that only active members drink here," he said. The name on his shirt identified him as Chet. "And the last time I checked the roster, you ain't on it."

"Same answer as before—we're not here to drink," I replied.

"My point being, you have no reason to be here at all. So, why don't you and Miss America do an about-face and march on out of here. If you leave voluntarily, it will save me the time and energy required to toss your ass out."

"Here's my counter offer. One vet to another vet, how about you sell us a soft drink? That's only fair, isn't it?"

"*You* served in the military? What...college ROTC for a semester?"

"Army, Twenty-fourth Infantry Division, first Gulf War, Operation Desert Storm. And I have the medals to prove it."

"Well, I don't hardly see how I can deny a war veteran a soft drink," he said, his shit-eating grin back in place. He opened a cooler under the bar, came out with two cans of Coke, laid two coasters on the bar, and placed the soft drinks on the coasters. "Did you see actual combat, or were you one of those back-of-the-pack support guys?"

"Ask the Iraqi Republican Guard, if any of them are still around." I took a drink of Coke. "So, does my military resume meet with your approval?"

An Army guy asking someone from the Navy for approval? How absurd is that?

"If it's true, sure, I have no issues with it." Chet grinned and shook his head. "You know, you're even more unlucky than you are persistent."

"You're speaking in riddles, Chet. I don't have a clue what that's supposed to mean."

"Rabbit practically lives in this place—hell, he could almost have his mail delivered here... yet you've showed up twice looking for him and he's not been here either time. That's like a guy in a whore house who can't find the pussy. You know what that says to me?"

"Not really, but I'm probably about to find out," I said.

"That maybe Rabbit ain't looking to be found. That maybe he's purposefully avoiding you."

"Why would he do that?"

"Probably because he don't like strangers asking him questions."

"Strangers? I've known Rabbit a lot longer than you have. We grew up together. And for your information, I never said I was looking for him."

"Why else would you be here?"

"To ask *you* a few questions, Chet."

"Well, Chief, that marks you as a two-time loser. Rabbit ain't here, and I'm in no mood to answer your questions." Chet looked straight at Angel but directed his words at me. "I guess that makes you one unlucky fuck."

Angel didn't react or respond in any way to what Chet said. Although she was silent, her eyes were locked onto his. I had the feeling she was sizing up which moves would be required to beat the crap out of a man who spoke in such a vile, ugly manner. But Chet was a big strong-looking guy, so I could only hope she didn't elect to make a move against him.

"Here's your choice," I said, quietly. "You either answer a couple of simple questions from me, or a whole series of questions from the FBI. It's your call, *Chief*."

This was, of course, mostly a bluff. And not one I thought was very persuasive. Why should it be? I'm a writer, not a cop. Turns out I was right.

"I'll tell you the same thing here and now that I'll tell the FBI if they show up," Chet snapped. "And that is...fuck off."

With that pronouncement, Angel's patience had reached its limit. Leaning forward, elbows on the bar, she said, "Were you born a complete asshole, or did you have to work hard to achieve that goal? If you did have to work at it, you certainly succeeded, because by any realistic standard of measurement you are most-definitely a world-class asshole."

Chet looked at me, grinned, and said, "Damn, Chief, I like her a whole lot more than I like you. She's got some brass balls on her somewhere." He shifted his attention to Angel. "Okay, Miss Brass Balls, for you I'll let your boyfriend ask—"

"My *father*."

"…your father ask a couple of questions. Go for it, Dad."

Not ashamed to follow my daughter's lead, I said, "Are you aware that on the night Luke Felton was murdered, Todd Brown was here with Rabbit?"

"Ah, Chief, Rabbit drinks with dozens of different people when he's here, many of whom pay for his booze." He swept an arm toward the seating area. "And that includes just about everyone here right now. How can I be expected to remember who anyone was with on a specific night months ago? That's damn near impossible."

"When we were previously here, you made a big deal about my daughter being underage, and therefore you wouldn't serve her alcohol for fear of 'causing trouble you didn't want or need.' Those were your exact words. Do you recall saying that?"

"Yeah, I said it and I meant it."

"Yet you served Todd Brown when he was in here with Rabbit?" I nodded at Angel. "And Todd is younger than Samantha. What's your explanation for breaking your own rule?"

"You're claiming he was served that night," Chet said defiantly. "I don't have any memory of him drinking alcohol. Do you have proof that he did?"

"Yeah, I do. Todd acknowledged it."

"The kid's a convicted murderer, Chief. Do you think he's beyond lying?"

"Why would he? He's already locked up for life. What reason does he have to lie about anything?"

"What else can I tell you, Chief? I don't remember Todd Brown drinking that night, but if he did, who cares? What difference does it make now?"

"But you do remember him being here that night with Rabbit, right?"

"Maybe. But I wouldn't swear to it."

"Todd says he went to the rest room while he was here. Says he was away from the bar for a few minutes."

"Big deal. Going to take a whiz ain't exactly a newsworthy event."

"Did you know Todd had a pharmacy of drugs in his system on the night Luke was killed?" I said. "The kind of stuff that might cause a person to have a complete memory loss?"

"How could I possibly know that?" Chet said. "And I hope you aren't suggesting that I or anyone else sells drugs here, because we don't. Drugs of any kind are strictly forbidden on these premises."

"Think hard, Chet. Is it possible someone slipped something into Todd's drink while he was in the rest room?"

"Like who? Rabbit?"

"You tell me. Is Rabbit capable of doing something like that?"

"Why are you asking me, Chief? You're the one who grew up with him. You know him better than I do. Those are *your* own words."

"People change over time. He may not be the same guy I remember."

"Rabbit would never spike someone's drink, not in a million years. He's an alcoholic and he's a little weird, but he's not evil. And only an evil person would do something like that."

"There's something we can agree on, Chet," I said. "What do I owe you for the two Cokes?"

"For a genuine war hero, they're on the house," Chet said, sarcasm dripping with every word. "But those two Cokes are all you get. Don't bother coming back again with more of your questions. Third time ain't a charm, Chief. If you do, I will toss your ass out, medals and all. You get my message?"

Out of the corner of my eye, I saw Angel's body tense up. Although I have never seen a live jaguar on the prowl for food, that's what Angel reminded me of at this moment. She was wired and ready to pounce on her prey. I gently reached out and took hold of her arm, making sure she didn't charge at Chet. She wanted to, that was obvious.

"Message received loud and clear, Chet. Whether or not I adhere to it, well, only time will answer that for us." I laid a five-dollar bill on the bar. "That's for the drinks. Keep the change as your tip."

~ * ~

I expected Angel to explode like a bomb going off once we were outside the Legion. But that didn't happen. She was quiet all the way to the car. I have to give her credit...she was cool and restrained, not allowing her anger to control her actions. Angel was the kind of warrior I'd want beside me in a foxhole when the shit hit the fan.

Using her fob, she unlocked the car and we both got in. She started the engine, turned to me, and said, "That guy is such a turd."

I buckled my seatbelt and said, "I thought you called him a world-class asshole."

"Well, yeah, that too." She backed away from the Legion, made a sharp turn, and we headed for town. "What's our next stop, Dad?"

"Check on my car, see if it's ready. If it is, we'll go back to the motel and hang out until it's time to eat."

The Lexus was ready when we showed up, fitted with four brand new tires, waiting for me to get in and drive it away. Rick came outside when he saw us pull up in front of the big bay door. He had the keys in one hand and a receipt and warranty papers in the other hand.

"Your timing is impeccable," he said, smiling. "We finished putting the last tire on not more than fifteen minutes ago. She's ready to roll."

After making a cursory inspection of the new tires, which all looked good, I took the keys and papers from Rick, thanked him, and shook his hand. Prior to getting into my car, I asked Angel if she needed to follow me to the motel. It was a question better left unasked.

"Are you joking, Dad?" she replied. "If I can navigate my way around L.A.'s freeway system, I'm pretty sure I can keep from getting lost in Central City."

What could I do other than agree with that declaration?

Angel didn't get lost, successfully navigating the three turns required to get from Pace Tire to Best Western, a trip that took fewer than ten minutes. You can't get anywhere in Los Angeles in such a short time, regardless of how close point A is to point B. In my hometown, point A *is* practically point B.

~ * ~

At the motel I once again parked next to Angel and got out. She was a couple of steps in front of me as we moved toward the building. When we reached the back door, she made a snide reference to Lewis and Clark. I think it was her way of boasting about being a pathfinder, but I couldn't swear to what she was trying to convey. Didn't matter; I ignored it.

Angel went to her room, I went to mine. I think both of us felt a need to spend some time alone. Like point A and point B in my hometown, we had practically been joined at the hip for the past several days. Don't get me wrong...I'm not complaining. I appreciate every second with Angel. But a little time apart would probably do us both some good.

In desperate need of a drink, I cursed myself for not stopping on the way to the motel and purchasing some scotch and soda. A major oversight on my part. In lieu of alcohol, I walked down the hallway, found a vending machine, and bought a bottle of Pepsi.

My cell phone was buzzing when I got back to the room. I set the Pepsi on a table, picked up the phone, and cringed when I saw who was calling. Karen Tucker.

The last person on earth I needed to speak with.

"Karen," I said, trying to drum up some fake enthusiasm. "I didn't expect to hear from you. Is everything okay?"

"Everything is fine," she said. "Are you alone? In a position to speak freely?"

Damn. Now I regretted not having Angel in the room with me.

"Yes," I said.

"Why don't you come over tonight? I'd love seeing you again."

"Not a good idea, Karen. Maybe when Mike gets back, Samantha and I will have dinner with you guys."

"Samantha won't come...she hates me. She made that perfectly clear at the courthouse."

"That's because she knows about us. She doesn't approve. And to be perfectly honest with you, Karen, neither do I. What we did was a mistake. It can never happen again."

"Come see me, Nick," she pleaded. "We'll talk, have a couple of drinks, nothing more. I promise to be a good girl."

"Can't do it, Karen," I said. "Sorry."

"Why? Because you betrayed Mike? Your best friend?"

"We both betrayed Mike, Karen."

"What about Mike betraying me? Did you ever consider that possibility? And would that factor in at all?"

"What are you saying, Karen? That Mike cheated on you?"

"That's exactly what I'm saying. And not *cheated*, *cheating*. Do you think for one second that he's attending his meeting alone? Well, here's a news flash for you… he's not. He's with his newest paramour. Her name is Cheryl and she's from Dallas. Hate to shatter Mike's image for you, Nick, but he's far from the saint you make him out to be."

I sat there stunned, letting her words sink in, unsure how to respond. But I didn't get the chance. Karen wasn't finished unloading her anger.

"And for your information, Nick, this isn't his first fling," she continued. "He was head over heels in love with a woman about three years ago. Unfortunately, I never got her name."

Three years ago. Sharon Anderson. Say it ain't so, Joe.

"If you didn't get her name, Karen, then maybe you're mistaken. I mean, how can you know for sure?"

"How can I know for sure? Here's how, Nick. For almost a year, Mike moped around like he was the saddest man in the world. He rarely spoke, lost weight, and had no interest in having a physical relationship with me. I don't know why the affair ended, or who broke it off, although judging by how he dealt with it, I'm betting she did. The man was totally devastated. I didn't think he was ever going to snap out of it."

"Look, Karen, your marriage is between you and Mike," I said. "You guys are the only ones who can work it out. What goes on between the two of you is none of my business."

"Work it out? Yeah, right, like that's gonna happen."

"I don't know what to tell you, Karen."

"Tell Mike that you and I talked. Tell him I know about his affair. His *affairs*. Tell him that if he doesn't drop Cheryl, I'm out the door. Tell him I'm done with his philandering. And tell him this is his last chance. That's what you can tell him, Nick."

Her spiteful oratory concluded, now in tears, she ended the call. I was thankful and relieved that she had. There was nothing else for me to say, and I'd grown weary of listening to her demolish Mike, which she did without painting a full or accurate picture of what had transpired. Mike cheated *on* his wife, I cheated *with* his wife. Way I saw it, there was plenty of blame to go around. But like I told Karen, the fate of their marriage wasn't in my hands. I didn't know how they could repair the damage, even if that was still possible. All I knew for sure was that I'm in no position to pass judgment on anyone. I have enough sins of my own to answer for.

Eighteen

Angel and I were in Philly's Restaurant sitting across from Anne Bishop. Anne had phoned earlier asking to meet and to exchange notes regarding the Todd Brown case. I had no idea what notes she might have... she hadn't appeared to be working the case very intensely the last time we met... but I agreed to see her. Anne struck me as a serious professional who genuinely had Todd's best interest at heart, even though I questioned the extent of her recent effort to help. However, before casting too many stones at her, I couldn't overlook the fact that any effort she put forth, then or now, had been seriously short-circuited by Todd's ill-advised early confession. She was hamstrung from the start.

Anne was almost finished with her salad by the time Angel and I finally showed up. We had eaten breakfast two hours earlier at Huddle House, so we only ordered something to drink. Angel had iced tea, I had a Pepsi.

"Anything new or important you have to share?" Anne said, before taking a drink of her tea. "I'm assuming you are continuing your research."

Angel nudged me in the ribs with her elbow before I could respond. "Look who just walked in, Dad," she whispered. "Coincidence or do you think we're being followed?"

Perry Jackson and Deputy McElwain, both men attired in full uniform, strutted in looking like they owned the place. Sheriff Andy and Barney Fife would've been envious. They were accompanied by a third man who looked to be a few years senior to his companions. He wore gray khaki pants, a blue Polo shirt, and Dockers. He moved like a man with high self-esteem, a man comfortable with giving orders while fully expecting each one to be followed to the letter.

"You've been reading too many spy novels," I said to Angel. "I doubt they are following us. This is a restaurant, and it's lunch time. The fact that we're here at the same time is pure chance. We have nothing to be concerned about."

"Who are you referring to?" Anne asked. Her back to the door, she had not seen the three men enter. She glanced over her shoulder to get a better look. "Oh, you mean Perry and Dorsey?"

"Dorsey? That's McElwain's name?" Angel said.

"Yes."

"Do you know the guy who is with them?" I asked.

They had taken a table in the back, which required Anne to shift in her seat in order to see them clearly. "Russell Barker," she finally said, settling back in her seat.

"What's his deal?" I inquired.

"Russell was the county sheriff prior to Perry Jackson," Anne answered. "He held the job for several years, a decade or more, if I recall correctly. Then about eleven or twelve years ago, he decided not to seek re-election. I guess he'd just become tired of the job. No one was going to beat him if he ran again; he was a lock to win. Anyway, after resigning he sat around doing nothing for a year or so, and then decided to run for magistrate. He won easily, and has been re-elected ever since."

"So he worked with Perry Jackson?"

"Yes, I'm positive their time in the sheriff's office overlapped. In fact, I'd say Russ hired Perry."

"Have you had any dealings with Russell?"

"No. I really don't know the man at all. But what I can tell you is that he's very powerful in this county." Anne pushed her plate away. "I'm so full I could explode."

I said, "I'd really like to speak with Todd again. Can you make that happen?"

"How soon would you like to meet with him?"

"What about this afternoon? Is that possible?"

"I don't see any reason why we couldn't. I'm his attorney of record, which gives me the right to meet with him anytime I see fit. All I have to do is call the warden and let him know I'm on the way. He'll have Todd waiting for us when we get there."

"What about Samantha?" I said. "Can she come with us?"

"If she wants to, sure," Anne replied.

"How about it, Angel?"

"You have to ask?" she said, standing. "Why are we waiting?"

~ * ~

Anne followed us from Greenville to the Best Western, where Angel and I got in her car for the drive to the prison. Angel sat up front with Anne, while I rode in the back jotting down questions I wanted to ask Todd.

At the prison we cleared security with no problems and were led to what was obviously someone's office. There was a desk, bookcase, table, and six chairs in the room. When we got there, we were told that Steve and Mary Sue Brown were visiting Todd, along with Todd's mother, Susan. Steve, who was facing the door, saw us, got up from the table, and came out to talk with us. He had a very distraught look on his face. Who could blame him?

"Good to see you again, Nick," Steve said, forcing a smile. "Are you guys here to speak with Todd?"

Anne said, "Yes, but don't let us rush you off. We're in no hurry."

"Why don't you come in with us?"

"I think they might frown on six people with him at the same time," Anne said. "It's probably better if we wait until the three of you leave."

I didn't know if what Anne said was true or not, but it did make sense.

Steve went back inside but remained standing. A short while later, the two women stood and gave Todd a long hug, Mary Sue first, followed by Susan. It was plain to see how difficult it was for them to say goodbye. I'm sure they would be perfectly willing to stay with Todd forever. As they walked out of the room, the tears they had been holding at bay while in front of Todd came streaming out. It was one of the most heart-wrenching scenes I've ever witnessed. I had tears in my eyes, and so did Angel and Anne.

I feared that Todd would be too weary to speak with us but I was wrong. He actually seemed pleased when we walked into the room. I think he was relieved that the weight of his family's pain had been lifted. Another reason why he was eager to chat was the presence of my daughter. He kept his attention focused on Angel, even after I introduced her and we were seated.

"How are you holding up, Todd?" Anne asked.

"Same as I was yesterday, same as I will be tomorrow," he said, wistfully. "What's the reason for this visit? Is something up?"

"Nick has some questions he'd like to ask you."

Todd shrugged and said, "I don't know how much more I can tell you than I did the first time you were here. But, yeah, go ahead, ask away."

"Todd, have you been able to recall anything at all about that night?" I said. "Anything?"

"No. It's all still a blank. Sorry."

"That's okay, Todd. Then let's go back to what you do remember. Back to when you first walked into the Legion. What about the bartender? What can you tell me about him?"

"He was a big burly dude with one of those droopy mustaches. I forget what you call them."

"Fu Manchu," I said. "What else can you tell me about him?"

"Nothing. He didn't speak to me at all."

"Who ordered the drinks?"

"Rabbit."

"Did the bartender make an issue of selling alcohol to you?"

"Not to me, he didn't. And I don't remember him hassling Rabbit about it. Maybe that's because they're good buddies."

"Did Rabbit talk to anyone else while you were there?"

"Rabbit talks to everybody."

"Did he have an especially long conversation with anyone?"

"If he did, I wasn't aware of it."

"I want you to close your eyes, Todd, and go back as far as your memory allows concerning that night in the Legion," I instructed. "Let your mind float around the place. Try to remember the sights, sounds, smells. Do you recall seeing anyone there that night that you were familiar with?"

Todd kept his eyes closed and was silent for nearly a minute before finally saying, "No, I don't...hey, wait a minute. I do remember seeing some people I knew. The Lucketts. Brenda and Richard. They were sitting with another couple at a table against the wall."

"How do you know the Lucketts?"

"Their daughter Kelli was in my class at school. We hung out together quite a bit back then. I met her parents when I would go pick her up at their house."

"Do they live in Central City?"

"Greenville."

I turned to Anne and said, "Do you know them?"

"Does Brenda Luckett work at the library?" Anne asked Todd. When he nodded, she said to me, "I don't know her well, but we've spoken on several occasions. She's a very nice lady."

"Where do they live, Todd?" I said.

"On the corner next to the old Greenville high school."

"We should go talk to them."

Anne looked at her watch, said, "The library is still open for another couple of hours. We should go there instead and talk to Brenda. Then later this evening we can talk to Richard, if necessary."

"Yeah, that's a better plan, Anne," I admitted.

"What are you going to ask the Lucketts?" Todd said. "I mean, I don't see how they can help."

"Maybe they can't help, Todd. But I want to ask them who they saw at the Legion while you were there. Hopefully, they'll give us a name or two. Perhaps they won't. But it never hurts to ask."

When we stood, Todd said, "Thanks for coming by, and thanks for believing in me. I don't know if I killed Luke or not, but I would like to know for sure either way."

Anne said, "You stay strong, Todd. Hang in, but don't let your hopes get too high. We're fighting a long uphill battle, one we're not likely to win. But who knows? Stranger things have happened. That's why we'll continue to fight for the truth."

~ * ~

When we were in the car I wasn't reflecting on our conversation with Todd. My thoughts were on Russell Barker, the man we had seen with Perry Jackson and Dorsey McElwain at Philly's earlier today. There was something about the man I couldn't quite pin down. He possessed a certain quality that eluded me, that I couldn't put a finger on. Was it arrogance, a sense of superiority, or simply supreme confidence? Maybe it was a combination of all three. But one thing I did know for certain...he was not someone to be overlooked or dismissed. He carried himself like a man who easily wielded power.

"What is the actual function of a magistrate?" I asked Anne.

"Primarily, they are responsible for handling the county's budget," Anne said. "They are the ones who appropriate funds to most county offices, including sheriff, county court clerk, jail, and the highway department. I'm certain there are others, but I can't name them. Here's an example: Say you need a street in front of your house paved over, your magistrate is the person you contact. He then recommends to the highway folks that the job needs to be taken care of. That's basically how it works."

"Who do magistrates answer to?"

"The fiscal court."

"What kind of money are you talking about?"

"I would estimate the county's budget is in the neighborhood of thirty million dollars. That's based on the county's tax rate, which the county sets. And that doesn't include the school tax, which is a different matter entirely."

"What's the length of a magistrate's term? And how much do they make?"

"Magistrates are up for re-election every four years," Anne said. "And they don't get rich at the job. I would say their salary is between eight hundred and a thousand dollars a month. Plus expenses, of course."

"How many magistrates are in Muhlenberg County?"

"Five. Why the sudden interest in magistrates, Nick?"

"Because Russell Barker intrigues me. Maybe it's because he strikes me as a guy who makes plenty more than a thousand bucks a month. Could be I'm aiming in the wrong direction, but I think he's worth a serious look."

"Nick, I don't know Russell any better than I know Isaac Newton, but I don't see him as a killer," Anne said, as we pulled in front of the library and parked. "I think you're making an insane stretch with that one."

"Maybe that just means he's clever enough to keep from getting caught," I said, after we exited Anne's car. "I can't explain it, but he's not a righteous guy."

Anne looked at Angel, and said, "Sam, is your father always this cynical?"

"If he's not cynical or skeptical, how can he be expected to find the answers he's looking for?" Angel replied.

"That's a good point, Sam," Anne said. Then to me: "Your daughter is very insightful, Nick. You should be proud of her."

"I am proud of her."

"But heed this warning, Nick," Anne said. "If you do go after Russell Barker, be prepared for some blowback. He won't be pleased if he finds out he's being investigated."

"Good to know," I said, entering the library.

A conservatively dressed woman with short auburn-color hair sat at a table demonstrating to an elderly lady how to thread microfilm into a microfiche machine, an ancient dinosaur that I thought had long been extinct. The woman, who looked to be in her forties, walked quickly toward us, wearing a smile on her face. She went straight to Anne. I assumed, correctly, that this was Brenda Luckett.

"It's great seeing you again, Anne," Brenda said. "And quite a pleasant surprise. How can I be of help to you?"

"Brenda, this is Nick Gabriel and his daughter Samantha," Anne said. "Nick is a writer… he's originally from Central City… and he's in town to research a possible book about the Luke Felton murder. If you can spare a couple of minutes, he would like to ask you a few questions."

"About a murder?" Brenda said, her demeanor trapped somewhere between surprise and terror. "I don't see how I can possibly be of any assistance regarding a murder."

I said, "We just came from talking with Todd Brown at the prison, Brenda. He claims to have seen you and your husband in the American Legion on the night of the murder. Were you there that night, and do you recall seeing Todd?"

"Why, yes, we were there that night. And I did see Todd. He came in with Rabbit."

"Were you surprised to see Todd there?"

"I wasn't surprised to see him there, but I was surprised that he was allowed to stay. Chet, the bartender, has a very strict rule when it comes to underage kids wanting to drink. He keeps a tight lid on whom he does or does not sell alcohol to."

"Why do you think he lifted that lid and served alcohol to Todd?"

"I can't say for sure, but maybe it's because…well, Todd does have something of a wild reputation. You know, drugs, drinking, that sort of thing. Could be it wasn't the first time Todd was in the Legion. I'm only there three or four nights a month, so maybe I missed him during those times he was there."

"Did you see Todd speak with anyone other than Rabbit? Or did anyone else speak with Todd?"

"You really ought to be asking Richard—that's my husband—these questions," she said. "I was sitting with my back to the bar that night. I only saw Todd because Richard pointed out that he was there."

"What time will Richard be home tonight?" I said.

"He won't be. Richard is a drill sergeant in the Army Reserves, and is at Fort Knox. He should be home this Sunday."

"One final question, Brenda. On that night, do you remember seeing anyone you didn't see on a regular basis, whether that person spoke with Todd or not?"

Brenda took a deep breath and slowly let it out. "God, that was so long ago, and it's not like I'm all that much of a regular, so don't hold me to this, because I might be wrong," she said. "It could be I have my trips to the Legion all mixed up. Having said that, I do recall seeing one person I had never seen there before."

"Who was that?"

"Dorsey McElwain."

My heart skipped about a dozen beats when I heard that name. A rush of air escaped my lungs. My blood pressure spiked. Was I overreacting? Probably. But the body's impulses sometimes have a mind of their own. Yes, I had to resist jumping to a conclusion that in all likelihood might be thinner than air. There was no logical reason for me to take such a leap. But sometimes logic flies in the face of logic, if that makes any sense.

However, if Dorsey McElwain was at the Legion that night, well, in my mind that makes it a whole new ballgame. True, McElwain might be more innocent than a newborn baby. Maybe he was just there like everyone else... to knock back a few drinks. And it's just as likely that Brenda Luckett was wrong and McElwain wasn't even at the Legion that night. Or she did see him, but on another evening. Those are possibilities that can't be dismissed.

And yet...

What if he was there that night? What if he was responsible for "doctoring" Todd's drink with a nasty concoction of drugs combined with alcohol that ripped away his ability to remember what occurred that fateful night? McElwain, Perry Jackson, maybe even pal Rabbit, were they involved in the murder of Luke Felton? I had no way of knowing for certain, but I damn sure was going to find out the truth behind what transpired that night.

If Todd was innocent, and if the law couldn't prove it, then it fell on my shoulders to get him out from behind those prison bars and back with his family.

Nineteen

"Everything possible to be believed is an image of truth."

When I was still toiling in Hollywood as a script doctor, I rewrote a huge chunk of dialogue for an A-list actor portraying a tough homicide detective. In the film, which was really little more than a glorified potboiler, I was somehow able to sneak in this William Blake quote. Both the actor and the movie's director later told me it was among the best lines that had even been written for a movie. In fact, they were so moved by the line that they were positive I would get an Academy Award nomination, which was impossible. I wasn't even listed as one of the screenwriters when the movie was released. I realized at the time that their nomination prediction was total bullshit. That's why I didn't feel guilty for not informing them that I swiped the line from Blake.

The reason I bring this up now is because Blake's words were, to quote the Prophet Jeremiah, "...in mine heart as a burning fire shut up in my bones, and I am weary with forbearing." Jeremiah then goes on to conclude his dark prophecy with "and I could not stay."

It would be folly for me or anyone else to disagree with Jeremiah's words, but can the same be said about what Blake told us? The more I thought about this, and as unhappy as it makes me to disagree with Blake, in this particular instance I think he might be wrong. At least, when it relates to the Todd Brown case, and to what I'm hoping to accomplish. Just because I believe in Todd's innocence, how close am I really to an image of truth? Conversely, I, like Jeremiah, am "weary with forbearing," while his "and I could not stay" is a directive I might be wise to follow.

Foolishly perhaps, I had wedded myself, heart and soul, to finding justice for Todd. But what was justice in this case? What if Angel nailed it when she wondered if maybe justice was already staring us in the face, and Todd was guilty of murdering and dismembering Luke Felton? Every shred of evidence points in that direction. Even Todd acknowledged that he may be Luke's executioner. What gives me, a second-rate script doctor, the audacity to believe I can magically turn all that evidence topsy-turvy and prove Todd isn't a killer?

You want an example of *chutzpah*? Well, look no further. There it is.

I can't decide whether to laugh or cry at what can only be called an absurd quest. Cry would probably be the best bet. And yet, I cannot bring myself to walk away until a resolution, good or bad, is found.

My immediate quest, however, was to locate Angel. I phoned several times and she didn't answer. Same thing when I sent text messages. I walked down to the breakfast area thinking she might be there. She wasn't. Then I went back to her room and knocked on the door. No response. Feeling a rising combination of fear, panic, and desperation, I went out back to the parking area. Her car was gone.

Now I was officially worried. I know she boasted about having a brown belt in Krav Maga, and how she could take care of herself in a dangerous confrontation, but none of that did anything to drive away my deepening concerns for her well-being. To me, she was still my seven-year-old daughter who needed her father's protection.

Where in the hell could she be? And why did she leave without informing me?

~ * ~

Back inside the motel I hurried to the front desk and ask if either of the two ladies on duty had seen her. Neither one had. But a maid standing nearby heard my question. She came over and told me that, yes, she had seen Angel leave about an hour ago.

"I had just finished cleaning a room when I saw her leave," the maid said. "She went out the back door, got in her car, and drove away."

"Was she alone?" I asked.

"I didn't see anyone with her."

"Did she appear to be frightened or stressed in any way?"

"She seemed perfectly normal to me. Have you tried phoning her?"

"She's not answering."

"Well, I wouldn't worry too much if I were you," she counseled. "She's probably just running some errands. I'm sure she'll be back in no time."

"I hope you're right," I said.

My concerns were hanging around like a bad cold as I walked back to my room. Sitting on the bed, I did my best to steady my nerves. My best failed to get the job done. Only then did I realize I was shaking all over. I was so caught up in my thoughts that I failed to notice that a late-morning rain had begun to fall.

When my phone buzzed, I was praying the call was from Angel. It wasn't. To my surprise...and disappointment...the caller was Mike Tucker. *Oh, shit*, was my first thought. His call launched a different set of nerves into overdrive. Was Mike calling to let me know he was wise to what had gone on between me and his wife? Surely not, I said to myself. Karen was too intelligent to share details of that misguided tryst with her husband. At least, I had to hope she was that intelligent.

Bracing myself, I decided there was no reason to delay gauging Mike's demeanor. Why wait, right?

"Hey, old friend," I said, aware that the tone of his reply would tell me all I needed to know. "Are you back in town?"

"Got back about an hour ago," he replied, sounding his usual chipper self. "How's the research coming along? Making any progress?"

"An inch here, two inches there, but I'm still moving forward," I said, breathing a sigh of relief. "Listen, Mike, since I've got you, I could use your advice on a matter of some importance."

"Okay, how can I help?"

"I want to interview Dorsey McElwain, but not in the presence of Perry Jackson. Any idea how I can make that happen?"

"Definitely. Dorsey works out every evening at the Convention Center," Mike said. "That's where the old high school building was located. He usually gets there between six and six-thirty, exercises for about an hour. Sometimes he'll stay longer if he goes into the gym and runs laps. It will take a death in his family or an emergency involving the sheriff's department to keep him away. You can talk to him then."

"That's perfect. I'll try to catch him tonight," I said. "One more thing, Mike. What can you tell me about Russell Barker?"

"Russ is unquestionably the most-influential man in this county. No one gets elected to any important office unless he or she has Russ's endorsement. They all owe him, and every one of them is in his pocket. He also has plenty of pull with certain bigshots in Frankfort. If you are his enemy, never turn your back on him, because he always has a sharp knife ready to use."

"What about you, Mike? Are you included among those in his pocket?"

"No, Russ and I are political rivals. We've clashed too many times in the past to ever be on the same side of the fence. In fact, the word making the rounds is that he is sharpening his knife to use against me. Rumor has it that when my term is up, he's going to run for this office. If that happens, he'll win."

"That's not a very positive outlook, Mike."

"But a realistic one." Mike paused, then continued, "Nick, the real reason I called is because Karen would like you and Samantha to join us for supper tonight. What do you say? You'd be crazy to turn down the invitation. Karen is a terrific cook."

Before I could answer, Angel opened the door to my room and came in. She was holding a big Walmart bag in one hand. As she was removing her raincoat, I pressed the phone against my leg and mouthed "Where have you been?" She responded by giving me the classic how-dumb-are-you-look, and then held up the wet Walmart bag.

"I'll get back in touch with you later today, Mike, and let you know about tonight. It'll depend on how long my talk with McElwain takes. Also, I'll need to check with Samantha, see what she says."

"Looking forward to seeing the two of you tonight, Nick."

Angel was staring hard at me when I ended the call. Shaking her head, she said, "What? The Tuckers want us to pay them a visit tonight?"

"Yes, to have supper with them."

"How do you define awkward, Dad? Wouldn't you agree that having dinner with your best friend and his wife who you recently had sex with is the perfect definition of awkward? I doubt Mr. Webster could improve on that. Please tell me you will decline their invitation."

"Is that what you want me to do?"

"Duh."

"He is my best friend, Angel."

"Whose wife you slept with."

"Which he doesn't know, nor should he ever find out that it happened." I'd had it with being grilled by my daughter. It was time to go on the offensive. "Why didn't you tell me you were leaving? I've been worried sick ever since I found out you were missing."

"I wasn't missing, Dad. I went to Walmart, which does not rank as a dangerous place, except on Black Friday. Then all bets are off."

"You could have been courteous enough to answer my calls or respond to my text messages."

"I left my phone in the car when I went inside Walmart," she pointed out. "And I was on my way home when I noticed the missed calls and text messages. There was no reason to call when I knew I'd see you in ten minutes."

"Well, it would've been nice to know you were okay," I said, my bark now meeker than a kitten's meow.

Angel grinned, said, "Being a full-time parent is not an easy gig, is it, Dad? Here's a news flash for you… teenage daughters are complex creatures. Only a fool wants to deal with them."

"I'm learning that lesson the hard way."

"Now you've had a brief taste of what Mom had to put up with all those years."

"You turned out great, Angel. Your mom deserves an A-plus for how she raised you."

"Agreed." Angel dug into her Walmart bag and came out with a can of Pringles barbeque potato chips. "In the mood for one of these?"

"Have you eaten yet?"

"Nope," she said, biting into a chip.

"Put those away," I ordered. "We'll go grab lunch and talk about the rest of today's agenda."

"That agenda better not include dinner with the Tuckers."

"Will you give it a rest, Angel?" I pointed toward the door. "You first."

~ * ~

We debated where to eat lunch before finally settling on a barbecue place in downtown Central City. We arrived at a little past noon. Several customers were there, none that I recognized, and the food turned out to be better than I expected. We stayed for almost an hour, then took a stroll down Broad Street, which, as I've already stated, is much different than the Broad Street I remember from my youth. For some unknown reason, Angel was keenly interested in seeing the place where Billy Hughes and I had our scuffle. Not wanting to disappoint my daughter, I led her up the alley to a narrow area that was being lorded over by two large Dumpsters. This was directly in the rear of the movie theater that was destroyed by fire.

"It was right about here that the fight took place," I said. "I remember there were five or six guys watching us. They were in a circle while we went at it. I'd say they got their money's worth."

"Did you shed any blood?" Angel asked.

"Not as much as Billy did."

"Was it a decisive win?"

"Yeah. When I walked away, he was bleeding on the ground."

"God, I wish I'd been there to see you in action."

"Why? Do you have a thing for violence?" I said.

"Not really. But seeing you fight, that would've been cool."

"Have you seen enough?"

"Yes, Rocky, I have," Angel said. "I have now visited the sacred site of your greatest pugilistic triumph. What more could a girl want from her father?"

~ * ~

The rest of the afternoon was spent back at the motel playing chess. One of Angel's Walmart purchases was a cheap checkers/chess board that couldn't have cost more than a couple of bucks. Cheap or not, we put the small board to good use, doing battle and matching wits for nearly four hours. When Angel was very young, I taught her the basic chess moves. I was surprised she remembered them. However, the bigger surprise was how good she was at the game. She was a smart, fierce opponent.

For me, chess is the greatest competitive game ever invented, bar none. It is an easy game to learn and an impossible game to master. I've played hundreds of games of chess against opponents whose skill level ranged from very high to below average. I've won my share, lost even more, but I have never ceased to marvel at the intricacy and the beauty that goes with moving those small pieces around the board. The invention of chess ranks as one of history's great miracles.

At five, after having won every match (much to Angel's growing frustration), I suggested that we freshen up, then go to the Convention Center and seek out Dorsey McElwain. Angel pleaded for one more game… "I know I can beat you,"… but I declined. Beating my daughter was one thing, humbling her bordered on cruelty. And I wasn't about to do that.

~ * ~

Dorsey McElwain was on a stationary bike pumping the pedals at a furious pace when Angel and I walked in. Judging by the amount of perspiration dripping from his face, I would estimate that he had been on the bike for quite some time. The buds in his ears indicated he was listening to music. He did not look pleased when he saw us approaching.

Removing the buds from his ears, he said, "You two again. I hope you aren't here to talk, because I don't have the time. As you can see, I'm otherwise occupied."

"Just a couple of quick questions and we'll be on our way," I said.

"Come to the sheriff's office. If I find the time, perhaps I can work you into my schedule."

"You've learned well from Perry Jackson."

"You want to talk, we do it in the office."

"It's better if we talk here, now."

McElwain stopped pedaling, wiped his face with a towel, and turned his attention to Angel. "Now, if this beautiful creature wanted to ask me a few questions, I just might agree to answer them," he said, his grin just shy of a leer. "But she's just your sidekick, and we all know sidekicks aren't allowed to say much. That's a shame."

Angel stepped in front of me, and asked, "Are you a regular at the American Legion?"

MeElwain was clearly stunned, and I couldn't decide if it was because of the question, or who had posed it.

"I've been inside the Legion maybe three times in my life," he managed to say. "So, no, I'm not a regular."

"But you were in the Legion when Todd Brown was there, weren't you? That's also the night Luke Felton was murdered."

"No, I wasn't there. Who the hell is spreading that lie?"

"A very credible witness puts you there that night. And if we ask around, I'm betting we'll find others who will corroborate what our witness saw. You may as well acknowledge you were in the Legion that night. Not being truthful might come back to bite you on the ass."

"What credible witness?" McElwain said. "Tell me. I have a right to know who that person is."

Angel pressed on. "You were there, Dorsey. And we believe that when Todd went to the rest room you put something in his drink. Whatever it was, when mixed with alcohol, it caused his memory to shut down."

"That's bullshit. I never put nothin' in his drink. And there is no way you can prove I did."

I said, "Did you drop Rabbit off at the Speedway station earlier that afternoon?"

McElwain's eyes widened, his face tensed. I had struck a nerve with that question.

"I'm done answering your stupid questions," he snapped. "The next time we talk I'll have my lawyer with me. Now, get the hell out of here and leave me in peace."

"Your lawyer? Why not call Russ Barker instead? He's the big dog around here, isn't he? Maybe he can save your ass." I tapped McElwain on the arm without waiting for his reply. "You have a good workout, Dorsey."

As Angel and I turned and walked away, McElwain muttered, "You'd better leave Russ Barker out of this."

"We'll be seeing you around, Dorsey," Angel said.

Once we were outside, I said, "Damn, Angel, you were just like Pepper Anderson in there."

"Who is Pepper Anderson?"

"Angie Dickinson's character on the TV show *Police Woman*."

"Never heard of Angie Dickinson or that TV show."

"You're kidding?"

"When was it on?"

"Sometime in the seventies."

"Duh, Dad, I'm nineteen, remember?"

"What is it with your generation? Don't you kids have any appreciation for history?"

"Yes, but not *ancient* history, which is what the seventies are."

"Okay, I'll cut you a break this one time. But only because that 'bite you on the ass' line was beyond perfect. Anyway, the point I was trying to make is that you were really terrific in there with McElwain. I can't tell you how proud I am of you."

"Just doing my job, boss."

Twenty

The bullet smashed into the tree two seconds before the crack of rifle fire carried the distance. Angel and I were standing in the parking area trying to decide which of us would drive when we reacted to the sound. We darted to a space between our two cars and ducked down behind hers. Staying low, we waited for more shots to be fired, although I was fairly certain the shooting had ended. I felt we were out of harm's way. At least for the time being.

I peeked over the car and saw a man coming around the corner of the building, a puzzled look on his bearded face. My initial impression of the man was that he probably worked for the motel in some capacity. Not in a managerial position, but more like a maintenance worker.

"Was that gunfire I just heard, or did a car backfire?" he asked, when he saw me.

"Gunfire," I answered. Having fought in Iraq, I definitely know the difference between the two.

"Oh, my goodness. Was anybody hurt?"

"No. But you should call nine-one-one, get the police here."

He reached into a hip pocket, took out his cell phone, and began dialing the three digits. Not willing to take a chance that the shooting had ceased, he stepped inside the back door to deliver his message. Can't blame the guy for being cautious.

"Stay down, Dad," Angel pleaded, still squatting behind her car. "The next shot might not miss."

"There won't be another shot," I said. "This one wasn't meant to kill...it was intended to scare us."

"Well, it worked."

Angel stood and nervously looked around. By this time word had spread and the motel's manager made an obligatory, albeit reluctant, appearance. He was absolutely mortified by what had just happened. And he had good reason to be. Having guests shot at isn't exactly good advertisement for future business. It would require a miracle of messaging to entice travelers to lodge in your motel if there's a chance they might get gunned down in the parking lot. But to the man's credit and to his professionalism, he did say the right things.

"Praise God everyone is all right," he said, walking in our direction. "Do you think it was intentional, or did someone accidentally fire the shot?"

Not wanting to go into great detail, I said, "Could be either one. We'll leave it to leave it to law enforcement to make that determination."

"Yes, yes, by all means."

After the manager left us, Angel commented, "There can be no doubt who did this, Dad. It had to be Dorsey McElwain."

"Maybe."

"Why do you say maybe? Who else could it be? We interviewed McElwain just last night, practically accused him of spiking Todd's drink on the night Luke Felton was murdered, and the next morning someone takes a shot at us? Come on, Dad. Common sense says McElwain was the shooter."

"I'm not saying you're wrong, Angel. But let's withhold judgment until we have more facts."

"Withhold judgment? Are you kidding me? You know I'm right."

~ * ~

The city police car, lights flashing, pulled into the parking lot with a loud nerve-shattering screech. It reminded me of a scene from that old *Starsky and Hutch* TV show, the one where those two guys drove like maniacs. I shouldn't have been surprised. Jimmy Martin was behind the wheel, and back in the day he was a notorious drag racer. He got out of the car, while a second officer, whom I had never seen, emerged from the passenger's side.

"Didn't I warn you about rattling cages?" Jimmy asked. "You should have heeded my advice and left well enough alone."

I pointed to my right. "The bullet is in that tree," I said, adding, "purposefully would be my guess."

Jimmy wandered over to the tree, trailed by his partner, who was about a foot shorter than his superior. He located the place where the bullet entered the tree, took out his pocket knife, opened it, and removed the damaged slug. He held it in his palm and inspected it.

"Not gonna learn much from this sucker," Jimmy said. "It's too badly damaged to accurately determine the make or the caliber."

"I'm not particularly concerned about those details, Jimmy."

Jimmy turned, looked behind him, and said, "I'd say the shot came from that clearing across the highway."

"I'd say that's about right."

"Do you have any idea who might've done this, Nick?"

"I don't know, Jimmy. You tell me. Do you have any idea who did this?"

"It certainly wasn't me, if that's what you're hinting at. I don't waste good ammunition shooting at trees. If I pull the trigger, it will be for the sole purpose of killing my target. So you can scratch me off your list of suspects."

"Not accusing you of anything, Jimmy. Just asking if you might point me toward the person who did fire that shot."

"Sorry, Nick, can't help you," Jimmy said, shaking his head. "You and your daughter need to come by my office and make a statement. Anytime today is okay."

"Making a statement isn't really necessary," I countered.

"Yes, it is. If there is no official record, I have no incentive to investigate. That's like saying it never happened. Also, this incident should be on record in case, God forbid, something bad happens to either you or your daughter."

"You're here, Jimmy. You are my witness. If something bad happens to Samantha or me, you can be the official record."

"Have it your way, Nick. But I'll be in my office until five in case you change your mind."

~ * ~

I returned to my room badly in need of some serious alone time. Fortunately for me, Angel went to her room rather than coming to mine, which had lately become standard procedure. I needed solitude, because the moment had arrived when I had to have a come-to-Jesus conversation with myself. A bullet being fired in our direction changed the dynamics. That bullet missed...intentionally I'm sure...but what about the next one? Maybe it wouldn't miss. I had put my daughter's life in danger. I didn't bring her here to get killed, or to witness her father being gunned down in front of her. And all for what? This insane mission I was on to somehow exonerate Todd Brown? What arrogance on my part! The smart thing for me to do would be to put Angel on a plane back to Los Angeles, then get in my car and return to the safety of Siesta Key. No one was likely to take a shot at me in the Old Salty Dog.

Angel rapped on my door, opened it, and came into my room before I had time to respond. She moved quickly to my bed and sat across from me. It was easy to see she was seriously charged up about something.

"We've been making a huge mistake, Dad," she said. "We're not looking in the right direction. We need to chart a different path."

"Okay, I'm listening. What's the mistake, and what direction should we be looking in?"

"We have totally focused all our attention on Todd Brown, on proving his innocence, and on who might be responsible for setting him up. But what about Luke Felton? We have completely overlooked him. We'd be smart to shift our focus and take a deeper look at him.

If we do, and if we catch a lucky break, maybe we can answer *the* key question... why he was in the car with Todd that night?"

Out of the mouths of babes. There is no way I can adequately describe what a "Perry Mason moment" feels like, but this had to be close. Mixed in with that feeling was the realization that I had been a blind fool, and that my daughter was more intelligent than her old man. Not that much of a stretch, I'll admit.

"Angel, when I told you I would like to have your eyes and ears here with me, I neglected to mention your brain. For that I apologize. You are correct. My focus has been too short-sighted."

I picked up my phone, rang Jimmy Martin's number, and waited for him to answer. It didn't take but a few seconds. It was obvious from the ambient sounds that he was in the car and on his way back to the office.

"You have a change of heart, Nick?" Jimmy said. "You guys gonna come in and file a report?"

"Maybe later this evening," I lied. "No, the reason for my call is to ask a question about Luke Felton."

"Goddammit, Nick, can't you leave all this shit alone?" A pause, then, "What do you want to know about Luke?"

"He had two kids, right?"

"Yeah. Jeff and Aaron."

"Do they live around here?"

"Aaron does...he has a house in Powderly. Jeff lives in Wyoming or Arizona, one of those Western states. I'm not sure which."

"Where does Aaron work?"

"He doesn't; he's on full disability. Some accident at his old job crippled him up pretty bad. His wife, Naomi, works in the lunch room at one of the middle schools."

"Thanks, Jimmy, you've been a big help," I said.

I ended the call before he could pose more questions or toss in additional commentary. Then I opened my laptop and began a search for Aaron Felton's address. It took a solid fifteen minutes before I came across his address and a phone number. And I only succeeded because Naomi Felton was on Facebook.

"Come on, Angel," I said, closing the laptop. "We'll take a pass on Mike's invitation, get a bite to eat, then go pay a visit to Aaron Felton and see if he can enlighten us about his late father."

~ * ~

Aaron Felton lived in a small but well-maintained brick house located several yards off U.S. 62 in Powderly, the halfway point between Central City and Greenville. The front yard was neat, highlighted by a lovely rose bush, and on the porch there was a swing and two metal chairs. A two-car garage was to the right of the house. Inside was a blue late-model Ford Fiesta.

It was a much better house than I expected from a man too disabled to work and a wife who probably didn't earn much money working in a school lunch room. Maybe Aaron had received a settlement for his injury, or it could be he filed suit against the Brown family and was awarded some remuneration for his father's death. The nice house, the two-car garage...the Feltons weren't starving.

Angel and I walked onto the porch and I knocked on the door. It took a few minutes before sounds could be heard coming from inside the house. Someone, Aaron I presumed, was moving slowly toward the front. He fiddled with a couple of locks, and then opened the door.

Aaron Felton was a virtual carbon copy of his father. He was shorter than Luke, maybe a little heavier, but in the face he was practically a dead ringer. When he spoke, if I closed my eyes and listened, I would swear it was Luke Felton's voice I was hearing. It was a true flashback moment.

"What can I do for the two of you?" Aaron said, his eyes darting between Angel and me.

"Aaron, this is my daughter Samantha," I said. "My name is—"

"I know who you are...Nick something or other. You're the writer working on a book about that damn drug-addicted kid who murdered my father. Your goal is to save his sorry ass, isn't it? What the hell do you want with me?"

"You're wrong, Aaron. Saving Todd is not why I'm here. Anyway, how can I save someone who is already behind bars? No, I'm only looking for the truth. You may not be aware of this, but I knew your father. When I was a kid, he often came to watch our baseball games. I also ran into him at the pool room. He was always a good guy around me. I am not against your father, Aaron, I'm for finding out what really happened."

"What you're doing is *dodging* the truth. The Brown kid is guilty as sin. He admitted to murdering my father."

"I understand that, Aaron. But I'm not as convinced as you are. There are too many pieces that don't fit into the puzzle for me to accept the tale being told."

"Such as?"

"What possible reason would your dad, who was almost seventy, have for being with a kid not yet twenty that late at night? That's the one question that haunts me the most."

"I have to admit that's always bothered me as well," Aaron said. "And I gotta be honest with you, I've never been able to come up with a good answer. I know what some people say, that Dad was either selling drugs to the kid, or he was gay and it was a sexual encounter gone wrong. That is nothing but horseshit. Dad didn't sell drugs and he wasn't gay."

"Can we come inside and discuss this, Aaron?" I inquired.

"I don't reckon it would do any harm." He pushed the door open. "Come on it. It ain't much, but it's a palace to us."

Angel and I followed Aaron down a short hallway and into the living room. Aaron walked with a decided limp...his left leg appeared to be shorter than the right leg...and he grimaced with every step he took. Whatever his injury, it wasn't minor. Seeing the pain he was in, I could understand why employment was obviously out of the question.

Aaron pointed to the couch and motioned for us to take a seat. He sat in a leather recliner and wasted no time kicking back and stretching his legs. Once again, he grimaced when he did this. Even comfort for him wasn't without pain.

"How did you injure your leg?" I said.

"Working construction. Big slab of concrete fell and crushed it all to hell. Damn lucky I didn't lose it, although if they had chopped it off I wouldn't always hurt so much." He grimaced once more and massaged his damaged leg. "But who cares about me being hurt? Let's get back to the real subject, talking about Dad. Do you really believe the Brown kid is innocent?"

"No, I'm not willing to go that far, but certain aspects of the case don't ring true for me. Like your dad being with Todd that night. Until I get some satisfactory answers, I'm keeping an open mind."

"But the kid confessed. In my opinion, that's the final answer."

"That's not entirely accurate, Mr. Felton," Angel corrected. "We watched the tape of Todd being interrogated by Sheriff Jackson and we were troubled by what we saw. Todd couldn't remember anything about what happened that night, so Jackson remembered for him. He filled in all the missing blanks, informing Todd what happened. Jackson dictated, Todd agreed. It was less like an interview and more like follow-the-bouncing-ball."

"Couldn't remember?" Aaron scoffed. "Am I supposed to believe that? Who forgets killing another human being?"

"We think Todd was drugged earlier that night while he was at the American Legion. That's why he can't remember."

"I've never heard that theory."

I said, "Where did your father live at the time of his death?"

"He owned a house in Greenville."

"Do you own it now?"

"No, Jeff and I sold it several months after Dad's death. Jeff is my older brother. There was no reason to keep the house, and we both needed the money. Why the interest in Dad's house?"

"What about his personal items? Keep any of those?"

"Yeah, a few," Aaron said. "Which ones are you referring to?"

"Did you find any papers when you went through his things? Notebooks, ledgers, documents, bills, personal letters? Things like that?"

"There are three boxes of his stuff in the second bedroom."

"Have you sorted through them?"

"They haven't been touched since I brought them home."

"Would you object to us giving them a quick look?" I asked.

"What are you looking for?"

"Anything that might be relevant to the case."

"If you think it might do some good, then I have no objection." He lowered his legs and slowly got out of the chair, once again grimacing with each movement. "Follow me. It's down this hallway to the left."

The three boxes were lying side by side in a corner between a bed and the wall. They were medium-size boxes but they were filled to the top by a mountain of papers. This wasn't going to be a quick project, I realized. Digging through the papers was bound to take some time.

"Would you be open to allowing us to borrow the boxes for a couple of days?" I asked Aaron. "We're staying at the Best Western in Central City. We can study the contents there. I'll return the boxes within twenty-four hours."

"No, I think it would be better if the boxes stayed here," Aaron responded. "It's not that I don't trust you. It's just that, well, you know, those things belonged to Dad, and I don't want to risk losing any of it. I'm sure you can understand where I'm coming from. It's important to me."

So important you haven't bothered to look through any of the contents.

"Sure, I understand," I said. "Do you mind if we rummage through the boxes for a few minutes?"

"Not at all. Take as long as you need. I'm not going anywhere."

That didn't turn out to be true. Aaron excused himself a minute later, saying his leg was throbbing, which necessitated taking a couple of Aleve for the pain, then getting back into his recliner and stretching out. He limped away, the pain written on his tortured face and in his body language.

~ * ~

An hour later, after rushing through the contents in the first box, I had come up with nothing even remotely interesting. Most of what I found was receipts for old bills Luke had paid, past tax information, personal letters, or commendations he'd received while he was in law enforcement. There were also dozens of photographs he had taken over the years, some of which were attached to newspaper articles that included the original photo. Luke was an excellent shutterbug, but unfortunately for us, his photography skills were of no help.

"Here, Dad, take a look at this," Angel said, handing me a single piece of paper. "I think this might be important."

"What is it?" I asked, taking the paper from her.

"Luke's final phone bill. Check out the date on those last three calls. Wasn't that the day he was murdered?"

I looked at the date. It corresponded to the last day Luke was alive, although the actual time of his murder could have been that day, or early the following morning. That particular fact had never been made clear to me.

Luke's final call, which he made at four-ten, was to a number in Jackson, Wyoming. That was obviously a call to his son, Jeff. However, the two earlier calls, one he made and one he received, spaced out about ninety minutes apart, captured my attention.

Especially the second call, the one he received. I recognized the number. Taking out my phone, I scrolled through the call list to verify that I wasn't mistaken. I wasn't.

"That twelve forty-five call was from Perry Jackson," I said to Angel.

"Are you positive? Maybe it's the sheriff's office. The call could have come from McElwain."

"Anne Bishop gave me Perry's cell phone number when we were at Philly's. I already had the number to his office."

"Perry Jackson calling Luke on the day he was murdered? That sounds more than a little suspicious to me."

"Let's refrain from immediately jumping to any conclusions," I warned. "It might have been a friendly call. Don't forget, Luke and Perry worked together. Maybe Perry just wanted to chat with his old boss."

"Yeah, and I just want to chat with Ryan Gosling. What are the chances?"

"The more important question for me is who Luke called at eleven-fifteen. That's what I'd like to know."

"Well, why don't we find out?" Angel picked up her phone, snatched the piece of paper from me, typed the number, and waited. Then: "Yes, is Lana there?...Isn't this the Del Rey residence?" At that moment, Angel's eyes widened and her jaw dropped to her chest. "Oh, gosh, I'm so sorry. Silly me, I've dialed the wrong number. I'm such a klutz."

She ended the call, stuffed her phone into her purse, and stared at me.

"You going to sit there like a dummy or tell me what it is that has you so jazzed?" I said.

"You'll never guess who I just spoke with."

"You're right, so why don't you save me from the guessing game and solve the mystery for me?"

"Dottie Barker, who, I'm assuming, is Russell's wife."

"Like you said, why don't we find out?" I picked up my phone and called Anne Bishop's number. When she answered, I said, "Anne, what is Russell Barker's wife's name? Thanks, that's all I needed to know."

I ended the call before she could cross examine me.

"Did I assume correctly?" Angel asked.

Nodding, I folded the paper listing the phone calls in question and tucked it into my pants pocket. Technically, I was committing the crime of larceny, or more accurately, theft of private property. But I wasn't too concerned about it, either from a legal or a moral perspective. This was information that might prove useful, and I wasn't leaving Aaron Felton's house without it. I would seek penance at a later time.

"Come on, Angel," I said, standing. "We need to get moving."

"Where to?"

"First, we make a quick stop at McDonald's to use the rest room and to get something to drink. Then we proceed to the American Legion, park close but not close enough to be seen, and then we wait until a certain individual named Rodney Adcock shows up."

"Who is Rodney Adcock?"

"The elusive Rabbit."

Twenty-one

We drove straight from McDonald's to the American Legion and parked in a spot that provided us with a dead-on view of the front door. We had been there for an hour, and during that time several members had come and gone. There was plenty of activity going on inside the Legion, but as of now no sign of Rabbit.

"This is my first stakeout, Dad," Angel said, finishing off her soft drink. "And I have to tell you, it lacks excitement. Do you think this is what a real stakeout is like?"

"Are you bored?"

"To death."

"Then, yes, this is exactly like a real stakeout."

"How do you know?"

"When I was working on a script for a cop movie, I spent three nights riding around with a couple of real Los Angeles detectives. On one of those nights, we kept watch on an apartment complex while waiting for a suspect in an armed robbery to show up. We sat there all night and never laid eyes on the guy. Yeah, it was boring."

"That settles it for me. I'll never be a cop."

"With your observation skills and insights, you would make a good one," I said, adding, "not that I want you to choose that as a career path. By the way, I really admired your Lana Del Rey reference. Kind of a risky thing to do, wasn't it?"

"Right, like there was any chance Dottie Barker has a clue who Lana Del Rey is. To be honest, I'm surprised you do."

"Hey, I might be an old dude, but I'm hip."

"Why do you think Luke phoned Russell Barker?" Angel asked, changing the subject.

"Good question."

"Then less than two hours later Luke gets a call from Perry Jackson. I would pay a million dollars to know what those conversations were about. They all had to be connected."

"That would be good to know."

"Is it possible Russell ordered Jackson to call Luke?"

"I'd say it's more than possible."

We were silent for the next few minutes. It was completely dark by then, but the front of the American Legion building and the adjoining parking area was well-lighted. The good lighting made it easy for us to see the people coming and going. Although it was not yet nine o'clock, a good crowd had already gathered inside the big Legion hall.

My first glimpse of Rabbit took me by surprise. He wasn't going into the Legion, as I had anticipated, he was coming out. Apparently, he had arrived before Angel and I began our stakeout, had concluded his drinking, and was heading home. His earlier-than-usual exit caused me to wonder if he was leaving for fear that I might show up and ask him a few tough questions. I didn't doubt for a second that he knew I had been there on two previous occasions. Chet, the unfriendly bartender, had surely given Rabbit the heads-up.

What Chet said or didn't say hardly mattered at this moment. Rabbit was in my sights, and I wasn't going to let him slip away. As the great Joe Louis once said: "He can run but he can't hide."

"That little pipsqueak, that's Rabbit?" Angel said, breaking the silence.

"You think he's small now, you should've seen him in high school. He's a monster compared to then."

Monster was a slight exaggeration, I must admit, but not totally inaccurate. Rabbit was several inches taller and a few pounds heavier than the kid I had grown up with. Back then he was really small, maybe five-four, tops. I recall he had brown hair, a sickle-shaped scar over his left eye, a slightly off-center nose, a small mouth, and a ruddy complexion. Except for the height and weight difference, I doubt much else had changed over the years. There was only one thing even remotely memorable about the guy...his eyes. They were constantly moving, wary, on the alert for possible danger.

Rabbit had always been paranoid about everything and everybody. He truly believed evil forces, dangerous men, or law enforcement personnel were forever tailing him, watching his every move, zeroing in on him, the target in their cross hairs. Because of his ever-present fear, and perhaps due to his small stature, Rabbit was a scrapper. He never backed down from a fight, and thanks to his hair-trigger temper, he usually threw the first punch.

Rabbit walked briskly toward the parking area, his head constantly turning, first left, then right, those eyes scanning the darkness for danger. For him, every shadow was a potential hiding place where one of those evil villains was preparing to spring out and attack with deadly vengeance. What Rabbit couldn't know or possibly suspect was that an attack was imminent. But it wouldn't come from a villain or with a deadly vengeance.

This attack would come from one of his oldest friends.

~ * ~

Angel and I got out of the Lexus and began walking in Rabbit's direction. He was heading straight to his car while we were approaching from his right. We had closed to within a few yards before he looked up and took notice of us. He immediately stopped in his tracks and began to furiously look over both shoulders, his eyes intently studying the darkness.

Rabbit held his arms straight out, palms facing forward in the classic don't-come-any-closer pose. His head swiveled side to side and his eyes were like two marbles rolling around inside a can. Finally, he focused those fear-filled orbs on me.

"You need to leave," Rabbit stated, his head again turning side to side. "I can't talk to you. Not now, not ever."

"Good to see you too after all these years, Rabbit," I responded.

"Believe me, Nick, you gotta go."

"You can't make time to reminisce with an old baseball teammate? Is that what you're saying?"

"We both know you aren't here to talk about baseball, Nick. You think I'm not aware that you've been looking for me? You want to ask me about Luke Felton's murder. Sorry, but I'm not getting into that with you, so you may as well hit the highway."

"This is not the reception I expected."

"Too bad, because it's the only one you get."

"What's preventing you from talking to me, Rabbit?"

"Take a wild guess, Nick."

"I'm not in the mood to play games, so why don't you explain it to me?"

"Because I'll end up just like Luke if I do. And so will you if you keep snooping around."

"Who are you afraid of?" I asked.

"Leave, Nick, please, I'm begging you."

"Not before you answer some questions."

"Shit, Nick, don't you get it? You are putting our lives in danger." He pointed at Angel as though he were only now realizing her presence. "Who is she, Nick? Why is she with you?"

"Samantha. She's my daughter."

"You sure about that? She don't look much like you."

"She caught a lucky break," I said. "We don't have to talk here, Rabbit. We're staying at the Best Western. We can have our conversation there."

"Oh, yeah, we all know how safe it is at that place, don't we? The next shot might not miss."

"How do you know about that?"

"Word gets around."

"Who's spreading that word?"

"I don't want to talk about it, okay?"

"Let's cut to the chase, Rabbit. You need to understand I'm not going anywhere until you answer my questions."

"I've already answered about a hundred questions. I don't have anything else to say."

"I'm talking about hard questions, Rabbit, not those softball lobs tossed at you by Perry Jackson."

"Perry never asked me a single question," Rabbit declared. "It's that FBI guy I'm referring to."

"Greg Harkins? Really, you were interviewed by him?"

"For almost three hours. I thought he was never going to cut me loose."

"But Greg Harkins had nothing to do with the Luke Felton case," I pointed out, my thoughts swirling. "If he interviewed you, it had to be about something else. Was it the Sharon Anderson murder?"

"I've said all I'm going to say about those murders, Nick. Hell, I've already said too much. I'll probably be a corpse in a few days."

"You're in this up to your neck, aren't you, Rabbit?"

"I'm not involved in anything."

"Did you murder Sharon Anderson?"

"I never murdered anyone," Rabbit said. "And that's the God's truth."

"But you know who did."

"I don't know anything. And that's exactly what I told that FBI guy."

"I have no reason to believe you killed Sharon Anderson," I said. "But you were involved in Luke Felton's murder. There is no question about that. You can protest all you want, Rabbit, but I know better. It's a fact."

"You're climbing the wrong tree, Nick. I don't know why you're so goddamn convinced I had anything to do with any of this shit. It's not true."

"Facts don't lie, Rabbit."

"Yeah, but they don't always lead to the truth."

"Who dropped you off at the Speedway station on the day you ran into Todd Brown?"

"My girlfriend."

"What? She just dropped you off and left?"

"That's right."

"Did you know Todd was inside Speedway?"

"No."

"You sure about that?"

"Yeah, Nick, I'm sure."

"How well do you know Todd?" I asked.

"Fairly well. We saw each other a few times, you know, here and there. He seemed like a nice kid."

"Were you aware that he had a serious drug problem?"

"I'd heard rumors, but I didn't know it for a fact," Rabbit said.

"Why did you take him to the American Legion? You had to know he was underage. Yet, you took a kid with drug issues there and you bought alcohol for him. Did you think that was a smart thing to do?"

"Once again, you've got your facts twisted into a knot. Todd did not drink alcohol while he was there."

"Two witnesses disagree with you," I pointed out. "One happens to be your pal, Chet. We both know he has no reason to lie."

"Don't be so sure, Nick. Chet's not always a truthful guy."

"Now here's the key question I have for you, Rabbit: Who put drugs into Todd's drink when he went to the rest room, you or Dorsey McElwain?"

"I don't know anything about drugs. All I can tell you is that I didn't do it."

"If it wasn't you, Rabbit, then it had to be McElwain. Were you aware that he was planning on doing it?"

"How the hell can I know what Dorsey was planning to do? I'm no mind reader. If he put something in Todd's drink, hell, if he pissed in Todd's drink, I didn't see him do it. I don't have anything else to say about that."

"Did Todd leave the Legion with you?" I inquired.

"No, I left before he did."

"How long before?"

"How can I answer that? I wasn't there when he left."

"You rode to the Legion in his car, but you left before he did. How did you get home?"

"With a friend," Rabbit replied. "We went to his house to watch TV and to do more drinking."

"So you left Todd, an underage kid, alone at the American Legion? What possessed you to do that?"

"He was deep in conversation with a young woman at the time. I didn't want to interfere with what he had going."

"Are you positive it wasn't Dorsey McElwain he was talking to?" I asked.

"No, it wasn't Dorsey. I know the difference between a man and a woman, Nick. Now for the final time, I don't know what more I can tell you."

"You can start by telling me what you know about Russell Barker."

"He's a magistrate. And he has plenty of money. That's all I know about him."

"What's his relationship with Perry Jackson?"

"I don't know. Why don't you go ask Perry?" Rabbit said, now virtually pleading.

"I intend to do just that, Rabbit."

"Great. But will you do me a favor, Nick? Please don't come to my funeral when I'm dead, which I'll likely be within the next several days."

"A funeral is the least of your worries, Rabbit."

"What's that supposed to mean?"

"You know damn well what it means."

"No, I don't. Why don't you explain it to me?"

"You're in the middle of a real mess, Rabbit, so let me offer you a free piece of advice. If you hope to avoid going to prison for a long time, you need to get with someone in law enforcement and tell that person everything you know. Every detail, big or small. Don't leave out a single fact. Prison is not a place you want to be, Rabbit. You won't exactly thrive there. That's why you would be wise to get out in front of this from the beginning. Don't keep what you know hidden away. The truth will eventually come out. You know that. It's to your advantage to take control of the narrative before the story takes control of you. Once that happens, all bets are off. You'll just end up a minor footnote in a long, sordid tale."

"Thanks for your unsolicited advice, Nick. I'll be sure to—"

"You take good care of yourself, Rabbit," I interrupted. "Angel, it's time to go. We've wasted too much time here already."

~ * ~

As we headed to my car, Angel said, "What a strange dude. If Central Casting was looking for someone to play a weirdo, Rabbit would be the perfect choice. He's just...odd. And for someone who says he doesn't want to talk, he rarely shuts up."

"Rabbit always was the chatty type," I said, getting in the car. "He's one of those people who can make a short story long."

"Has he always been so paranoid?"

"Not to this extent, no. But he's never had a pair of brutal murders riding on his shoulders."

"Are you going to talk to him again, Dad? I mean, you almost have to, don't you? You have to get him to tell what he knows."

"Can't do it, Angel. I'm a writer, not a member of law enforcement. I don't have the authority to persuade him to say anything he isn't inclined to say."

"You can't leave things like they are now," Angel said. "You have to make something happen."

I took out my cell phone and began punching in a number.

"Maybe I don't have the authority to move things forward," I said, "but I know someone who does. We'll let him question Rabbit."

Twenty-two

We were at the door of the Huddle House when I recognized a familiar voice calling out my name. Turning, I saw Karen Tucker coming toward us, several steps ahead of Mike, who was getting out of his car. I cringed, knowing Angel and Karen in the same place was like a powder keg that could explode at any moment.

"We were on our way to invite the two of you to have breakfast with us when we saw your car pull in here," Karen said. "The gods must be smiling at us."

From my past reading, the gods rarely ever smiled on anyone. More often than not, they were inflicting pain and causing mayhem for us poor mortals. If the gods are smiling it's in anticipation of the fury they might unleash inside Huddle House.

When Mike caught up with Karen, he said, "Since you guys won't come to us, we decided to come to you. Let me buy your breakfast. What do you say?"

How was I supposed to respond? No, we'll take a pass, but thanks anyway? How unappreciative would that be? How inappropriate? Angel and I were like a pair of trapped animals with no way of escaping. There could only be one response, whether Angel liked it or not.

"Sure, Mike, we would love to," I said. "You picked a good time, too. The place isn't all that crowded."

Five minutes later the four of us were ensconced in a booth by the window. Angel was sitting directly across from Karen, which only increased my fear of a potential explosion. I could only hope my daughter had the good sense to keep her feelings in check.

"How is your research coming along, Nick?" Karen asked, peeking over her menu. "Are you finding enough good stuff for a book?"

"I'm uncovering nuggets every day," I replied. "Whether or not I have enough for a book I can't say at this stage of the game. The jury is still out."

"Well, here's hoping you do write the book," Karen said. "I know it would be a great read."

The waitress came to take our orders. Karen and Mike must have been famished; they both went with a full breakfast. Perhaps because she wanted to get the hell out of this uncomfortable situation (for her), Angel ordered only orange juice and toast. I split the difference, opting for scrambled eggs, sausage, and orange juice.

"Tell me, Samantha, has your father taken the time to drive you around and show you where he grew up?" Karen asked, after the waitress departed. "Or has he been too occupied with his research to give you the nickel tour?"

"No, he's driven me around and pointed out a few important sites," Angel said, sounding surprisingly pleasant. "Like the alley where he was involved in a big fight."

"With Billy Hughes, right?" Mike said, excited by the memory. "Up behind the old movie theater. I was there that night. Your dad kicked the shit out of Billy."

"That seems to be the consensus," Angel agreed.

"What's your impression of the area?" Karen asked Angel. "How would you characterize our town?"

"Wicked."

Karen was clearly startled by Angel's response. "Wicked? That's a peculiar term to use," she said. "Why on earth would you say that?"

"Give me a more appropriate word to describe a town where your tires get slashed and someone fires a shot at you. For my money, that's the essence of wicked."

"Are you telling me those incidents actually happened?" Karen practically screamed. "Did they, Nick?"

"Yes," I replied.

Karen turned to Mike, and said, "Did you know about this?"

"I heard about it yesterday," Mike admitted.

"And you didn't think it was important enough to share with me?" Karen snapped.

Before Mike could defend himself with what was certain to be an unacceptable excuse, two things happened simultaneously: the waitress brought our food, and my cell phone buzzed. I had a pretty good idea who was calling—Heather Anderson. Prior to leaving the motel I had phoned her, got the answering machine, and left a message for her to give me a call when she had time. I checked the Caller ID. The call was from Heather.

"Thanks a lot for getting back with me so promptly," I said, leaning back as the waitress distributed the plates.

"Not a problem," Heather said. "What can I do for you?"

"In our past discussions I failed to ask you what Sharon did for a living."

"She was a beautician."

"A beautician, huh? That's good to know."

"I could have told you that, Nick," Karen mumbled.

"Did Sharon have her own salon?" I asked Heather, ignoring Karen's remark.

"No, she worked in a beauty shop downtown," Heather answered. "She was very successful, too. Her chair was rarely ever empty. And she had five or six women who would have her over to their house after hours to do their hair. She was normally gone three or four nights a week doing those jobs."

I took a drink of orange juice, then said, "By any chance, Dottie Barker happened to be one of those women?"

"Oh, yes, Dottie loved her. Sharon was at her house two or three times a week, come hell or high water. She was Dottie's favorite. And my sister told me Dottie paid twice as much as her other customers."

"This is good information, Heather, just what I need," I said. "And I will stay in touch with you. If I learn anything new, you'll be the first person I contact."

After ending the call, I poked at my scrambled eggs. They looked tasty, but I was in no mood to eat.

"Why are you inquiring about Dottie Barker?" Karen asked, taking a bite of her omelet. "What's your interest in her?"

"Just collecting information," I said. "Do you know her?"

"Dottie is on the college's Board of Regents. I teach a Saturday class there, and that's when I occasionally bump into her. We've chatted several times, usually about the college, but we are far from being anything other than acquaintances."

"What's she like personally?"

"Arrogant, aloof...she gives off the feeling that she's superior to everyone else."

"I'm sensing a negative vibe coming from you. Am I right?"

"Have you heard anything about Dottie?"

"By anything, what are you getting at?"

Karen looked at Mike, who shrugged his permission for her to continue. "Dottie has a reputation for being...ah, how shall I put it?...a rather open-minded lady," Karen stated. "*Extremely* open minded."

"You mean sexually?" I said.

"Yes, that's what I mean. Putting it bluntly, she is quite sexually active. And not only with men. She likes women as well. According to the rumor mill, she doesn't always limit the number of participants to two. I've heard she prefers threesomes."

"Does Russell know about his?"

"Know about it? Sure, he does. He's involved. Those threesomes I mentioned often include him and another woman. Sometimes it's him, another guy, and Dottie. On other occasions, it will be two women and Dottie. He watches those encounters. And Russell records everything."

"You can't possibly know if all this is true, Karen," I said.

"Ask your friend Anne Bishop if it's true. I'll wager she will know."

That was one of those statements you want to pull out of your ears before it registers in your brain. But, of course, that's not possible. Your brain is like Las Vegas…what goes in there, stays in there.

I didn't want to know the answer, but I had to ask the obvious question. "Is Anne one of Dottie's playmates?" I said.

"It would be more appropriate if you ask Anne that question," Karen remarked.

"How old is Dottie Barker? I get the feeling she's younger than Russell."

"Russell is at least twice her age. I would guess him to be in his mid-sixties, Dottie in her mid-thirties."

"Is it possible Todd Brown was involved in their hanky-panky?" I said.

"I have no knowledge of that either way. But what I can tell you is that I heard from a solid source that Dottie does recruit college students on occasion. If that's true, those kids would only be a few years older than Todd, so I suppose it's not beyond the realm of possibility that he was a participant."

"What spurred your interest in Dottie Barker?" Mike asked, repeating an earlier question from Karen.

"My main interest is Russell Barker. Dottie's name just happened to come up."

"Have you come across anything interesting about Russell?"

"You mean, other than what Karen just told me? No, not really."

"This has been a most-naughty breakfast conversation," Mike said. "And despite my love for salacious gossip, I need to get moving. I'm already late for work. No doubt, people are screaming at me."

~ * ~

Mike paid the bill as promised. Although most of the food was left uneaten…except for Mike; he cleaned his plate…we went outside, said our goodbyes, and headed toward our respective vehicles. I was silent, my thoughts vacillating between what I'd just heard about Anne Bishop and my relief that Angel had behaved in a mature manner despite being in the presence of a woman she had little respect for.

"I find it laughable that Karen is so outraged by Dottie Barker's sexual activities," Angel said, bringing an end to her mature behavior. "Has the woman looked in a mirror lately?"

I started to respond, but didn't. What could I say? Whether she intended to or not, Angel's condemnation of Karen was also a slap in my face. A well-deserved slap, I might add. After all, I was equally guilty.

When we were in the car, Angel said, "If you're worried that Anne was involved with the Barkers, don't be. Trust me, she wasn't."

"How can you know that?"

"The same way I know she will never sleep with you. I realize such a statement may crush your ego, but it's true. I knew it the first time we met her. Anne is a highly moral, highly principled woman. She is not the type to leapfrog from bed to bed, sleeping around. And she's certainly not into anything kinky."

"Only one way to know for sure." I picked up my cell phone and placed a call to Anne. She answered after several rings. "Anne, this is Nick Gabriel. I was wondering if you were free for dinner tonight. If I remember correctly, it's my turn to pay."

"I have a better plan," Anne said. "Why don't you and Sam come over to my house for dinner? Lasagna, a salad, a bottle of good Merlot? Does that sound tempting?"

"Yes, it does. But Samantha won't be able to make it. She has other plans for tonight."

"Sorry she won't be joining us, but I'm glad you told me. I'll cook for two rather than three. Will six-thirty work for you?"

"Perfect. I look forward to seeing you then."

Angel was grinning when I ended the call. "Don't get your hopes up, Dad," she teased. "You've got no shot with Anne."

"Here's a thought: How about you stop concerning yourself with me and focus instead on what you have to do tonight? Think you can do that?"

"Relax, Dad, I've got this."

I wanted to believe her, but...the mission we had planned wasn't without peril.

~ * ~

Angel peeled off and disappeared into her room once we returned to the motel. Presumably, she required the alone time to get mentally prepared for tonight's task. Being more apprehensive than my daughter, and therefore more nervous, I sought a distraction from my justified concerns about what was in the works for tonight. So I grabbed my laptop, strolled down to the front lobby, and sat on the big sofa. Except for the lady working the front desk, I had the area to myself, which saved me from the kinds of distractions I *didn't* need.

My goal was to learn all I could about Russell Barker. It was hard for me to believe he wasn't involved in some capacity with one, possibly two, homicides. A deep dive into his background could provide a glimpse into what that involvement might be.

Of course, I had to face the fact that there was no guarantee I would find anything about the man on the Internet. Not everyone has a past worthy of national or international social media exposure. In fact, only a small percentage fit into that category. Fortunately for my purposes, Russell did.

There were several Russell Barker-related articles on the Internet. Most were brief, but one was quite lengthy. And that one included a detailed biography of Russell. Precisely what I was hoping to find.

Russell Barker was born in Baton Rouge on April Fools' Day in nineteen fifty-two, thus making him sixty-eight, or slightly older than Karen Tucker guessed him to be. His parents divorced when Russell was ten, and he moved to New Orleans with his mother. In nineteen-seventy he enlisted for a two-year hitch in the Army, spending nineteen seventy-one serving as a rifleman for an infantry company in Vietnam. After leaving the military he took several stabs at college life, but failed to graduate.

Russell married Gloria Stafford in nineteen seventy-eight, a union that ended when she and their ten-year-old son died tragically. Mother and son were on their yacht when it exploded and was consumed by flames. This happened in nineteen-ninety while they were living in Palm Beach. It was ruled an accident. According to the authorities, the explosion occurred when a faulty gas line ignited while Gloria was cooking dinner in the cabin. Russell was not on the yacht at the time of the explosion, which turned out to be a twin blessing for him. Gloria happened to be the heiress to one of the big clothing companies, while Russell, as her surviving spouse, inherited virtually all of her fortune.

Russell relocated to Muhlenberg County five years after the death of his wife and son. No reason was given for his move from a super-wealthy area like Palm Beach to the economically challenged home of dead coal mines. Then in nineteen ninety-five, despite having no background in law enforcement, Russell decided to run for sheriff. Bolstered by his enormous wealth, and his combat experience in Vietnam, he easily won the race. He held the office for twelve years, then stepped down, choosing instead to run for magistrate rather than seek another term as sheriff. Once again he won with ease.

Dottie Barker, previously Dorothy Conrad, was mentioned only once in the article. This came in a reference to her marriage to Russell at age nineteen in two-thousand-four. If my math is correct, this makes her thirty-five, not quite half as young as her husband. I have to believe Russell has to work double time keeping up with her.

Closing my laptop, I contemplated what I had just learned about Russell Barker. Two points in his biography stood out. First, there's the sad tale of his wife and son's tragic death. Was it truly an accident, or could there be more to the story? That was worth looking into. Second, why did Russell leave Palm Beach for Muhlenberg County? No one is his or her right mind makes a move like that unless there is a compelling reason, and I can't begin to fathom what that reason might be. This was another question begging to be answered.

"Okay, Dad, I'm taking off," Angel said, snapping me back to the moment, and to my concerns for her safety. "Lose the worried look. Nothing bad will happen. I'll be fine."

"You don't have to do this, Angel," I said. "We can always find another way."

"Nope, this was my idea, and I'm going through with it. There is no backing out now."

"Promise me you will be careful. And don't take any dumb chances. The first sign of trouble, you walk away."

"Relax, Dad. Have a pleasant evening with Anne. Like I told you, I've got this."

I had a single thought as she walked out of the Best Western: *I certainly hope so.*

Twenty-three

Cars were entering and leaving the Convention Center when Angel arrived at six-thirty. The parking area was lined with vehicles of all sizes and shapes, many on the prowl for a place to park. Angel hadn't expected this much activity, mainly because she wasn't aware of the outdoor swimming pool, which was packed with people. The sounds of laughter, splashing water, and blaring music, typical for a crowded swimming pool, came through loud and clear on this warm summer night. Angel had her doubts about finding a parking spot, and she only did when a large truck pulled away from the space it occupied. She cut the engine, grabbed her equipment bag, got out, locked the car, and headed for the Convention Center door.

Inside the big building, she stopped at the desk, introduced herself, and then informed the young lady behind the counter that she was on vacation from California. Then she inquired about the possibility of swimming in the indoor pool. The young lady said a ten-dollar fee was required for a guest to utilize the pool. Angel paid the ten bucks, signed in, thanked the young lady, and moved off toward the pool. She hadn't lied about wanting to swim, but that wasn't her main reason for being there. She had come to meet someone.

And that required making a detour to the exercise room.

Dorsey McElwain had just stepped down from a treadmill and was wiping sweat from his face with a towel when he saw Angel come into the room. He picked up an orange-colored energy drink and took a long swig. He was breathing hard, his face was red, and a vein in his neck was pulsating. It was obvious to Angel that he had put himself through a strenuous workout. And judging by his physique, he was no stranger to serious exercise. Only then, seeing him in gym shorts and no shirt, did Angel see how ripped Dorsey McElwain was.

"Kind of lost, aren't you?" Dorsey asked.

"Nope, I'm right where I want to be," Angel replied.

"Why are you here?"

"To swim. I'd heard about the Olympic-size pool and thought I would like to check it out."

"How can you do that? You aren't a member here."

"I paid the ten-dollar guest fee."

"If you are here to swim, where's your bathing suit?"

"Underneath what I have on."

Dorsey emptied the bottle and tossed it into a recycle container. "Hope you are a competent swimmer, because there's no lifeguard on duty," he said. "Hate to see you drown."

"Don't concern yourself with that, Dorsey. I swim like a dolphin," Angel said. "And, no, you wouldn't shed a tear if I did drown. We both know that."

"That's your big problem. You think you know everything."

"Here's a suggestion, Dorsey. Rather than argue or debate my problems, why don't we make an attempt at getting along? Bury the hatchet, as they say."

"I don't think that's likely to happen anytime soon."

"Why not? Come on, follow me. We'll talk while I swim."

"What's with this attitude change?" Dorsey wanted to know. "Why are you suddenly being so friendly to me?"

"Because I'm a friendly girl, that's why. Is that too hard for you to believe? Life is too short to waste precious time arguing or fighting." Angel walked to the door. "Swimming? You in or out?"

"Out."

"Tell you what. If you don't want to swim, that's okay. No problem. You can sit on the side and watch me swim. That way, we can still talk. And when I'm finished, I'll shower, get dressed, and we'll go somewhere, have a soft drink, and continue our talk. Does that sound like a plan?"

"I don't know. Maybe."

"It would be a lot better if you'd swim with me," Angel said.

"Can't. I didn't bring my bathing suit."

"You know, Dorsey, it's too bad we aren't at a lake or a river. If we were, we could go skinny dipping."

"Like I'm supposed to believe you would swim naked with me? Not a chance in hell that would that ever happen."

"Why not? I've done it countless times."

"Swim naked? I don't believe it."

"Dorsey, as a true California girl, I can assure you that there are two things we can't tolerate... pubic hair and tan lines. And tan lines aren't possible if you don't wear a bathing suit. I'm going to the pool. You coming or not?"

Angel walked away, Dorsey nipping at her heels. Inside the pool area she removed her Tee-shirt, shorts, and sandals, slipped on her goggles, and jumped into the water. Dorsey eased to the side, took off his running shoes, peeled off his sweat socks, sat, and dangled his feet in the water. He kept his eyes glued to Angel's every movement as she effortlessly swam laps. So did a half-dozen other male swimmers who were present. Angel's skimpy two-piece bathing suit was not something they were accustomed to seeing. Although none of them would dare complain, her suit was probably a little too risqué for the Central City Convention Center pool.

When Angel finished her laps, she swam to the side and dog-peddled in front of Dorsey. "Still worried about me drowning?" she said, removing her goggles. "Or did I successfully pass the swim test?"

"There's something not right about all this," Dorsey said, shaking his head. "You're working an angle, aren't you?"

"Why are you so suspicious? Don't you think it's possible that I just want to talk? For us to be friends?"

"Want to know what I really think? Your father sent you here to grill me for information. That's the only reason you are being so friendly."

"Boy, you must really hate my father," Angel said.

"You got that right. Your dad is a jerk and a sorry piece of shit."

"Dorsey, a minute ago I told you that under different circumstances I would swim naked with you and what do you do? You verbally rip my father. How dumb is that? You really need to recognize a winning hand when you have one."

"Well, maybe I shouldn't have said those things. It's just that I don't trust your dad. He's always pumping me for information. I don't like that."

"You can relax, Dorsey. My father is not going to question you again. You are officially off the hook."

"Yeah, why's that?"

"He has concluded that you don't know anything that would be helpful to his research," Angel said. "So you can rest easy."

"That's what he believes?" Dorsey said.

"Yes. He told me that earlier today."

"Well, he just might be wrong about that."

"In fact, my father is planning to speak with someone else tomorrow at noon. He's certain this individual will have plenty of information to share."

"What individual are you referring to?"

"A high school pal of Dad's. I don't know his real name, but everyone calls him Rabbit."

"Rabbit? That squirrelly little douchebag? That's the guy your dad is going to speak with?"

"That's his plan."

"Hell, I know ten times more than Rabbit ever will," Dorsey said.

"Doesn't matter now. Anyway, Dad doesn't seem to think you do."

Angel swam to the ladder and climbed out of the pool, all eyes continuing to focus directly on her. Picking up her towel, she briefly dried off, and then wrapped a second larger towel around her, effectively ending the show that had kept Dorsey and those other men so spellbound for the past forty-five minutes.

"Let me make a quick change, then we'll go somewhere," Angel said, using her hands to wring water from her hair. "Meet me outside the locker room. Shouldn't take me more than ten minutes."

Dorsey didn't protest or show any signs that he planned to leave. He stayed put, firmly planted a few feet from the locker room door. Just exactly where Angel knew he would be.

~ * ~

While Angel was hanging out with Dorsey McElwain, her new BFF, I was at Anne Bishop's house. We had just finished an excellent meal and were well into a second bottle of Merlot. In private, Anne was even easier to be around than she was in public. I was perfectly comfortable in her presence, and genuinely enjoyed being in her company.

Prior to leaving for Anne's house, I made a follow-up call to FBI agent Greg Harkins in Owensboro. I wanted to confirm that our noon meeting tomorrow in my motel room was still on. Greg said it was. Good, I thought, after ending the call. We had much to discuss.

Unlike most women I've been around, Anne lived a rather Spartan life. At least, judging by the interior of her house, that was the only conclusion I could come to. There was nothing extra or extravagant in the entire place. Just the necessary furniture and nothing more. We were in what she called the family room, yet there wasn't a picture, plaque, trophy, or any other item that gave the room even the tiniest hint of personality. There wasn't even a clock on the wall. This certainly didn't resemble any family room I'd ever been in.

"Why don't you have any photos?" I finally asked her.

"Well, who would you recommend that I have photos of?" she answered.

"I don't know. Family, I guess."

"I never had a family. My birth mother was barely fifteen when she had me. Too young, she felt, to keep a kid. That was probably a good decision on her part. Long story short, I ended up being raised by several foster parents, none of whom I ever really bonded with."

"Did your mother ever try to contact you?"

"I have never laid eyes on the woman."

"Living with different foster families. That must've been tough."

"It was rarely easy or pleasant, but as you can see, I survived," Anne acknowledged.

"You not only survived, you thrived," I pointed out. "College, law school...those aren't cheap. How did you manage to handle the cost?"

"Scholarships, grants, loans, and I worked my ass off. From the age of fifteen until I earned my law degree, I never had fewer than two jobs. There were many times I had more than two. After an uphill struggle like that, this lawyer gig is like being on vacation."

I replenished my glass with more wine, not necessarily out of need, but rather as a way to fortify myself for the road I was soon to embark upon. You know, the old liquid courage thing. I'm not sure how much wine was required to achieve that goal, but after taking a sip I decided it was time to wade into dangerous territory.

"I did some digging on Russell Barker and what I found was intriguing," I stated. "What more can you tell me about him?"

Her smile indicated she knew where I was heading with this. "Intriguing, in what way?" Anne said.

"The death of his wife and son, for starters."

"I didn't know Russell had previously been married and had a child. What happened to them?"

"They were on a yacht that exploded and burned up."

"Where did this happen? And how long ago?"

"Palm Beach in nineteen-ninety."

"Wow, this comes as a complete shock. I had always assumed Dottie was his only wife. However, given their age difference, I don't know why I never considered that Russell might have been married before."

"His first wife came from an extremely wealthy family," I said. "That's how Russell ended up with so much money."

"You think he was responsible for her death?" Anne asked. "That he murdered her?"

"He wouldn't be the first man to murder his wife for her fortune. Many men have done it for much less than what he got."

"Maybe so, but...his son? He'd have to be really sick to do something that evil."

"Could be the son wasn't supposed to be on the boat. Maybe he was sick and stayed home from school that day and Russell wasn't aware of it. Or maybe Russell wasn't inclined to share the money with his son. With the kid out of the picture, Russell got every penny."

"Takes a twisted bastard to do something like that."

Twisted. The perfect word for seguing to...

"Dottie Barker," I said. "I've heard some wild stories about her."

"I was wondering when you would get around to her," Anne said, still smiling. "And I'm betting my name has been mentioned in those wild stories currently making the rounds. Am I right?"

"As a matter of fact, you are."

"And you want to find out if they are true or not, right?"

"Angel says there is no way they are true. That you aren't the type of woman to participate in sexual games like that."

"You are desperate to believe your daughter is right, but somewhere in the back of your mind, you just aren't completely sure, are you? But that's understandable...you're a typical guy. You have all those mental images of me involved in a threesome with Dottie and some other sexy chick. Maybe we're in a swimming pool, or we're all soaped up in the shower. One of those obvious clichés. Well, if you do, you need to wipe them away. Sam is correct...I would never lower myself in such a way. I'm no prude. Every consenting adult is free to do whatever he or she wishes to do, and with as many partners as they desire, but I'm far too traditional for that kind of behavior. Now, here's the big question: Are you happy to hear that, or are you disappointed?"

"Happy. Want to know what else Angel said?" I asked. "That you would never sleep with me."

"I'm not sure Sam is right about that," Anne said. "Under certain circumstances I might consider it."

"What circumstances?"

"We would have to live in the same city. Long-distance relationships never work."

"Just so you know…I own a house on the beach in Florida. On Siesta Key, to be precise."

"As far as bribes go, that's not a bad one," Anne said. "I've certainly had worse offers. I'll keep yours in mind."

"You owe it to yourself to do that," I said, standing. "I should get going, Anne. If I drink another drop of wine, I'll be spending the night with you whether you want me to or not. Thanks for having me over. Dinner was great."

"Maybe we can do it again in the future. Hopefully, next time my chief defender can join us."

"Don't worry about that. I'm sure Angel will be all in."

I wasn't expecting a goodbye kiss from Anne, but I was pleasantly surprised to get one. It was on my cheek and not on my lips, which I would have preferred. But beggars can't be choosers, right? And being a beggar, I was content to receive what was offered. You'll hear no complaints from me.

Twenty-four

For more than two-thousand years, the verdict on Judas had been clear and final—guilty as charged. He betrayed Jesus to the Roman overlords for the infamous sum of thirty pieces of silver, then identified his Master in the Garden of Gethsemane by bestowing upon him what would later become known in Mafia lore as the "kiss of death." For decades, the word Judas has been synonymous with betrayal.

However, in more recent times, say the past sixty years or so, many scholars have begun to re-evaluate Judas and the set of circumstances that led to his fatal act of handing Jesus over to the hated Romans. Several scenarios have worked their way into the conversation, but among scholars and biblical experts, two have risen to the top of their list.

The first of these, and the simplest, maintains that if it was God's plan all along to dispatch his son to Earth and then allow him to be humiliated and murdered by fellow humans, in this case the Romans, why should Judas wear the cloak of blame? After all, he was simply playing his designated role in the Almighty's big drama?

Nothing could be simpler, right? God sent Jesus to die, his death was meant to atone for the sins of all mankind, someone had to betray Jesus, and poor Judas was handed that dark part to play. If you want someone to blame, many scholars argue, then look no further than God himself. He was the Martin Scorsese who directed that movie.

The second scenario regarding this re-evaluation of Judas is more complex, and it harkens back to what the Jews expected their long-awaited Messiah to be once he finally arrived. Most Jews envisioned a Messiah in much the same vein as David, a warrior-king who would unite the Twelve Tribes of Israel, drive the enemy from the Holy Land, rebuild the Temple, and rule over Israel and the Jewish people in peace forever. At the time Jesus lived, many of his followers were certain he was the Messiah. There is no reason to believe Judas doubted this. And yet Jesus was nothing like the Messiah those followers were anticipating. Rather than challenge the Romans, Jesus preached that Jews should turn the other cheek and love their enemies, a doctrine that disappointed and baffled Judas, who was looking for an ass-kicker, not a soft-hearted snowflake. Judas became convinced that all Jesus needed was a little push, a gentle nudge that would force the Messiah's true nature to the forefront. How best for Judas to accomplish that goal? Simple. Turn Jesus over to the Romans. Once Jesus was shackled in chains, once he realized his life was in imminent danger, he would strip away his robe of peace, pick up his sword and shield, and fulfill long-held Messianic prophecy by driving the Romans out of the land of Israel. But when none of that happened, when meek Jesus was tried, humiliated, and crucified, Judas, crushed by guilt and acknowledging that his plan had failed, threw down the thirty pieces of silver, then committed suicide by hanging himself, thus cementing forever his reputation as the most reviled villain of all-time.

For those scholars who ascribe to this re-evaluation scenario, Judas was a sympathetic character rather than the guilty betrayer he had long been believed to be.

Why am I bringing this up now? Because it relates to me. I have already betrayed one friend by sleeping with his wife, and now I am on the verge of betraying a second close friend. How will I be judged for these two deeds? For the first one, sleeping with my friend's wife, I know exactly how I will be judged… harshly. I'll be seen as a traitor, and rightfully so. That stain can never be washed away.

The second one, though it has yet to happen, isn't so clear-cut. In all likelihood I don't think it will be viewed in a negative light within the court of public opinion, especially after all the facts are uncovered. Truthfully, I'm not persuaded this act qualifies as a betrayal. Granted, I may be throwing a friend under the bus, but failure to do so would be, in my mind anyway, the greater betrayal. With this one I'll take my chances when Judgment Day comes.

~ * ~

When there was a knock on my door I checked the time on my cell phone and saw that it was only ten-thirty. This concerned me because my meeting with Greg Harkins wasn't until noon. If he was this early, it meant communication between the two of us was less than ideal. Or perhaps he was eager to get the meeting started early, which was perfectly fine with me.

But it wasn't Greg Harkins standing there when I opened the door. It was Jimmy Martin and his much-shorter deputy, whose nametag identified him as Hall. My initial thought was that Jimmy had showed up to inform me he had located the spot where the shooter stood when taking his shot at us, and no evidence had been found that would lead to the shooter's identification. But that thought quickly faded when I saw the look on Jimmy's face. He was here in his role as an investigator. Delivering a message was not on his agenda.

"What's up, Jimmy?" I asked.

"Mind if we come in, Nick," Jimmy said. "We need to talk."

"Absolutely." I opened the door wider and motioned for them to come in. "What's on your mind, Jimmy?"

"Is your daughter available? She's really the one I need to speak with. Care to get her for me?"

"Not until you tell me what this is all about. Beginning with, why do you want to talk to her?"

"Dorsey McElwain is dead. He was murdered late last night or early this morning in his house on West Second Street. When I retraced his movements yesterday, I discovered your daughter was the last person he was seen with. Naturally, I have questions for her."

"What are you saying, Jimmy? That you believe she murdered Dorsey?"

"I'm saying I need to question her, that's all."

"I'll get her."

"Maybe it would be better if I got her," Jimmy suggested. "Unless you have a problem with that. Do you have a problem with it, Nick?"

"No."

Jimmy went across the hall and knocked on Angel's door. It took several seconds before she opened it. If she was surprised to see Jimmy standing there, she didn't show it. Jimmy told her he wanted to ask her a few questions, and would she mind answering them in my room. She quickly agreed, not bothering to ask Jimmy what this was all about.

"Where were you last night, Miss Gabriel?" Jimmy asked, once they were back in my room.

"Why do you care where I was last night?" Angel answered, defiance in her tone. "What business is that of yours?"

"Let me clarify how this works, Miss Gabriel. I have the badge, which entitles me to ask the questions. Your job is to answer them. Once again, will you please account for your whereabouts last night?"

"I went to the Convention Center to swim."

"What time was this?"

"About six-thirty."

"And how long were you at the Convention Center?"

"Approximately an hour, I'm guessing, maybe a little longer."

"Did you speak with anyone while you were there?"

Angel nodded, said, "The young lady at the desk who checked me in."

"Anyone else?"

"Yes, Dorsey McElwain. But you knew that already, didn't you?"

"Did Dorsey swim with you?" Jimmy said, ignoring her question.

"He did not. But we did talk while I swam."

"What did the two of you talk about?"

"Nothing substantial, just talk." Angel looked at me, then back at Jimmy. "What's with all the questions about Dorsey McElwain?"

"Dorsey was murdered sometime last night, Miss Gabriel," Jimmy said. "And you were the last person seen with him while he was still alive."

"Not the last person," Angel corrected. "That would be the person who killed him."

"Did you and Dorsey leave the Convention Center together?"

"We left at the same time, yes, but we weren't together."

"What does that mean?"

"When we left the building, he got into his truck, I got into my car, and we drove away separately."

"Was that the last time you saw him?" Jimmy inquired.

"No, we met at Dairy Queen. I was hungry after swimming, so I had some fries and a soft drink. Dorsey had a chocolate sundae. When we finished eating, we left. Separately."

"How long were you at DQ?"

"No longer than forty-five minutes."

Before Jimmy could ask his next question, he was startled to see Greg Harkins open the door and enter the room. I could only imagine what Jimmy must have been thinking. Why the hell was an FBI agent in my room?

"And what time did you leave?" Jimmy finally said.

"Around ten," Angel answered.

"What happened next?"

"I came to the motel and went straight to bed. As for Dorsey, I don't know where he went when we left. Home, I would assume."

"Just to be clear, Miss Gabriel. The last time you saw Dorsey McElwain was when the two of you departed Dairy Queen? Is that accurate?"

"Yes. Now will you tell me how he died?"

"Broken neck. He was sitting on the sofa...someone approached from behind, and snapped his neck like a twig. He died instantly."

"What time did this happen?" Angel wanted to know.

"According to the coroner, death occurred between eleven-thirty last night and one-thirty this morning."

"Well, that rules me out as a suspect. I was here at that time."

"Can you vouch for that, Nick?" Jimmy said to me.

"I didn't get back to the motel until around eleven," I said. "Angel's door was closed when I got here."

"Where were you last night?"

"I had dinner with Anne Bishop at her house."

"So you can't vouch for your daughter, right? You don't know for sure if she was in her room or not?"

"No, but I believe my daughter is telling the truth. If she says she was in her room, that's where she was. Besides, what reason would she have for murdering Dorsey McElwain?"

"What reason did she have for talking with him at all? To me, that's the big question. And if you think I buy the notion that she just happened to accidentally run into him at the Convention Center, then you've been smoking too much crack, because I don't buy it, not for a second. I happen to believe she purposefully went there to question him, most likely on your orders."

"Question him about what?" I said.

"The Todd Brown case. Apparently, you aren't going to leave that one alone."

"Do you have more questions for us, Jimmy? If not, we need to cut this short. I have an important meeting scheduled."

Jimmy cut his eyes toward Greg Harkins, no doubt wondering now more than ever why an FBI agent was standing two feet away with a stern look on his face. Jimmy had to be perplexed.

"We're done for now," Jimmy said to me. "But neither you nor your daughter should even think about leaving town until I get this mess sorted out. We clear on that?"

"We're not going anywhere, Jimmy."

~ * ~

"Don't look at me like that, Dad," Angel groused, once Jimmy and his deputy were gone. "I can see what you're thinking and you are wrong. I did not kill Dorsey McElwain."

"The thought never crossed my mind," I lied, hoping she didn't see through my mendacity. "But the timing of his death tells us something, mainly that someone knew he spoke with you and wasn't happy about it."

"Obviously."

"Did Dorsey reveal anything important during your conversation?"

"I didn't think it wise to press him with a bunch of questions last night. That would've made him even more suspicious than he already was. We were going to meet again tonight at the Convention Center. That's when I planned to dig a little deeper. But one thing I can tell you is that he possessed plenty of knowledge about what's been going on around here."

"How can you be so sure if you didn't probe for answers?"

"When I told him you no longer had any interest in questioning him again, that you had determined he had nothing helpful to offer, and that you were planning to query Rabbit for information, Dorsey became very agitated. I would go so far as to say he was offended. He told me he knew ten times more than Rabbit ever would. And now he's dead, which means we'll never know what he might have told us."

Greg Harkins was seated in one of the chairs, quietly listening to this exchange between Angel and me. His interest level seemed to kick up several notches when he heard Rabbit's name mentioned.

"Rabbit? That's who we're going to discuss today, isn't it?" Greg asked.

"Yes, it was," I said. "But Dorsey McElwain's murder throws a blanket over that plan."

"Not necessarily."

"What are you thinking, Greg?"

"During my investigation into the Sharon Anderson homicide, I spoke with Dorsey several times in Sheriff Jackson's office. I got the feeling he wanted to be kept in the loop, to stay on top of what I was learning. Individuals who behave in that manner are always worth a second look. And he went out of his way to be helpful. For instance, when I wanted to interview Rabbit, Dorsey was the person who brought him in." Greg paused, then continued, "I might be mistaken, but you've always given off a vibe that you believe the Anderson-Felton murders are related?"

"Yeah, but that vibe is not much more than a gut-level hunch. Why are you asking that?"

"Maybe it's time for me to make a serious effort at linking the two cases."

"How would you go about doing that?" I asked.

"By investigating the Dorsey McElwain homicide. If what your daughter says is true, that Dorsey had knowledge of certain events, then he might be the connection between those previous two murders. That may be the reason why he was killed. He knew too much. Therefore, he had to be silenced."

"Can you get assigned to the McElwain investigation?"

"Not unless someone reaches out and enlists my assistance. That would have to be either the chief of police or the county attorney. And I think we both know Jimmy Martin is never going to ask for my help. But Mark Robinson might. During our meetings, he came across as a decent guy."

"Will you reach out to him?"

"I could, but going through a back channel might be the more appropriate approach to take."

"Am I to be the back channel?"

"Unless you wouldn't feel comfortable in that role."

"I have no problem doing it," I said. "I'll contact Mark later this afternoon and let him know you are willing to help."

"Great," Greg said, standing. "It's past noon. I'm starved, so let's go find some nourishment. We can talk about your friend while we eat. Does that sound like a plan?"

Neither Angel nor I objected. Seconds later we were out the door.

Twenty-five

"Who do you think murdered Dorsey McElwain, Dad?" Angel asked. We were in the Mexican restaurant near Best Western. "I can tell you who my prime suspect is...Perry Jackson."

"That's because you detest the man," I said.

"You're telling me you don't think he's involved?"

"Maybe he is, but let's get the evidence that proves it before we put the noose around his neck."

Greg laughed, said, "Having evidence to bolster your case is always a good idea, Angel. Your father—"

"My father should introduce me as *Samantha*, my real name," Angel interrupted.

"Oops, sorry about that, Samantha," Greg said. Then to me: "About the Florida thing you mentioned yesterday, I phoned Juan Perez, the Miami SAC, and asked him if he would look into the incident. But I'd completely forgotten that Juan's first assignment as a young agent was in the Miami office. He didn't work the Barker case, but he remembers it quite well."

"And what did he tell you?" I asked.

"Because the yacht was completely destroyed by the explosion and fire, no evidence survived that would lead investigators to conclude if what happened was an accident or a homicide. But based on the amount of money he walked away with …"

"Wait a minute," Angel interrupted. "Who are you talking about?"

"Russell Barker," I said.

"That sick, perverted bastard? Why …"

I held up my hand to cut her off. Then I nodded at Greg to continue.

"As I was saying, Russell walked away with a mountain of money… upwards of forty-million bucks…which sent up a red flag for the investigators. However, with no way to prove a homicide had been committed, no charges were ever filed. Another factor worked to Russell's advantage… his son perished in the explosion. And the way Juan remembers it, Russell was pretty torn up by the death of his son. The investigators just couldn't convince themselves he would kill his own child."

"Unless Russell wasn't aware that the boy was on the yacht at the time," I pointed out.

"That's definitely a real possibility," Greg conceded, adding, "I guess we have to chalk it up as a mystery that will never be solved."

Angel plucked a chip from a basket sitting on the table, dipped it into a bowl of salsa, and took a bite. "Why are you discussing Russell Barker, Dad?" she said, wiping a crumb from the corner of her mouth. "I thought we were here to talk about Rabbit."

Greg responded to her question before I did. "The answer to that is simple, Samantha," he said. "Your father is certain Russell was involved in these murders. Am I right, Nick?"

"Murders? I don't know," I said. "But I'm reasonably certain he was involved in Sharon Anderson homicide."

"What about this latest homicide? Was Russell also in on the murder of Dorsey McElwain?"

"If what I believe is close to the truth, I'd have to say yes."

"The floor is all yours, Nick. Lay out your version of the truth."

"Heather Anderson told me Sharon spent quite a bit of time at the Barkers' house, ostensibly to do Dottie's hair. But after what we learned about the Barkers' sexual proclivities, I believe... "

"Whoa, Nick, let me stop you right there," Greg said. "Sexual proclivities? Details, please."

"Apparently, the Barkers tend to have a very liberated view of the marriage contract," I said. "That's especially true of Dottie, who has shared her bed with numerous partners of both sexes. Word is, she has a strong preference for threesomes. Russell often joins in, other times he's a spectator. His greatest joy comes from watching his wife with two women. And every encounter, whether he is involved or not, is recorded."

"Salacious, I grant you, but how do you go from threesomes to murder?" Greg asked.

"What if those trips Sharon Anderson made to the Barker house were to take part in the sexual escapades rather than to labor over Dottie's hair? According to Heather, Sharon was madly in love with someone at the time of her death. What if Russell was that someone? What if?"

"Jesus Christ, Nick, you're killing me with what-ifs," Greg said. "If you hope to persuade me you have to give me more than pure speculation."

"It is speculation, Greg, I'll admit that. But let me finish before you dismiss what I'm saying. Will you grant me that favor?"

"Okay, request granted. Keep going."

"Sharon spends so much time at the Barkers' house that she eventually develops strong feelings for Russell. They carry on for a few months...it's outside-the-marriage fun for him, but not for her. As for Dottie, she couldn't care less. She's off having her own fun. Anyway, Sharon is madly in love with Russell, wants him all to herself and begins nagging him to dump Dottie and marry her. At some point, Sharon becomes overly possessive and begins to lay down ultimatums. Maybe she threatens to go public with the sexual stuff unless Russell marries her. Or she wants more money. But Russell isn't about to capitulate to her demands. And he's damn sure not going to allow Sharon to go public with what goes on inside the Barker house. Suddenly she has become a threat, not merely a sexual plaything. She has to be done away with."

"So Russell kills her? Is that what you're saying?"

"No, he hires someone to do the dirty work."

"Let me take a wild stab at who that someone is. Dorsey McElwain, right?"

"Dorsey for sure, perhaps with assistance from Perry Jackson."

"I can see why those movie people want you as a writer, Nick," Greg said. "That's some tale you're spinning. I'll give you credit for that."

"What part do you see as being so outlandish?" I asked.

"Quite frankly, Nick, most of it, I'm sorry to say. You start with Russell, then you bring in Dorsey McElwain, and for the final cherry on top of the plot, you include Perry Jackson. That's a wild conspiracy you've got working. About the only person missing from the group is Lee Harvey Oswald."

"Make a joke, Greg, but Dorsey McElwain is dead. That's not funny. One conspirator has been permanently shut up. Do you really believe his death is a coincidence? I don't. He was a threat to Russell. Therefore, he had to be eliminated."

"A minute ago you claimed Russell wouldn't get his hands dirty by committing murder. Now, all of a sudden, he's willing to dirty his hands? Come on, Nick. You can't have it both ways."

"Russell hired someone to kill Dorsey, just like he hired someone to kill Sharon Anderson," I said.

"Who? Perry Jackson? If that's so, how long will it be before Perry is murdered? And who is going to eliminate him? If my calculation is correct, once Perry is gone, Russell has officially run out of local henchmen to do his dirty work. He'd have to go out and hire a new crew of killers, wouldn't he?"

I remained silent, sensing Greg wasn't quite finished with his lecture. I was right.

"You want to know the gaping hole I find with your wild theory, Nick?" Greg continued. "Dottie Barker. What role does she play in any of this? Do you expect me to believe all these homicides are occurring and she's clueless? Well, I don't. I'm not buying her innocence. And here's one of your what-ifs that you conveniently overlooked. What if Sharon was madly in love with Dottie and not with Russell? That theory is as plausible as the one you laid out. Maybe Dottie is the mastermind behind these homicides."

"Dottie Barker snapped Dorsey McElwain's neck like a twig? That's what you want me to believe? Really? Now who's being outlandish?"

"Who's to say she didn't hire it done? She has access to Russell's money."

"A clever diversion, Greg," I said. "But you're way off base. Russell is behind the murders."

"Okay, Nick, you've solved two murders, Sharon's and McElwain's. But what about the one in the middle, the one that brought you here in the first place? The Luke Felton murder? Haven't you maintained all along that these homicides are linked in some way? Where's the link? What's the link? *Who's* the link?"

"Dorsey McElwain. Solve his murder and you'll see that I'm right. That's why it's imperative that you handle the investigation."

"Which I can't do unless my assistance is requested." Greg looked at Angel and said, "What's your opinion on all this, Samantha?"

"I don't know if Dorsey was the link or not, but the timing of his death so soon after speaking with me is more than a little suspicious," Angel said. "His death needs to be thoroughly investigated."

At that moment Greg's cell phone chirped. He picked it up, checked the Caller ID, frowned, looked across the table at me, and whispered, "Talk about serendipitous."

Before I could ask Greg what the hell he meant, he put the phone to his ear and spoke. Hearing his first words told me all I needed to know.

"Yes, Mark, it's good to hear from you," Greg said. "In fact, I have heard about it. Yes, it is sad. Sure, I'd be more than happy to help in any way I can. Really? You don't see my involvement as possibly starting a turf war? Actually, I'm in town now. I'm with Nick Gabriel and his daughter at the Mexican restaurant near the Best Western.

West Second Street? I'm sure Nick knows where that is. We can be there in fifteen or twenty minutes. Okay, Mark, I'll meet you there."

"Mark Robinson, I presume," I said, as Greg put his phone away.

Greg nodded. "He wants me to take complete charge of the investigation. Naturally, Jimmy Martin is less than thrilled, but Mark isn't concerned about Jimmy's hurt feelings. He said Jimmy is good at handling routine matters, but a homicide investigation is out of his league."

"That's a good call by Mark," I said.

"Do you know where West Second Street is?"

"Of course."

"Did I lie, or can we make it in fifteen or twenty minutes?"

"We can be there in ten if we leave now."

"Then let us tarry no longer." Greg stood. "Let me pay the bill and then we'll be on our way."

~ * ~

We made it to West Second Street is under ten minutes. West Second, a short street located between Reservoir and Center Street, was currently the epicenter of more activity than neighbors had probably ever witnessed in the past. There were several police cruisers, a sheriff's vehicle, two sedans, and a fire truck parked on the street in front of the house. Yellow tape, ubiquitous at every crime scene, was wrapped around the small front yard, put there to cordon off the house from inquisitive rubberneckers. Two uniformed officers stood on the front porch, while Jimmy Martin's diminutive Deputy Hall closely monitored the scene for anyone who looked like he might be planning to sprint past the yellow tape.

Dorsey's house of residence, fourth on the right if you turned left off Reservoir onto West Second, appeared to be a typical three-bedroom, two-bath wooden structure. There was a front yard and a back yard, both small, and a porch. The house itself needed work. Back when it was first built, the house had probably been one of the nicest homes on the block. But that wasn't the case anymore, and it hadn't been for years. The passage of time and long-term neglect rendered it one step above a true eyesore.

Greg and I exited the car and headed toward the house. Angel stayed behind, hopping up on the hood of the car to get a better look at what was taking place across the street.

Greg badged Deputy Hall, who immediately lifted the tape for the FBI agent to enter. But Hall didn't feel compelled to be so accommodating to a writer, and it was only after Greg ordered him to grant my entrance that Hall reluctantly raised the tape.

I followed Greg onto the porch and into the house. I'm no cop but even I was quick to realize that too many people were milling around in what was obviously a crime scene. Most of them would have to go. Jimmy Martin and Perry Jackson were standing against the wall, while Mark Robinson, the county attorney, stood behind the sofa, where, I presume, Dorsey had been sitting when he took his final breath. His body had been removed, but the way Mark was inspecting the area left little doubt that Dorsey had died sitting there.

Greg acknowledged Jimmy and Perry with a nod, then went over and shook hands with Mark. I planted myself against the wall opposite Jimmy and Perry, both of whom glared at me with disdain in their eyes.

"With the exception of Mark, Jimmy, and Perry, I want everyone else out of here," Greg announced. "I have put in a call to my forensics team. They should be arriving within two hours. It would be nice if they could work a relatively undisturbed crime scene, which won't be the case if all you folks continue strolling around like you're visiting a museum. Try not to touch anything on your way out. Thanks."

Greg hadn't mentioned my name when ordering people to leave, but I stayed put just the same. There was no way I was leaving unless directly ordered by Greg to do so. Call me nosey, but I wanted to know what was going on. This was research, remember?

Greg continued to confer with Mark, then motioned for Jimmy and Perry to join them. Once they did, the foursome went on a recon mission through the house. I toyed with the idea of tagging along with them, but decided that probably wasn't the wise thing to do. No sense unnecessarily pressing my luck.

Instead, I went over to a wooden table that had stacks of CDs piled on top of it. Curious, I began browsing through them. The vast majority were music recordings, heavy on Country and Western, while a few cowboy movies were included. Nothing unusual or out of the ordinary for a guy Dorsey's age. However, there was one that did catch my attention. It was the only one not in a case. But the main reason it drew my interest was because the word "Personal" was written on it in red ink.

When Greg and his gang came back into the room, I went over and handed the CD to him. "This might be interesting," I said.

Greg went to the TV, studied the equipment until he had it figured out, turned on the TV, put the CD in, and pressed the Play button.

The TV screen sprang to life, first with nothing but snow and the familiar low buzzing sound that normally comes when your cable has been disconnected. I feared I had given Greg a dud. But I was wrong. Seconds later, a picture, bright and in full color filled the screen, and the movie began. The stars were two women and a lone male, all completely nude, and judging from the moaning and groaning on the soundtrack, each one was clearly enjoying what they were doing. The trio was arranged in a circle, their contorted bodies a miracle of flexibility, which reminded me of a serpent eating its own tail.

"Did you know Dorsey was involved in this, Perry?" Greg asked.

"No, I didn't," Perry answered. "I'm as shocked as you are."

"How about you, Jimmy?"

"Hell, no."

"You're both sure about that?" Greg said. "Now is the time to come clean if you did know."

"Are you calling me a liar?" Perry said, taking a step closer to Greg. "I hope for your sake that's not the case."

"Did either of you ever participate?"

"In that sick, twisted shit? No way." Perry turned to Mark. "You want to put this guy in charge, Mark, that's your call. But he'd better start directing his stupid questions to someone other than me. For his own good."

"My job is to find answers, Perry, not to worry about pissing you off," Greg said, forcefully. "I'll ask you or anyone else one hundred fucking questions if I think they'll help me find the answers. As for my own good, you let me worry about that."

The atmosphere had suddenly become tense and highly volatile. There was a moment when I really thought Greg and Perry were going to clash. Mark must have sensed the same thing, because he eased in between Greg and Perry, both of whom dwarfed him in height and weight. I'm not sure Mark could have done much had the two men decided to tangle. And I'm even less sure whose side Jimmy would be on.

I ended the silence and softened the tension by posing a question. "I recognize Dorsey, but who are the two women?" I asked.

"Dottie Barker and Sharon Anderson," Mark replied.

Greg looked at me, smiled, and said, "Your theory might not be so outlandish after all, Nick."

I didn't respond, but inwardly I was beaming.

"Jimmy, I'm leaving to speak with the Barkers," Greg said. "You are more than welcome to come along. This is also your investigation. I have no desire to cut you out."

"What about Perry?" Jimmy inquired.

"Perry has no role in this investigation. He can't come with us."

"I'll pass," Jimmy said, answering my silent question about whose side he would be on.

"Suit yourself, Jimmy. I will fill you in if I learn anything important at the Barker house."

"You are wasting your time," Perry noted. "Russell's not the talkative type."

"Then I'll have to win him over with my charming personality," Greg said, turning to Mark. "Leave one officer posted at the door with orders to let no one in until the forensics team arrives."

"You got it, Greg. And let me know how things go with Russell and Dottie."

Greg and I left the house, ducked under the crime scene tape, and met Angel at the car. She noticed the CD in Greg's hand, but waited until we were in the car before inquiring about it.

"Are we listening to music or watching a movie?" Angel asked, only half-kidding.

"You don't want to know," I said. "Anyway, you're too young to watch it."

"It's that bad, huh? Who's in it? Anyone I know? Wait...that was Dorsey's house, wasn't it? Yeah, it was. Is he the star? He is, isn't he?"

"Yes."

"Now it's must-see TV. Great. I'll provide the popcorn." She laughed out loud. "My pal Dorsey, the big porno star. Who would've thunk it?"

Twenty-six

Russell Barker's house was located two miles from downtown Greenville on several acres that had once been rich farmland. Calling Russell's place of residence a house was doing it a great injustice. It was by any assessment a massive three-story stone mansion that would not be out of place in such wealthy enclaves as Palm Beach, Malibu, and the Hamptons. The entire estate probably cost twelve million bucks at the very least, or a substantial chunk of the money Russell received following his first wife's death.

The main house was located at the center of the full estate. Also, on the grounds were a covered swimming pool, a tennis court, a putting green, a guest house, and a garage large enough to accommodate a fleet of vehicles. A circular driveway with a stone water fountain in the center snaked its way around the front of the main house. I had to give Russell credit...he had put his fortune to good use, whether he came by it as the result of an accident or by committing murder.

Greg pulled his car behind a red Porsche convertible, killed the engine, and the three of us got out. When turning onto the property I was surprised by the absence of a gate. In my experience, virtually every house this large had one in place as a means of keeping out those not deemed worthy of setting foot on holy grounds, which included about ninety-nine percent of the population. Looking around, I was also surprised by the lack of security cameras. Only two were noticeable, but that didn't mean there weren't others hidden from view.

The next surprise came when Greg pressed the buzzer and moments later Russell opened the door. I fully expected a maid or butler to perform that task, not the owner of the place. But there was Russell wearing a purple jogging suit over a white undershirt, with a pair of white sneakers rounding out his leisurely clothing ensemble. Russell stood about five-ten, with snow-white hair and cobalt-blue eyes. He looked to be in very good physical shape, a requirement no doubt for any man who knew he was going to be filmed performing sex acts with much younger participants.

Initially, Russell seemed genuinely perplexed when Greg introduced himself, but then I saw a flicker of recognition in his eyes when he noticed me standing behind Greg.

"What an eclectic trio of visitors," Russell commented. "A federal agent, a local boy who went off and conquered Hollywood, and an absolutely stunning young woman, who, I must confess, is like a rose between two thorns. What an honor to have such distinguished guests. How can I help you?"

"If you could spare us some of your time, I would like to ask you a few questions," Greg said.

"I doubt you know this, but I was once the sheriff of this county. As a proud former member of law enforcement, I am always more than happy to assist in any way I can. Please, come in."

Russell led us into the house and down a brightly lit hallway that appeared to be the length of a football field. There seemed to be no end to it. Along the walls, there were several framed pictures, all of which could have been originals, and if they weren't, they were near-perfect reproductions. After we passed a winding marble staircase that led to the second floor, Russell branched off and took a left into his library. I'm not sure the Central City Public Library could match the number of books in this massive room. Three floor-to-ceiling bookshelves were crammed full with hardbacks and paperbacks of all shapes and sizes. How many of these books had Russell actually read? I wondered. Not many would be my guess. And what about Dottie? Could she be the reader? Not likely, given that so much of her time was spent being recorded by her husband while cavorting with fellow sex partners. It's difficult to read when one is busy engaging in sex.

Once we were all seated around an oak table, Russell said, "Okay, Agent Harkins, fire away with your questions."

"Would your wife happen to be available?" Greg asked. "If she is, I would appreciate it if she could join us."

"I'm afraid she's not here at the present time."

I pegged this as a lie. That red Porsche parked out front had to be Dottie's. Since the car was here, that meant she was also here. Either Russell didn't want her with us, or Dottie declined to make herself available.

Russell's smugness dissipated slightly when Greg placed the CD on the table. At the very least, it caught his attention. But I have to give Russell credit. He showed no outward signs of concern or apprehension.

"One of mine?" Russell asked Greg.

"It is."

"Do you mind telling me where you got it?"

"Dorsey McElwain's house," Greg said. "Have you heard what happened to him?"

"Yes, Perry Jackson phoned me a few minutes prior to you showing up. He told me Dorsey was dead. That's too bad. He was a decent kid."

"Did Perry give you details concerning Dorsey's death?"

"No, he did not. But I'm assuming it was a suicide."

"Why would you make that assumption?"

"Remember, Agent Harkins, I was the sheriff for almost twenty years, so I'm familiar with the statistics. The suicide rate among law enforcement personnel is very high. Why? Are you saying Dorsey didn't take his own life?"

"Dorsey McElwain was murdered, Russell. Someone broke his neck."

"I hope you don't suspect me of killing Dorsey."

"Did you?"

"I most certainly did not," Russell replied firmly. "Like I said, Dorsey was a decent kid. I would never do anything to harm him."

"Where were you last night between eleven-thirty and one-thirty?" Greg inquired.

"Right here in this house. And I have several friends who will vouch for me."

"I'm sure you do. How well did you know Dorsey?"

Russell pointed at the CD. "Have you viewed what's on it?" he asked.

"Yes, I have."

"That sums up how well I knew Dorsey. Aside from his participation in our adventures, I didn't have much interaction with him. All I can tell you is what I've already said—he was a decent kid. If you really want to know more about him, I would suggest talking to Perry. They were close."

"What's your relationship with Perry Jackson?" Greg said.

"Well, I hired him and we worked together for several years. But we rarely had much contact away from the job."

"Did he participate in your adventures?"

"Oh, no, Perry would never go in for that kind of fun." Russell picked up the CD and looked at both sides. "Obviously, Dorsey was on this one. Did you identify the others who participated with him?"

"Your wife and Sharon Anderson."

"Just as I suspected. Dottie and Sharon were Dorsey's favorites. He always asked for them."

"I take it from your comment that Dorsey was a regular."

"For the past three or four years, yes, that's true."

"How long have you been entertaining in such a way?" Greg wanted to know. "And how many people are involved?"

"Oh, we've been entertaining for ten or twelve years now. Number of participants? There has been a revolving door over the years, but I would estimate the figure to be around a hundred, give or take a few. You may not approve of what we do... most people don't... but there is no law against consenting adults enjoying themselves by having sex."

"It is against the law if any of those individuals, consenting or not, is underage," Greg pointed out.

"You need not concern yourself with that, Agent Harkins. I monitor the age of each new participant with a sharp eye. That's a role I take very seriously."

"But Dottie does recruit from the college, doesn't she?"

"You've obviously done your homework. My compliments, Agent Harkins. Occasionally, yes, Dottie does find individuals at the school, usually females, who are willing to participate. But the ones she does recruit are all over twenty-one. You have my word on that."

"How many CDs do you have?"

"That's hard to say. My guess would be three hundred, maybe more."

"Your first wife died, didn't she?"

I thought that was an odd question for Greg to ask at this time. The only reason I could come up with was that he sought to break Russell's rhythm by tossing him a curveball. If the question was meant to rattle Russell, it didn't work.

"Yes, she died in an explosion," Russell said calmly. "My son also perished that day. What does her death have to do with anything?"

"Did she participate in these adventures when the two of you were married?"

"No, never. She was not that kind of woman."

For once, I believed Russell. These so-called sexual adventures... orgies to most folks... began after he married Dottie. Their union served as the genesis for what was currently going on. The age difference undoubtedly caught up with Russell, who was no longer the stallion he'd once been, and it forced him to find alternative venues for Dottie's sexual fulfillment. Group sex, either as participant or voyeur, obviously did the trick for both husband and wife.

"Isn't it true that your first wife was rich?" Greg said.

"Yes, she came from an extremely wealthy family," Russell answered. "I am not comfortable talking about her, Agent Harkins, other than to say it was a dark and difficult period in my life. So, if you don't mind, let's change the subject."

"Sure, not a problem. What can you tell me about Sharon Anderson?"

"Very little, other than it's a real tragedy she was taken from us. The woman gave good head."

Sharon Anderson had been beheaded, but I doubt Russell saw the terrible irony in his statement.

"Sharon didn't just die, Russell," Greg said. "She was murdered. Do you know who killed her?"

"I do not," Russell said, pointedly. "Why don't we stop waltzing around like two drunken dancers crashing into each other, Agent Harkins? What you really want to know is did I murder my first wife for her money, and am I behind the murders of Sharon Anderson and Dorsey McElwain? Isn't that what you're asking me?"

"Were you involved in those homicides?"

"No, I was not. And for your information, my wife's death was ruled an accident." Russell stood. "I have given you more than enough of my time. If you have further questions, you can ask them with my attorney present. Now, I don't mean to be rude, but we are finished with this meeting. Follow me. I will show you out."

As Russell opened the front door, I said, "One final question, Russell. Has Rabbit ever participated in your adventures?"

"Rabbit? Are you joking? The Virgin Mary has a better chance of being invited to participate than Rabbit does. You can watch my CDs until the end of time and you won't see Rabbit on any of them. No, he did not participate."

This was the second thing Russell said that I believed.

~ * ~

"How much of what Russell said was true?" Greg said. "Some, all, none?"

"He's a perverted lying scumbag," Angel answered, though the question was directed at me. "I can't say what's true or not, but I can promise you he knows more than he told us."

"I don't think there is any doubt about that," Greg agreed.

We were sitting in Philly's Restaurant killing time before departing for our next mission...to hunt down and question Rabbit. It had taken a good deal of persuasion on my part to get Greg to finally agree that talking to Rabbit might be worthwhile. Greg was hesitant, arguing that when he questioned Rabbit about the Sharon Anderson murder, he determined Rabbit was evasive, and that he lacked information which was beneficial. I countered by reminding Greg that he had more information to throw at Rabbit now than he had back then. However, the big selling point came when I informed Greg that Rabbit was terrified of certain unknown people, and now with Dorsey dead, those individuals would have no qualms about coming after him, which could very well be sooner rather than later.

"I can point to one thing Russell lied about," I said. "Dottie was in that house. I'd bet she heard every word that was spoken."

"I'm having a difficult time determining her role in all this," Greg admitted. "I doubt she's involved in the murders, but that doesn't mean she's clueless as to who did commit them. I'd love nothing more than to get Dottie in a room and grill her. See how she handles the pressure."

"She would most likely recruit you to join their adventures," Angel said.

"You really despise those people, don't you, Samantha?"

"Yes, Greg, everything about them."

Greg looked at his watch, said, "It's almost three-thirty. How much longer do we wait before we look for Rabbit?"

"We'll leave at four," I said.

"Where do we start?" Angel asked. "At the American Legion?"

"No. Jimmy Martin was kind enough to give me Rabbit's home address. He lives in a small house on Reynolds Street. We'll start there."

"If we do locate him, he'd better not waste my time playing the artful dodger again," Greg said.

"We won't allow him to waste our time, Greg. We'll scare the truth out of him."

Twenty-seven

Our timing couldn't have been more perfect. As we turned onto Reynolds Street, Rabbit was leaving his house and walking to his car. Greg parked on the street in front of the house, which I thought was a tactical mistake. Had I been driving, I would have pulled in behind Rabbit's car, thus preventing him from leaving until our vehicle was moved.

When Rabbit saw us coming in his direction, his entire body began to shake uncontrollably. He had always been nervous and fidgety, but this was different. It was almost like his body had been seized by a sustained spasm. I knew he would be less than thrilled to see me show up accompanied by a federal agent, but I never expected this extreme reaction.

Rabbit closed his eyes and took several deep breaths in an effort to calm his breathing and slow his racing heartbeat. He'd done exactly the right thing, I thought, given what was soon to take place. The next few minutes were sure to be difficult for him, possibly even life-altering, but I had no desire to see my old friend keel over from a stroke or a coronary.

When Rabbit opened his eyes, he looked at Greg, then at me. His shaking and his breathing were closer to normal, but the look on his face was one of great sadness. I couldn't swear to it, but I thought I saw tears in his eyes. He knew what was coming.

"Dammit, Nick, what the hell are you doing here?" Rabbit asked. "I begged you to stay away and leave me alone. I don't have anything to say, yet you not only show up, you bring the Feds with you. Unfucking believable."

"We have to talk, Rabbit," I said. "There is no avoiding it."

"Why? Do you have more of your lame-ass questions for me?"

"I don't, but Greg does."

"Yeah, I remember him from three years ago. When he questioned me then, he didn't stop for three hours. I don't have time for that nonsense a second time. So, here's what he can do with his questions... shove them straight up his ass. With all due respect, of course."

"Remember what I recently told you, Rabbit?" I reminded him. "About how you need to get out in front of the story before the story gets out in front of you? Well, this is your chance. And you'd better not blow it. The walls are going to crumble, Rabbit. If you are on the inside looking out, you'll be crushed in the rubble."

"I don't have anything to say to you, Nick, or to the FBI."

Greg stepped forward and said, "On the contrary, Rabbit, like it or not, you are going to answer my questions. You are a material witness to three homicides I'm in the process of investigating. As such, you have an obligation to speak with me. It's beginning to drizzle, and I have no desire to get wet, so let's all go inside your house and remain dry. You lead the way, please."

"You are going to get me killed, Nick," Rabbit said, pointing a finger at Angel. "Just like your daughter got Dorsey killed."

"What the hell are you talking about?" I snapped.

"Hey, you're the smart guy, Nick. You figure it out."

"Inside, Rabbit," Greg said, taking charge before I could defend my daughter. "No more talk until we are inside the house. Now, move."

The interior of Rabbit's house bore a close resemblance to Dorsey McElwain's. There was a small den, an even smaller kitchen, two tiny bedrooms, and a bathroom. About the only discernible differences were Rabbit's house was messier than Dorsey's, and his TV was older and much smaller. Of course, Rabbit, unlike Dorsey, had no need for the large-screen TV, since he didn't star in any of Russell's homemade sex movies.

There was no couch in the den/TV room, only a love seat that could comfortably accommodate two people, and a single wooden chair. Rabbit sat on the love seat, and Angel took the chair, leaving Greg and me standing. I asked Greg if he wanted me to bring in two chairs from the kitchen, but he said no, he didn't mind standing. I decided that if he was willing to stand, so would I.

Once we were settled in, the expression on Rabbit's face changed from sadness to defiance. He was bracing himself for a battle of wills against Greg and me, certain in his belief that he could outwit both of us. Or perhaps he counted on outlasting us. Either way, I knew he was fighting a losing battle. Greg wasn't leaving without getting some answers.

"Who are you afraid of, Rabbit, and why are you fearful of them?" Greg asked.

"I'd rather leave names out of it," Rabbit replied. "As for the why? That's easy. I don't want to end up like Dorsey McElwain."

"Know what troubles me about you, Rabbit?"

"No, I don't. Why don't you tell me?"

"On the one hand, you claim to be in possession of such a vast amount of knowledge about these homicides that it puts you in danger of being killed if you share what you know with me. And then you turn around and tell me you don't know anything, and you don't want to talk with me. Sorry, Rabbit, but you can't have it both ways."

"If I do talk to you bastards, it will get me killed."

"Not if you tell the truth. You do that and I'll make sure you're protected. I give you my word on that. However, if you don't come clean about what you know, you'll end up behind bars. You also have my word on that."

"Behind bars? For what? I haven't committed any crimes."

"Rabbit, there have been three homicides," Greg pointed out. "The way I see it, at a bare minimum you are on the periphery of two of those murders. And you are without any doubt an accomplice in one. Jail time is staring you squarely in the face."

"Accomplice?" Rabbit said, shaking his head. "You fucking guys don't have a clue about anything."

"That's why we're here, Rabbit, so you can enlighten us and put us on the same knowledge level as you are. But before you decide to hit us with lies and deception, make no mistake about this... we aren't quite as clueless as you might think."

"Really? Why don't you tell me what you *think* you know?"

"I'll ask the questions, Rabbit, beginning with why did you say Samantha got Dorsey killed?"

"Because he was seen talking with her last night at the Convention Center. Certain people were afraid of what he might tell her, so they shut him up for good."

"Perry Jackson shut him up, isn't that what you're saying?"

"You think Perry murdered Dorsey?"

"He's the logical candidate," Greg stated.

"And you're the logical candidate for the loony bin. Perry didn't kill Dorsey. Perry was like Dorsey's father, or his older brother. If Perry knew who murdered Dorsey, he'd be on the warpath looking for the killer. Why would you even think Perry killed Dorsey?"

"Because Perry and Dorsey murdered Sharon Anderson. And like you just said, when Perry got word Dorsey talked to Samantha at the Convention Center, he had no choice but to silence him."

"Well, you are half right about the Sharon Anderson murder. But only Dorsey was involved, not Perry."

"You want me to believe Dorsey killed Sharon all by himself? That's a big pill you're asking me to swallow."

Rabbit shrugged. "I didn't say he acted alone, did I?" he said.

"Who was with him, Rabbit? You?"

"I've never killed anybody."

"You know what, Rabbit? I believe you."

"Well, hallelujah, you finally see me as I really am…an honest man. You've cleared me, so if it wasn't me, who's next on your list?"

"I'm positive Russell Barker was behind the murders, but I don't see him as a hands-on killer," Greg noted. "Are you saying Russell helped kill Sharon?"

"Man, you guys are way more clueless than I ever imagined. You really think Russell was involved in the murders?"

"It had to be Russell. Who else could it have been?"

"Why would Russell kill her?"

"Sharon Anderson had something on him. Maybe she threatened to expose what was going on in the Barkers' house, or perhaps she was squeezing him for money. She was working some angle that Russell couldn't let continue. So he had her killed. When Dorsey became a liability, Russell had him taken care of."

"Nick, did you come up with this insane plot?" Rabbit said to me.

"It's not insane, Rabbit, and I think you know it isn't," I said.

"And what about Luke Felton? Was Russell also behind that murder?"

"You tell me, Rabbit," Greg said. "That's the one you're directly involved in."

"How do you figure I'm involved?"

"None of it would've happened if you hadn't taken Todd Brown to the American Legion that night. Once you had him there, either you or Dorsey McElwain drugged him and set him up as Luke's killer. Then one of you, most likely Dorsey, actually murdered Luke."

"You're forgetting that I left the Legion before Dorsey and Todd did. I'd say that clears me of murder."

"It might," Greg agreed. "But you are still an accomplice, even if it was Dorsey who doctored Todd's drink."

Rabbit looked directly at me and said, "If me and Dorsey didn't put anything in Todd's drink, and we didn't, yet someone did, then who does that leave?"

"Enough with the riddles, Rabbit," I responded.

"Think about it, Nick. It'll come to you."

"Chet," Angel interjected. "It was Chet, wasn't it?"

"Finally, someone who truly understands the picture," Rabbit said. "Your daughter is smarter than you, Nick."

"Wait a second, I'm lost," Greg said. "Who is Chet?"

"Bartender at the American Legion," I replied.

"What reason would this Chet have for doctoring Todd's drink?" Greg asked.

"Do I have to spell everything out for you?" Rabbit answered.

"Yes, please do."

"Chet murdered Luke Felton. He also murdered Sharon Anderson and Dorsey McElwain."

"On Russell Barker's orders, right?" I said.

"God, no, Russell never killed anybody." Rabbit shook his head. "Haven't you put the pieces together yet? Dottie was behind the murders. All of them."

Though I had been convinced the murders were done at Russell's behest, I wasn't completely surprised to learn that Dottie was the one who ordered them done. I'm not sure I have a good explanation for why I wasn't shocked by this news. After all, I had never met the woman in person, only seen her in action on the TV screen. But for some strange reason I wasn't surprised.

"Why would Dottie have those three people killed?" I inquired.

"She and Chet were lovers."

"How does that lead to Sharon's murder?"

"Something must have gone wrong involving Sharon and she had to be eliminated. Don't know about you, but that's how I see it."

"How do you know this, Rabbit?"

"Dorsey told me."

"Dorsey actually told you that he and Chet murdered Sharon Anderson?" Greg asked.

"Yes, he did."

"What is Chet's last name?"

"Woodward."

"If you knew all this, Rabbit, why did you seek out Todd at the Speedway and then have him drive you to the Legion?" I said. "You had to know you were delivering him to his executioners."

"No, you're wrong, Nick. I was asked to take Todd there because he owed Chet some money."

"That didn't sound fishy to you?" I said.

"No, not at all. Chet often sold drugs. I just figured Todd failed to pay Chet what was owed. That's the only reason I took Todd to the Legion. I certainly never suspected they were planning to set him up for murder. Hell, I don't know why they did, or why they killed Luke."

"How did Chet and Dorsey lure Luke to the murder site?" Greg said.

"I can't answer that question," Rabbit said. "You just need to believe I had nothing to do with those murders."

"Why didn't you tell me about Sharon Anderson's murder three years ago?"

"I didn't know everything then. It was only later that Dorsey told me about it."

"Was it Dorsey who told you about Dottie's involvement?"

"Yeah, he did. See, Dorsey had a thing for Dottie. He'd do anything she wanted him to do. He couldn't say no to her."

"And you expect me to believe Russell wasn't aware of this?"

"Russell is more clueless than you are. The only difference is he doesn't want to know anything; you guys want to know everything." Rabbit stood and looked at me. "Are we done here? I've told you all I know. Can I go?"

I turned to Greg. He nodded his consent.

"Go with God, Rabbit," I said.

"Yeah, well, if certain people find out I spoke with the FBI, God will be seeing me a lot sooner than I planned," Rabbit said, walking out the door.

Twenty-eight

"What is truth?" Wasn't it that murderous thug Pontius Pilate who posed this infamous question? According to Scripture, yes, he was the guy. Was he being sarcastic or profound? Only he could answer that for us. Why am I thinking about that at this moment? Because it is a question I'm now asking myself. Was Rabbit telling the truth, or was he simply spewing out more of his usual steady stream of bullshit? Only Rabbit, like Pontius Pilate, has the answer.

I sensed that Greg believed Rabbit. Me? I'm not so sure. Yes, I'm positive there were elements of truth in what Rabbit told us. I do believe his narrative about Dottie being the mastermind behind the killings, and how she used Chet to actually do the dirty work. I also think he was truthful about Dorsey McElwain's involvement in the murders. Those aspects of Rabbit's story rang true to me.

However, other parts of his story came across as false, misleading, or perhaps more to the point, they led to further questions. For instance, did Rabbit lie about his involvement in any of the killings? I don't think he did, but how could I know for sure? Was he being truthful about leaving the Legion before Dorsey and Todd did, or was that another lie? What about Perry Jackson? Was he truly not one of the killers? And are we to believe that Russell Barker was completely blind to all that was taking place around him? Is it plausible that he didn't know his beloved trophy wife was bumping people off with regularity? Or that she and Chet were lovers? Was he really that tuned out?

Answers to those questions would come later, if they came at all. But there was one question that could be answered once we got back to the Best Western. I would put in a call to Richard Luckett, husband of Brenda, with whom I had spoken last week. Brenda was the lady who verified that Todd and Rabbit were in the Legion on that fateful night. But according to her, she had been sitting with her back to the bar, and therefore was unsure if Todd spoke with anyone else, or when he actually departed. She suggested I speak with her husband, who was serving as a drill instructor with his reserve unit at Fort Knox when we talked. Brenda said his seat faced the bar when they were at the Legion that night. Hopefully, he could give a more precise time when Todd departed, who he left with, and did he at any time interact with Dorsey McElwain.

"Are you going to the Barker house to interview Dottie?" Angel asked, breaking more than five minutes of silence. We were in the car driving through soggy downtown Central City. "Or is Chet at the top of your list?"

"Right now, we're going back to the motel," Greg answered. "I need to find out more about Chet before I speak with him. My laptop is in the trunk. I'll take it to your father's room and see what I can find out about the guy. I want to have every possible advantage when I do interview him."

"How much of Rabbit's tale do you believe?" I said to Greg.

"Surprisingly, most of it. Why? You didn't buy it?"

"I'm more skeptical than you are, Greg. Maybe my view is skewed because I've known Rabbit all my life. He has always had a loose relationship with the truth. He had a knack for saying things that served his best interest, true or not. Why do you believe he was being truthful?"

"For starters, he didn't hesitate to point the finger at Dottie and Chet. No way was he lying about that. Giving them up put his life in danger, and I don't see Rabbit as a guy who wants a bullseye on his back. He's right about one thing… if those two find out he talked to me, he'll be victim number four. And that's the reason why we don't have to worry about him alerting them to what we know. It's also why we need to nail this thing down today."

"You may be right, Greg, but even if Rabbit was telling the truth, there are still plenty of questions left unanswered."

"Which ones trouble you the most?"

"Why was Luke murdered? How did they get him to the murder site? Where is the murder weapon? And finally, how were the killers able to get Todd to his room without anyone hearing them? Two men lug a drugged teenager up the stairs and no one wakes up? How did they manage that trick?"

"The answers are out there," Greg said. "We just have to find them."

As we were nearing McDonald's, Angel said, "Would it be okay if we stopped for something to drink? I'm dying of thirst."

"Go inside, or the drive-thru?" Greg asked.

"Drive-thru works for me."

Several cars were lined up, but it didn't take long to place our orders and pick up the drinks. Once we left McDonald's, we drove the final mile to the Best Western. Unlike Angel or me, Greg chose to park in front of the motel. Maybe he felt there was less chance someone would fire a shot at us if we parked in the front lot.

As the rain began to come down more forcefully, Greg popped the trunk, grabbed his backpack, closed the trunk, and ran toward the motel. Angel and I were already inside when he came in. He was dripping wet. One of the maids who happened to be standing a few feet away pulled a towel from the big linen basket she was pushing and handed it to him. He thanked her profusely, slung the backpack over his shoulder, and began drying his hair as we headed down the hallway.

Angel went to her room to freshen up for what lay ahead. Greg followed me into my room, opened his backpack, took out the laptop, set it on a desk, and turned it on. Within seconds he was embarked on his mission to find out everything he could about Chet Woodward.

With Greg's attention focused entirely on his research, I decided to head back to the main lobby and make my call to the Lucketts from there. Greg didn't need any distractions, and me questioning the Lucketts would almost certainly interfere with his concentration. We both needed space to do our thing.

Sitting comfortably on the sofa, I phoned the Lucketts. Brenda answered quickly, put me on hold, and went to get her husband. It wasn't long before Richard was on the phone. Brenda must have informed him about our previous conversation, because he didn't bother with introductions or small talk. He cut straight to the chase.

"You bet I saw Todd Brown at the American Legion that night," Richard Luckett said. "He showed up with Rabbit, which I thought was odd. Rabbit is a regular, and he drinks with just about everybody, but I'd never seen Todd there before. And for Todd to be drinking? That was really strange. He's not a member at the Legion, and he's the same age as our oldest daughter, which means he's too young to be served alcohol. Chet never sells to minors, yet he definitely served Todd that night. I have no idea why he did."

"You said Todd and Rabbit arrived together," I stated. "Did they also leave at the same time?"

"No, Rabbit left first. I'd estimate at least half-an-hour before Todd did."

"Who did Todd leave with?"

"Dorsey McElwain. But Todd really didn't leave. It's more like Dorsey carried him out."

"Dorsey carried Todd?"

"No, he didn't physically carry Todd, but he was holding him up as they walked out. You know, he had an arm around Todd to keep him from falling down. I figured Todd had too much to drink, or he couldn't handle his booze. He looked like he was really loaded."

"Was Todd putting up any kind of struggle?"

"Todd was in no shape to do much of anything."

"Todd told me he went to the rest room at some point while he was there," I said. "Did you happen to see him leave, then come back a short time later?"

"It didn't register with me if I did," Richard said.

I knew my next question was a longshot at best, but I had to ask it. "Did you see Chet or Dorsey slip something in Todd's drink?"

Richard paused momentarily, then said, "No. Are you implying that Todd was drugged?"

"In your estimation, was Todd there long enough to get so hammered that he had to be carried out of the place?"

"Time isn't the real issue, is it? It would all depend on how much alcohol Todd consumed, and how well he could hold his liquor."

Richard checkmated me on that one. "You're right, Richard. Those are the key factors. Thanks for sharing your thoughts with me. You've been a big help."

"I pray you get that poor kid's conviction overturned," Richard said. "I know he's had his problems, but I've never believed he was capable of murder."

I started to remind Richard that Todd's conviction came courtesy of his confession, but I didn't. Instead, I thanked him a second time, ended the call, and traipsed back to my room. I was eager to find out what Greg learned about Chet, the homicidal bartender.

~ * ~

"Chester Arthur Woodward was born in Nashville in nineteen fifty-three," Greg read from notes he'd scribbled down. "His parents divorced three years later, he and his mother moved here, and she eventually married a coal miner. Chet dropped out of school after the eleventh grade and enlisted in the Army, where he served for three years, including one in Vietnam. He was given an honorable discharge upon his release from service. He's been married and divorced twice, and he has a daughter he seldom sees. His criminal record isn't bad, but it's far from perfect. It includes a DUI he got not long after leaving the Army, and three assault beefs, all of which were dismissed when the men he allegedly attacked dropped the charges. All three of those incidents occurred within a five-year period in the nineteen-nineties.

Following his time in the Army, he went to work as a brakeman for the Illinois Central Railroad. When he retired after twenty-five years on the job, he started working at the American Legion as a bartender. He is now considered the Legion's manager. Like I told you, Nick, there's not much in his past that stands out, and certainly nothing that would identify him as a potential killer."

"Those three dropped assault charges sound suspicious," I responded. "One, I might say, 'okay, the guy changed his mind, didn't want to go through the hassle of a trial.' But all three? No way. That tells me Chet got to them, made threats, either to the person pressing charges, or to his family and they dropped the charges out of fear."

"That very well could be the case. I've seen it happen before."

Angel made her standard entrance, barging in without bothering to knock. I wasn't sure if that's the California way or not, but it didn't matter to me. I was just overjoyed she was here. It wouldn't have bothered me if she had flown in through the window like a movie vampire.

She cleaned up well, I'll give her that. Wearing fresh blue Levis, a white Tee-shirt with Tom Petty's picture and 1950-2017 on it, red tennis shoes, and her still wet hair pulled back into a ponytail, she was a world-class beauty. And I'm not making that judgment because I'm her father. She's a work of art. Seeing her standing there was a painful reminder of the wonderful daughter who had been absent from my life for twelve long years, while also forcing me to once again admit what a fool I had been for allowing such a thing to happen. Shame on me.

~ * ~

Greg's plan was one I didn't agree with. I know how insane that sounds, a writer challenging an experienced federal agent's strategy, but, hey, isn't a lowly scribbler allowed to have an opinion, even if it's a lousy one? And yes, I know the old saying about opinions. However, this particular writer was wise enough to keep his disagreement to himself.

The plan Greg laid out called for us to sit outside the American Legion until the place closed, then go inside and confront Chet Woodward. This approach, Greg said, would be more likely to catch

Chet off guard, and perhaps rattle him to the extent that he lets important information slip out. A surprise attack was the reason Greg opted for this approach.

The surprise element wasn't why I disagreed (silently) with Greg's plan. I just felt the smart thing to do would be to enter the Legion when the place was busy and grill Chet in front of his peers. If I were in Chet's shoes, being questioned with multiple eyes watching would rattle me more than being questioned by a lone FBI agent with no one else around staring at you. But my approach was one I undoubtedly had seen in a movie, so it was for the best that I didn't openly challenge Greg.

Sitting around waiting has never been my forte (unless it was on a bar stool), but it didn't seem to bother Angel or Greg. They were in the front seat of the car chatting like lifelong friends while sharing a bag of pretzels. Mostly, I stayed quiet, preferring to think rather than talk. As always, my thoughts seemed to land on my Divine Rebel, William Blake. "Expect poison from standing water" was his apothegm that kept coming to mind. Somehow it seemed appropriate for the occasion. Would Chet Woodward poison us with his lies and false statements? More than likely he would, I quickly concluded.

~ * ~

The Legion officially closed at midnight. A handful of hardcore drinkers stayed around until closing time, but most of the customers were gone by then. By twelve-thirty, most of the lights inside had been turned off. We had no way of knowing for sure if Chet was alone, or if others were inside helping him with clean-up duties. It didn't matter. The time had come for us to move.

Greg banged on the locked front door for several minutes before it was opened. We were disappointed to see someone other than Chet standing there. He was a small guy with a full beard, shaved head, and creepy eyes.

"Sorry, folks, we're closed," the man said. "We open again tomorrow at noon. You're welcome to come back then."

Greg held up his credentials and said, "I need to speak with Chet. Is he around?"

The man eyed Greg's credentials with a wary look. "Yeah, he might be." He opened the door a little wider, but not nearly enough for us to enter. "Why do you want to talk with Chet?"

"That's none of your concern, sir," Greg said. "Are there others inside, or is it just you and Chet?"

"Ain't nobody but me and him."

"Then please stand aside and let me in. I'll want to speak with Chet in private, so why don't you call it a night and head home?"

As the man reluctantly granted us entrance, a voice called from the back. "What's going on up there, Carl?"

Greg put a finger to his lips before Carl could respond, indicating that Carl should remain silent. Then Greg nodded at the open door, his way of ordering Carl to decamp. Carl left without speaking.

"You deaf or what, Carl?" Chet yelled. An overhead row of lights was turned back on. "You know the rules. No one gets in after midnight. Send them on their way, lock the damn door, get your sorry ass in gear, and help me. I don't intend to be here all night."

"I'm afraid Carl has called it a day, Chet," Greg announced.

Chet turned around, eyed the three of us, grinned, and said, "I've met your two companions, but who the hell are you?"

"Greg Harkins, FBI," Greg said, holding up his credentials. "I'm here to ask you a few questions."

"I don't have time at the moment. As you can plainly see, I'm busy. Check back with me tomorrow."

"Make time, Chet. I'm not going anywhere."

Chet picked up a chair, turned it upside-down, and set it on a table. He did the same thing with the other three chairs around the table.

"What is it you want to talk about?" Chet asked, moving to the next table. "Did I serve alcohol to a minor? Is that it?"

"As a matter of fact, it is. But we'll get to that later. How about we begin with the murder of Sharon Anderson?"

"I don't know anything about that."

"On the contrary, Chet, you know all about it."

"Is that a fact? Okay, tell me what I know."

"You and Dorsey McElwain murdered her."

"That's bullshit. I didn't kill Sharon."

"I've met more than my share of liars, Chet, and you aren't a very good one."

"I'm not lying."

"Why did Sharon have to die?" Greg asked.

"How would I know? I didn't kill her," Chet replied.

"Chet, you not only killed Sharon, you also murdered Dorsey."

"Man, you are completely out of your fucking mind. I can't believe they'd give a badge to someone as crazy as you are."

"Want to hear another crazy notion, Chet? You killed Luke Felton."

"Now I know you're pissing in the wind. That kid confessed and was sentence to life in prison for murdering Luke."

"Todd Brown never killed anyone," Greg said. "He was drugged, then you and Dorsey killed Luke and set Todd up to take the fall."

"Chief, you've really gone off the deep end."

"What I don't understand is why Luke had to be killed."

"Are you going to stand there and blame me for every murder?" Chet asked, seriously.

"No, just those three."

"You've got the wrong guy, Mr. FBI Agent."

"Make my life easier, Chet. Confess to what you did. Admit you murdered those three innocent people."

"I'm not going to admit to something I didn't do."

"Admit it or not, you're going down for those homicides."

"But you have a big problem, don't you? You can't prove any of it."

"I wouldn't bet on that if I were in your shoes, Chet. Wait until I talk to your lover. Dottie Barker will give you up in two seconds. Trust me, she'll lay all the blame on you. And she has the money to hire the best legal minds to handle her case. You know the ones I'm talking about. Those sleazy well-dressed lizards who will stop at nothing to keep her from going down for those homicides. No, Chet, your ass is cooked."

As the two men were confronting each other, Angel and I were positioned on opposite sides of Greg. I was to his right, Angel to his left, which placed her just a couple of feet away from Chet. I didn't pay attention to her close proximity to him. As events soon unfolded, I should have.

"Dottie is a tough broad," Chet stated. "She won't say anything against me."

"Maybe she is," Greg said. "Maybe she won't rat you out. But what about e-mails and text messages? I'll bet there are hundreds of them. What will I find when I check them out?"

"Nothing, that's what."

"I'm betting I find a treasure trove of rich, salacious bedroom chat between you and Dottie. I might even be turned on by what I read. How about it? Will it turn me on?"

"Won't make a goddamn bit of difference," Chet snapped before making a series of surprisingly quick moves for such a burly guy. First, he dug into his pants pocket, pulled out and opened a switchblade knife, darted behind Angel, threw his right arm around her neck and pressed the knife against her throat. "I'm walking out of here, or this pretty bitch dies."

Greg's weapon was out and pointed at Chet. "Let her go and drop the knife, Chet," he ordered. "You aren't going anywhere, and neither am I. But let's talk. No one needs to get hurt."

"Don't test me. I've already killed three people. A fourth won't make any difference."

The next few moments, which couldn't have lasted more than five seconds, are the scariest and the proudest I've ever experienced in my life. It was a scene I've watched a hundred times in movies, but never in real life. And trust me, what transpired was real life.

Angel grabbed Chet's right arm with both hands, and then in an explosive move, she simultaneously pulled his arm away from her neck, ducked her left shoulder down, a move that also had the knife aimed toward the floor. With her right shoulder raised and Chet's body bent forward, she slipped out of the headlock, twisted the arm holding the knife, which was positioned blade-first toward his ribs, jabbed the knife into his side, and then kicked him twice in the face while taking the knife from his hand. When she released Chet, he fell forward on the floor, moaning and groaning, blood leaking from the small wound to his side.

I could only marvel at the scene I had just witnessed. A knife-wielding, two-hundred-fifty-pound three-time killer, a Vietnam vet to boot, had just been totally annihilated by an opponent who maybe tipped the scales at one-twenty. And she had taken him down without the first hint of fear or hesitation. Had I scripted this scene for a movie, I doubt it would have made the cut.

Greg put the handcuffs on Chet, who was still too woozy to stand. The injury inflicted by Angel was little more than a nick, but Greg, being a considerate law enforcement officer, took out his handkerchief and pressed it against the wound. When he was certain the bleeding had stopped, he stood and glanced at me.

I could tell from the look on Greg's face that he was equally impressed by what he'd just seen. He stared at Angel for a while, then shifted his eyes back to me. There was a minimum of ten questions behind those eyes, but he only asked one.

"Where the hell did she learn how to do that amazing shit?" he said.

"Brown belt in Krav Maga," I replied.

"Hey, I say give her the black belt. She just earned it."

"I second that motion."

Angel listened but didn't chime in. And most important of all, like a proud warrior she didn't gloat. She seemed to know instinctively that real heroes don't have to gloat or brag. Real heroes let their actions do the talking.

And my beautiful daughter *was* a real hero.

Twenty-nine

Well, this story ends where it began, me sitting at the bar in the Old Salty Dog on Siesta Key and Rory Killion peppering me with questions about my friendship with Anthony Hopkins. No matter how hard I try, I can't seem to get it across to Rory that the Oscar-winning actor and I are not friends, only working acquaintances, and barely that. I've tried and failed to make Rory understand that sitting in on a reading of my play or observing a few rehearsals does not a friendship make. None of my arguments mattered. Rory granted me friendship status with Sir Anthony and nothing was going to persuade him differently. You have to admire someone that stubborn and hard-headed.

It's only four-thirty on New Year's Day, but the bar was doing a bang-up business. Outside, the temperature is barely in the fifties, which necessitated adding a windbreaker to my normal beach wardrobe... shorts, Tee-shirt, and tennis shoes. The New England area is currently being blanketed with snow, so you won't hear me complaining about the cooler weather in Florida.

This Christmas past was the best I've had in, well, the past thirteen years. I say this because Angel was here. She and her college roommate flew down and spent ten days with me. We had a blast, trust me. The two ladies immediately fell in love with this entire area… Siesta Key, Sarasota, Longboat Key, Bird Key, and especially St. Armands Circle, where they shopped for hours each day.

Angel now claims that, after graduating from college, she intends to move here and live on Siesta Key. I was quick to say that was fine with me. She has decided to forego creative writing and stick with psychology, which, in my opinion, is a wise decision. It's much less risky. In my case, I got lucky. Few writers are fortunate enough to land good-paying gigs as a script doctor, or to pen a play that becomes a big critical and financial success. I reminded her that a guaranteed steady income is not a bad thing.

Speaking of *Divine Rebel: An Evening with William Blake*, the play is doing better now than ever. In London, Jeremy Irons replaced Jonathan Pryce as Blake, and from all I've read and heard, he is spectacular in the role. In September, I hooked up with Angel in Los Angeles and we attended the production at the Mark Taber Theatre that featured Brian Cox as Blake. Cox didn't disappoint; he was excellent. I know that a parent is not supposed to favor one child over another, but in my case I'm guilty of that transgression. Of all the productions of the play I've seen… and with the exception of the one in London, I've seen them all… my absolute favorite is the one I saw at the Steppenwolf Theatre in Chicago. John Malkovich was Blake, and Gary Sinise directed. I judged it to be beyond perfect. It's impossible for me to adequately explain why I felt this way, only to say there was something different, unique, about that production. Maybe it had more energy, or perhaps it's because Blake, for the first time, was portrayed by an American actor. There has been some chatter making the rounds that if Malkovich and Sinise can work it into their busy schedules, the Steppenwolf production might move to Broadway. I hope that works out. New York theatre patrons would love it.

~ * ~

Earlier, I stated that this had been a special Christmas because Angel shared it with me. Her presence made it truly special. There was also a second reason why it was so much better than normal.

On Christmas evening, I received a phone call from Steve Brown. We only spoke for a brief time, with Steve doing most of the talking. He thanked me again and again for never losing faith in Todd, and for never relenting in my effort to prove his innocence. I told Steve the real credit should go to FBI agent Greg Harkins, which was true. Without him, none of those three homicide cases would have been solved. Certainly not by a writer with no authority to investigate a series of murders. Steve promised to give Greg a call and thank him for his work on the case.

Steve said Todd was doing well, and that as incredible as it might seem, during the time Todd was incarcerated he made positive strides toward overcoming his drug addiction. According to Steve, his son had completed a one-month stay in a drug rehab facility, landed a job with the highway department, and was planning to enroll in the community college later this month.

What I didn't tell Steve was that I had previously been given this information. Todd called in early October, we spoke for almost two hours, and he shared with me all the positive things that were going on in his life. He seemed to be in good spirits, his thought process was sound, and he was eagerly looking forward to the future. My conclusion: He was happy and at peace with himself. Now he faced the real challenge... not straying from this path he's on.

What Todd couldn't do, however, was remember what had actually taken place on the night Luke Felton was murdered. He'd racked his brain countless times trying to recall those events, but always came up with blanks. So, it was left for me to unfold the story for him.

And that's what I did.

~ * ~

This whole sordid mess began when Sharon Anderson made the mistake of confiding to Chet that she was pregnant with Russell's child. Chet went straight to Dottie and told her. This sent Dottie into a panic. She didn't love Russell, but she did love his money. She feared that if Russell learned of the pregnancy, and after having lost his only child in that explosion in Florida, he would demand that Sharon keep the baby. That would be bad enough, Dottie knew, but what if Sharon wanted Russell to get a divorce and marry her? Or what if Sharon decided to blackmail Russell for big bucks, really hit his bank account hard? Neither one of those scenarios was acceptable to Dottie. There was but a single solution to this problem... Sharon and her unborn child had to go.

Naturally, Chet, Dottie's lover, was enlisted to put an end to this potential threat. He agreed to help... there was nothing he wouldn't do for Dottie... but said it would be difficult to pull off alone. Dorsey McElwain could be recruited, he told Dottie, if she agreed to pay him five grand, which for her was chump change. Dottie wrote the check right on the spot.

Two nights later, Chet met with Sharon under the guise of advising her how she should approach Russell with the good news that he was soon to be a father. When they arrived at the previously arranged destination, Dorsey was there waiting. Dorsey held her down while Chet strangled her with a rope. Then, per Dottie's orders—"I'm sick of hearing how great her blow jobs are"... Chet cut off Sharon's head, stuffed the rest of her body in the trunk, then he and Dorsey attempted and failed to completely submerge her car in the pond. Chet and Dorsey drove away... only those two know where they discarded Sharon's head... certain they had pulled off the perfect crime.

Which was true...for three years, anyway.

Dorsey McElwain was murdered because, just as Rabbit said, he was seen speaking with Angel at the Convention Center. That individual, and we don't know who it was, went to the American Legion and told Chet what he had just seen. This was not news Chet wanted to hear. When the Legion closed that night, Chet paid Dorsey a visit. No big deal, just two friends shooting the shit. Then at some point while Dorsey was sitting on the sofa Chet came up from behind and snapped Dorsey's neck, killing him instantly. Dorsey had become a problem; Chet took care of it. It was no more complicated than that.

This brings us to the one question that puzzled me the most— why was Luke Felton murdered? But before I lay the specifics on you, let me tell you how I found out.

~ * ~

Chet Woodward's bravado and his certainty that Dottie Barker would be his savior lasted about as long as all of us expected it to. Upon officially being arrested and charged with three homicides, Chet hired a local lawyer, a gentleman named Boyd Riley, who was a skilled ambulance chaser but far from skilled as a defense attorney. To say he was ill-prepared for the challenge was putting it mildly. In fact, he had never represented a client charged with a single murder, much less with three. Yet, this putz was all that stood between Chet and prison. Good luck with that.

Initially, when being questioned by Greg Harkins and Mark Robinson, Chet denied that he had confessed to the three homicides. He tried to make it sound like Greg pulled that admission out of his ass. That Greg needed a scapegoat and Chet got the part. Apparently, Greg conveniently forgot that Angel and I also heard his confession. When Greg pointed out this little detail, Chet's reply was, "If that's what they claim, then they're liars."

In a final burst of false bravado, Chet said he planned to have his attorney file a massive lawsuit against Angel, Greg, the FBI, and me for a series of offenses, including false arrest and police brutality. I'll win an Academy Award before that lawsuit sees the light of day.

"How are you gonna make that stick, Chet? I never touched you. Tell Mark who did kick your ass," Greg prompted. "Don't want to? Then let me. It was Samantha Gabriel who pinned Chet to the mat in less than five seconds. A female kicked his ass, Mark."

"Is that what happened, Chet?" Mark asked.

"Fuck both of you," Chet snapped.

Chet's will to fight the charges began to fizzle when he got word that Dottie was cutting him loose. Chet mistakenly believed his lover would persuade Russell to cough up the dough necessary to hire an experienced attorney to represent him. That didn't happen. As expected, Russell forked over a small fortune to enlist the services of two high-profile New York defense attorneys to represent Dottie, but not a penny was paid to help Chet. If that wasn't devastating enough for Chet, he later found out that Dottie was denying any involvement in the homicides and was laying all three murders on Chet and Dorsey McElwain. So much for true love.

When Chet got wind of Dottie's betrayal, he instructed Boyd Riley to get in touch with Mark Robinson, the county attorney, and let him know the time had come to play let's make a deal. But Chet had a major problem... after having already admitted to committing three murders, his stack of bargaining chips was virtually depleted.

"I'll give you Dottie's head on a platter," Chet promised.

"Not enough, Chet," Mark said. "With what we read in those e-mails and text messages between the two of you, her involvement is not in question. No, Dottie is going down, just like you are."

"Those big-shot lawyers might get her off. You ever consider that?"

"The best they can do is drag things out for as long as possible, or until Russell gets wise, sees what is waiting at the finish line, and decides to put in the plug that stops the money flow. But it won't matter what Russell does or doesn't do. Dottie Barker will spend the rest of her natural life behind prison bars."

"Come on, man, work with me here," Chet pleaded to Mark. "What can I give you that will keep me away from a lethal injection? I don't want any part of that damn needle."

"You tell us the truth and I'll take the death penalty off the table," Mark said.

"I've told you everything I know," Chet said.

"There is one thing you haven't shared with us, Chet," Greg pointed out. "And I have no doubt you know what I'm talking about."

"Luke Felton?"

"Exactly."

"What do you want to know?"

"Everything, from beginning to end."

"Well—"

~ * ~

In Chet's version of how events unfolded, Luke was the unwitting architect of his own death. It began one night at the Legion when Luke heard snippets of a conversation between Dorsey and Rabbit. At one point, Dorsey said, "It was really creepy seeing her body without a head. Dude, it seriously freaked me out." Rabbit scoffed at what Dorsey was saying, but to Luke, a former cop, it sounded liked Dorsey was being truthful. Remember, Sharon Anderson's headless body had been found three years earlier, which, for Luke, only added credibility to what Dorsey was relaying to Rabbit.

The next day, Luke chased down Rabbit and asked him if he thought Dorsey was bullshitting or telling the truth. Rabbit said he didn't believe a word of Dorsey's story. But Rabbit must have believed it, because he went to Dorsey and let him know Luke was sniffing around asking questions. Dorsey informed Chet, who then informed Dottie. Her dictate was simple and concise: Luke Felton had to be eliminated.

First on their agenda was putting together a plan that would fulfill Dottie's demand while not leading the cops back to their doorstep. What they needed was a fall guy to take the rap, and this was when Todd came into the picture. It was Chet's idea to make Todd the patsy. And Todd's previous drug use was the key to this plan.

Luke had occasionally sold weed to Dorsey in the past. Dorsey knew Luke wouldn't hesitate to meet with him and Todd for the purpose of selling them some weed. Luke was aware of Todd's drug use, so his being there wouldn't be a big deal. Dorsey and Todd had never made a drug purchase together, but this new arrangement wasn't likely to bother Luke. He agreed to meet them. Once the meeting time had been finalized, the next problem was how to set up Todd as the killer. Chet's solution... load Todd up with drugs.

The next afternoon, Dorsey and Rabbit cruised around town for two hours before they laid eyes on Todd, who was entering Speedway. Dorsey pulled into the lot, told Rabbit to hook up with Todd, and then have Todd drive them to the Legion. And what's what happened.

Chet plied Todd with enough beer and shots of bourbon to fill up his bladder in no time. When Todd went to the restroom, Chet put the drug into his drink. The impact of the drugs and booze was instantaneous... Todd began to wobble and stagger like a boxer who had just been tagged with a solid right cross. Anyone seeing him would conclude that he was drunk, and they wouldn't give a second thought to seeing Dorsey helping him to the door. After putting Todd in his car, Dorsey drove to his house, carried Todd inside, waited a couple of hours, took out his cell phone, sent a text message to Luke. He asked if they could buy some top-notch weed at the usual rendezvous site, a barren scar of land the Peabody Coal Company left like an open wound after all the coal had been removed. Luke agreed to the meeting. Now all Dorsey had to do was sit tight until the Legion closed and Chet showed up.

By then, Todd was slowly beginning to come around so they hit him with another shot of the drug. He was asleep in the back seat of Dorsey's car when Luke arrived at the site. Dorsey slid in on the passenger's side, all smiles, all happy-go-lucky. Luke was buckled up behind the steering wheel, unaware that he was living the final moments of his life. Dorsey grabbed Luke by his shoulders and pinned him against his seat. This happened so fast Luke didn't have time to put up a struggle. Chet opened the driver's side door and began repeatedly stabbing Luke with his knife. It was later reported by the coroner that Luke received thirty-one wounds, including two directly to his heart.

Chet unbuckled Luke's seat belt and laid the dead man's body on the ground next to the car. He then took a rag, dipped it in Luke's blood, and smeared the blood on Todd's clothes. For his final act, Chet cut off one of Luke's fingers, removed his ring, and put it on Todd's finger. Before leaving, Chet tossed Todd's driver's license on the front seat floorboard in Luke's car.

It was still dark when they drove past Todd's house and parked on the street several hundred yards away. They waited there until shortly after sunrise. That's when Todd's father left for work. Maybe a half-hour later, Todd's mother came out of the house with his two younger siblings, they all got in the car and headed off to school. With the coast clear, they pulled the car into the driveway, up behind the house, got out, lugged Todd up the stairs to his room and then put him in his bed. Job completed; they drove away. Later that morning, after Luke's body had been found, Perry Jackson and Jimmy Martin showed up in Todd's room with his driver's license in hand. They took him into custody, questioned him, and in less than two hours, Todd confessed to murdering Luke Felton.

Case closed. End of story.

"It was the perfect murder," Chet commented, after completing his narrative.

"Until it wasn't," Greg replied.

Thirty

There was a chill in the air as I walked out of the Old Salty Dog and into a new year. The air was crisp, clean, not unlike how I imagined it to be on Adam's first day on Earth. I wonder if he was fearful when daylight slowly gave way to the darkness of night. I'm sure he must have been. He had no way of knowing what darkness was, what terrors it held, or if the light would return again. He was but a child alone and frightened with no one to offer comfort. But there was one terror I know for certain that Adam never faced...the annoying sound of a buzzing cell phone. Until very recently in our evolution from Homo sapiens to Techno sapiens, Adam and I had that in common.

The call was from Mike Tucker. When I answered, Karen's voice could be heard in the background, which meant the phone was on speaker. In unison they wished me Happy New Year...I returned the sentiment...and then Mike asked if the book was nearing completion. It had been a little more than six months since the events in Central City, a fair amount of time for most writers to finish a book. Or more than enough time, in Mike's estimation.

Mike went silent when I informed him that I had decided against writing the book. Karen's reaction was much different, I found. She had expressed genuine disappointment...maybe even a hint of anger... that I chose to pass on what had originally been her idea. She spent ten minutes berating me for my decision, saying there was a story to be told and I was the logical person to tell it. This part was true...no one knew more about the details of what had gone on at the time than I did.

Once she calmed down, the conversation returned to a more normal flow. Mike told me about an old teacher of ours who recently passed away, and Karen said she was retiring at the end of the school year but would continue to teach her class at the community college. The conversation went on for a few more minutes, then we exchanged invitations to visit and ended the call.

While it was nice hearing from Mike, and especially pleasing to get the feeling that their marriage seemed to have miraculously survived past indiscretions, the damn call brought back to life the guilt I felt for having slept with his wife. I have a hunch this particular shame will always stay with me. And I must admit it's a punishment I deserve.

After everything was taken care of in Central City, I paid for Angel's and my motel rooms, purchased a plane ticket for her flight back to California, took care of her rental car bill, and gave her three hundred bucks in cash for incidentals. Her trip to my hometown cost me a pretty penny, but I'm not complaining. It was money well spent.

Back on Siesta Key, I gathered and organized the notes and recordings I had made while researching the book, fully intending to immediately begin work on the project. However, before I wrote the first word, two famous Hollywood producers called to inquire if I would help them whip their respective scripts into shape. I had vowed to cease doing that crappy work, but the damn money was so good I couldn't refuse. What can I say? I'm a prostitute willing to sell my soul for a giant payday.

It was while I was laboring over those scripts that I had a change of heart regarding the book. The change came in a most unexpected way, while I was watching a two-night TV documentary about the 1959 Clutter family murders, which was the basis for *In Cold Blood*, Truman Capote's classic non-fiction novel that was to serve as the template for the book I planned to write.

During the four-hour documentary several surviving Clutter relatives were interviewed, along with close friends of the family and members of the Holcomb, Kansas community where the murders took place. Not a single person who spoke on camera had anything positive to say about the book or about Capote. In fact, they were unanimous in their regret that Capote sensationalized such a tragic event, and that he shed a negative light on their tight-knit community.

They also pointed out that Capote's book was littered with inaccuracies about the Clutter family, and that his portrait of the four victims, especially Mrs. Clutter, was far from true. Conversely, they felt Capote was overly sympathetic toward the killers, Perry Smith and Richard Hickok (Smith in particular, whom Capote seemed to have a crush on), and that the fortune Capote made from his bestseller amounted to nothing more than blood money.

Watching the program I couldn't help but wonder what the folks in Central City and Muhlenberg County would think when they read my book, were I to write it. What would be their opinion of me? Would they approve of the picture I painted of my hometown? Or would they despise it? Truman Capote wasn't from Kansas, so he had no skin in the game. He couldn't have cared less what those folks thought of him. But I'm from Central City. People know me. I have friends who still live there. If I wrote the book and it became a bestseller, would they view what I earned as blood money? Maybe yes, maybe no. But in the end, that was a chance I had no desire to take. So I canned the idea of writing the book.

Yes, I'll grant you that my book would've had enough positive elements to maybe offset the negatives. Three people were dead, true, but the killers were in custody, the Anderson and Felton families finally had some answers, and most-important of all, Todd Brown was released from prison and the murder charge against him removed from his record. When I ponder those details, I think maybe I should have taken my chances and written the book. But that feeling passes seconds after it arrives.

It's almost midnight now, I'm lying in bed, and a favorite saying of mine keeps running through my head. Somehow it seems appropriate to Todd Brown and the terrible ordeal he endured, although nothing can ever blot out the horror he experienced. I can only hope the experience doesn't damage him for life in negative ways.

You'll likely be surprised to hear that this saying did not come from William Blake. No, these profound words date back much further, to the Old Testament's Amos, first of the writing prophets:

"But let judgment run down as waters, and righteousness as a mighty stream."

Not even my Divine Rebel could improve on that.

Meet Tom Wallace

Tom Wallace is the award-winning author of ten previous Jack Dantzler mysteries, including: *88, The Journal, Heroes For Ghosts, Murder by Suicide, The Poker Game, The Fire of Heaven, The List, Gnosis, The Devil's Racket* and *What Matters Blood*. He also wrote the thriller, *Heirs of Cain*.

His novel, *Gnosis*, won the prestigious Claymore Award at the Killer Nashville Writers Conference, and *The Devil's Racket* captured the Mystery Writers top award. *Murder by Suicide* was an Amazon best-seller.

Tom, a former sportswriter, has written several successful sports-related books, including *The Kentucky Basketball Encyclopedia* (now out in its fourth edition), *So You Think You're a Kentucky Wildcats Basketball Fan?*, *Golden Glory: The History of Central City Basketball, Big Blue Dream* and *Heart of a Champion*.

While sports editor for the Henderson *Gleaner*, Tom was twice honored by the Kentucky Press Association for writing the Best Sports Story in Kentucky.

Tom is a Vietnam vet who currently lives in Lexington, Ky.

Visit Our Website

For The Full Inventory
Of Quality Books:

Wings ePress, Inc

Quality trade paperbacks and downloads
in multiple formats,
in genres ranging from light romantic comedy to general
fiction and horror.
Wings has something for every reader's taste.
Visit the website, then bookmark it.
We add new titles each month!

Wings ePress Inc.
3000 N. Rock Road
Newton, KS 67114

www.ingramcontent.com/pod-product-compliance
Lightning Source LLC
Chambersburg PA
CBHW070636100726
47907CB00007B/2007